Before Another Dies

Before Another Dies

Book 2

ALTON GANSKY

GRAND RAPIDS, MICHIGAN 49530 USA

ZONDERVAN™

Before Another Dies
Copyright © 2005 by Alton Gansky

Requests for information should be addressed to:
Zondervan, *Grand Rapids, Michigan 49530*

Library of Congress Cataloging-in-Publication Data

Gansky, Alton
    Before another dies / Alton Gansky.
        p. cm.—(A Madison Glenn novel; bk. 2)
    ISBN-10: 0-310-25935-5 (softcover)
    ISBN-13: 978-0-310-25935-0 (softcover)
    1. Women mayors—Fiction.   2. California—Fiction.   I. Title.   II. Series.
  PS3557.A519B44 2005
  813'.54—dc22

                                 2004030065

All Scripture quotations, unless otherwise indicated, are taken from the *New American Standard Bible*®, Copyright © 1960, 1962, 1963, 1968, 1971, 1972, 1973, 1975, 1977, 1995 by The Lockman Foundation. Used by permission.

All rights reserved. No part of this publication may be reproduced, stored in a retrieval system, or transmitted in any form or by any means—electronic, mechanical, photocopy, recording, or any other—except for brief quotations in printed reviews, without the prior permission of the publisher.

Interior design by Michelle Espinoza

Printed in the United States of America

---

05 06 07 08 09 10 11 12 /❖ DCI/ 10 9 8 7 6 5 4 3 2 1

Before Another Dies

chapter

He was in my parking place.

And that was the least of my worries.

Last week, I began my third year as mayor of Santa Rita. Prior to that, I served two four-year terms on the city council. After eleven years in public life, I thought I had seen everything.

People are attracted to the city. Maybe it's because Santa Rita is snuggled next to the Southern California ocean. Maybe it's because our nights are warm and our days only slightly warmer. We don't do hot; and we certainly don't do cold. The ocean serves as our personal heat sink. Our restaurants are exceptional, and our ocean is blue enough to make the sky envious. People come to Santa Rita to escape Los Angeles to the south. Some just pass through on the way to Santa Barbara to the north.

As I said, people are attracted to the city. Most are reasonable, civil, and normal people, but we have our share of fringe personalities. We have transients who wander our streets content to stay as long as their restless souls will allow. We have homeless who sleep in our parks and between downtown buildings. We even have our share of social gadflies. Some have burning messages for their civic leaders. Most are harmless; a few are scary.

Last week, Bobby "Street Dog" Benson was waiting for me when I arrived at city hall. I had chosen to park in front of the building as I usually do in the mornings. In the afternoon, I hide my car in the back lot. Fewer disruptions that way. Street Dog—he named himself—had been sent by some alien race or another to warn me of an impending invasion. The mother ship was due to land on the beach just south of the pier at precisely 3:10 that afternoon. Street Dog hears voices. I thanked him and rewarded his civic contribution with a five-dollar bill I hoped he'd use to buy an Egg McMuffin. Street Dog left satisfied. The mother ship never arrived.

Yes, I've seen it all. Or at least I thought I had until, under a bright January sky, I pulled into the front lot of city hall and aimed my car toward the reserved space with the sign that read, "The Hon. Mayor Madison Glenn." That's me, except I prefer the name Maddy. Madison sounds too . . . I don't know—something. My father, a history professor at the University of Santa Barbara, named me after a dead president. He likes dead presidents.

I directed my silver Lincoln Aviator up the drive and down the lot. A second later, I saw it: a lime green AMC Gremlin hatchback that appeared as if it had been traveling nonstop since the day it rolled off the assembly line sometime in the early seventies.

"Great." I'm not stuck on my title, nor do I think the citizens who elected me to be their first full-time mayor should treat me like royalty. I had moved beyond feeling that a reserved parking space made me important. The principle of the thing, however, bothered me. After all, the space was, well, reserved, and it had a sign that said so. Just like the space next to it for the city manager, city attorney, and the members of the council.

I had a choice to make. I could simply drive around to the back of the building and park there, or I could confront the space thief. Most days, I would have chosen the former. This day, I stopped my

SUV a few feet from the Gremlin and waited for the driver to catch my hint. I was ready with my patented how-dare-you scowl.

He didn't move. I gunned the engine and let the eight cylinders roar slightly less than a polite, "Hey, buddy." Nothing. Was he asleep? The urge to honk grew but I chose a more diplomatic approach, one fitting an elected official, especially one facing an election.

I exited my car and started forward. It was still early, just seven thirty, and the sun was crawling up the eastern sky, just beyond the coastal hills. Most of the city employees would not be around for another half hour. A brief but pungent fear rolled over me. What if the guy was off his rocker? I mean, he *was* driving a Gremlin. I considered calling security, but I was afraid I'd sound petty. A lot of things have changed in my life over the last six months, but I was still in a wrestling match with pride.

I approached the driver-side door and tapped the glass with the knuckle of my index finger. "Excuse me, sir." I tried to sound as pleasant as a woman could at seven thirty and one cup of coffee shy of contentment. "May I help . . . ?"

The driver was slumped in his seat. I assumed he was snoozing, perhaps having overexercised his right to knock back cold ones at the local bar.

He wasn't asleep. Spiders crawled down my spine, and I took a step back.

Returning to my car, I pulled the cell phone from my purse and dialed a number well known to me. Ringing was replaced by a curt voice. I made myself known. "This is Maddy Glenn. I don't suppose Chief Webb is in yet." The cop who answered assured me that Webb was in but that he was in some sort of early-morning meeting. "I need to speak to him right away."

"It might be better if we wait for the meeting to end. He hates interruptions. Trust me; he *really* hates to be interrupted."

"I understand. Please tell him *Mayor* Glenn needs him on the phone." There was a pause, then I was in the never-never land of hold.

"Webb." Chief Bill Webb had a gruff voice that matched his face. He sounded even crustier than usual, something I attributed to the early hour and my having yanked him out of his meeting.

"Chief Webb, it's Maddy."

"Madam Mayor." What little courtesy there was in his voice evaporated. Webb and I have history. He doesn't like me and never has. The feeling is mutual which is a bit awkward since he saved my life a few months back. I owe him a lot but he never brings it up. He is too professional. Regardless of our mutual misgivings, I know him to be an excellent police officer and superior administrator. Our problems have to do with politics and money and goals and money; and to make things worse, we've disagreed over money. He wants more; I don't want to give it.

"I'm sorry to disturb you so early, but this is important." I took a deep breath. "I just pulled into the front lot, and there is a car in my parking space—"

"You didn't just pull me out of an officer review meeting to evict some guy from your parking space, did you? Unbelievable. Call security. That's their job. Call a tow truck."

"You don't understand, the driver is in the car—"

"Then tell him who you are and tell him to beat feet."

"I would, but he's dead." Silence. I could hear people talking in the background and the chief breathing. "You there?"

"I'm here. You sure he's dead?"

I sighed. "Head tilted to one side, cloudy eyes open and unblinking, mouth agape . . . Oh, did I mention that he doesn't appear to be breathing?"

"I'll be right there." He hung up.

I closed my flip phone and forced myself to the Gremlin again. The man hadn't budged, but then I hadn't expected him to. I've seen dead people before and he looked like a classic case. Once, out of some sense of misplaced loyalty, I attended a friend's autopsy—well, most of it. There are some blurry spots, and the crystal-clear images I kept locked in a mental dungeon.

The man in the car looked to be in his mid-thirties, maybe a couple years younger than my thirty-nine. He wore a white dress shirt that I doubted had ever been touched by an iron and blue jeans. His hair was sandy brown and curly. I didn't get close enough to see the color of his eyes. That was more information than I wanted.

I could see my reflection in the driver-side window. I saw the same shoulder-length brown hair, narrow nose, and hazel eyes that were several degrees wider than they were in my bathroom mirror this morning—perhaps because there wasn't a corpse on the other side of the mirror.

The sound of rubber tires on asphalt caused me to turn. A patrol car with a uniformed officer stopped a few feet away. A moment later, a city-issued Lincoln Continental—the chief's car—arrived. The Santa Rita police station sits less than fifty yards across the back parking lot that separates it from city hall. At best, it was a sixty-second drive. The uniformed officer stepped from his car and walked slowly in my direction. He took a moment to nod and offer a friendly, "Mayor," before returning his gaze to the macadam. It took me a second to realize that he was making sure he wasn't about to step on some piece of key evidence. I wondered what I had stepped in.

Satisfied that no shell casing or other evidence littered the lot, the officer walked to the Gremlin. Webb was two steps behind him as was another man I knew, Detective Judson West. When I saw Webb, my stomach soured. When I saw West, my heart stuttered.

"Madam Mayor," West said, with a wan smile. He stood a well-proportioned six foot two, had hair black enough to shame coal and teeth that were whiter and straighter than piano keys. His dark eyes twinkled. At least I think I saw a twinkle. West is our lead robbery-homicide detective. He came to the city from the San Diego PD a little over six months ago. He's never talked about why he left the big city.

"Did you touch anything?" Chief Webb asked.

"I knocked on the window with my knuckle."

"That's it? You didn't try to open the car door?"

"It's locked. Besides, I know better than to put my fingerprints where they don't belong."

"How do you know the door is . . . ?" I saw his gaze shift to the lock button on the door—it was down. Webb leaned over and peered through the side window to the door on the other side. I had done the same. He frowned.

West gave me a knowing smile. He knew of the tension between the chief and me and always seemed to find it entertaining. He turned to the officer. "All right, Bob, let's get the area taped off. In fact, I want the whole parking lot secured. No one in or out until we've searched the place and taken photos. You'd better call for some help. In the meantime, block the entrance with your car. The lot should start filling up any time now."

"Got it." Officer Bob reached for the microphone attached to the shoulder of his uniform and starting talking as he walked away.

"Not the way I planned to start the day," I said.

"You okay?" West asked.

"Fine. Just wasn't expecting a dead man in my parking spot."

I caught Webb looking our way and scowling. He was shorter than West, and his mane had grown comfortable with gray. He kept his hair combed back and held in place with some magical hair tonic. His eyes were an unhappy blue, and his face seemed frozen in disgust, as if he were on a castor oil diet. Red tinted his cheeks and the end of his nose.

Detective Judson West gave me one of his now famous smiles and inched his way over to his boss. I was still close enough to hear, but far enough away that I didn't have to see the dead man's face. I had seen enough of that.

"I don't suppose you've seen him before," Webb grumbled.

"No, and I'm pretty sure I'd remember."

"Not even during council meetings?"

The city council met every Tuesday evening at seven. It was a public meeting held in the chambers of city hall. Attendance was usually sparse with only a handful of citizens interested enough to pull themselves away from the television. Occasionally, a city measure would come up that would pack the place, but I could count those times on one hand. "Still no. I don't recall seeing the car either. I *know* I would remember that."

Even the chief nodded at that. He studied the car a little longer, then turned to West. "It's all yours, Detective."

"Gee, thanks," West said. He smiled for a moment, then the grin disappeared. He was slipping into professional mode. I had seen it before. Half a year ago, I was embroiled in a mess of abductions and a murder. It ended badly, and I was still having nightmares. West had just started with our department, and I was his first case. I had seen what he could become when a mystery loomed before him.

Webb took a step back and watched West. The chief's chest seemed to swell as if watching his only son show up the neighbor's kid on the Little League field. West walked around the car, examining the paving, tires, door handles, windows, and everything else his eyes could fall upon. Then he stepped to the front of the car and placed his hand near the radiator grille. "Cold," he said. "It's been here for a while." He tilted his head to the side. "Anyone else hear that?"

"Hear what?" I asked.

He paused before answering. "Music. I hear music."

I shook my head. I didn't hear anything. I stepped closer and picked up the hint of a tune. It was low, just loud enough to hear that something was there, but not enough to make out words. West walked to the passenger side of the car and looked in. "The keys are in the 'on' position. The music is coming from the radio." He straightened and turned at the sound of another police car arriving on the street. He waved the officer over. "Hey, Mitch, you got a Slim Jim in your patrol car, right? Bring it to me. Bring some gloves, too."

A moment later, the officer was by West's side. He was holding a long, flat piece of metal and a box of disposable latex gloves. West donned the gloves, then took the flat tool. "Call the coroner, tell him we have some work for him, and then give Bob a hand with the crime-scene tape."

He studied the Gremlin again and then returned to the passenger-side door. Without a word, he slipped the metal strip down between the window and rubber trim. He pushed, pulled, wiggled, and twisted the tool. "This is why I had to become a cop; I never could break into a car."

"It was a good choice," Webb said. "Benefits are better."

"Got it." He pulled up, and the door unlocked. He looked at me. "You want to guess why it is illegal for regular folk to own these?"

"I think I know."

"Yeah, but did you know there's an urban legend about police officers being killed while using them?" I admitted that I didn't. "The story goes that cars with side-collision air bags have shoved these devices into officers' heads. It's not true, of course. It makes a good story at a party."

"But you're still glad that a car this old doesn't have side air bags."

"I'll never admit it in public." He removed the tool and set it on the roof of the car. Using just one gloved finger, he pulled the handle and opened the door. I don't know what I was expecting, but I steeled myself for whatever came my way. The only difference I noticed was that I could now hear the music. The volume was weak.

"He must have had good ears," I said.

Webb looked at me and fought back a frown.

"I think the battery is dying," West said. He leaned in the car. I took a step back and shuddered. I couldn't see what he was doing. Seconds chugged by like hours and finally West came up for air. "I was wrong when I said the key was in the 'on' position; it's turned to 'accessories.'"

"Meaning?"

"Meaning that he pulled into your space, switched off the car, but left the key turned enough so the radio would still work."

"What else have you got?" Webb didn't say it, but even I knew what he was asking.

"Body indicates that death is recent, maybe six hours or so. The coroner will have to tell us that." West squinted at the corpse. "He certainly hasn't been sitting here over the weekend. The city hires private security for city buildings; don't they patrol the parking lots?" He looked to me for the answer.

"They're supposed to, but I don't oversee their work, the city manager does."

"I'd check into that."

"I plan to. Any clue as to why he died? I assume he died of natural causes—stroke, heart attack, something like that."

"Why would you assume that, Mayor?" Webb asked.

"The car was locked," I said. "It's a two-door hatchback. Only three ways in or out. It's like a locked-room mystery."

"Ever lock your car without realizing it?" Webb asked.

I felt stupid. It wasn't hard to lock and close a door. If someone had murdered the poor man in the Gremlin, the murderer could easily have locked the door after exiting. I looked to West for help, but he only offered a raised eyebrow.

"Do you need me for anything else?" I asked. It was time to get out of Dodge before I said anything else stupid.

"Not now," West said, "but I'm sure I'll have questions. I just don't know what they are yet."

I pursed my lips and tried to act unflappable in front of the boys. "I need you to keep me apprised, Detective. Everyone in city hall is going to have questions. I need information if I'm going to sound intelligent." I caught Webb grinning. He was enjoying an unspoken joke.

chapter 2

My prophecy had been correct. As the morning wore on, employees who worked in the city hall building stopped by to say hi. Some were coy, not asking directly but hoping I'd offer information about the police hubbub in the front lot. Others, especially council members, were more direct. I told them what I knew, which wasn't enough to make more than a column inch in the Santa Rita *Register*. We had only one local newspaper and at times I thought it was one too many. I admire the press. I think they do a great job—usually. Politicians like me need the members of the Third Estate, but it is an uneasy marriage. What sells papers isn't what gets people elected, and what brings in the votes seldom sells papers or ad space.

My office has two compartments: an outer office for my aide who was missing in action at the moment, and my inner sanctum, the place where I spend my days trying to pilot the good ship Santa Rita. I sat behind my wide cherry desk. It had been a gift from my husband before his death. It was big enough to serve as a bomb shelter and at times I've been tempted to use it as such. Behind me was a matching credenza which doubled as my computer workstation.

Seated opposite me in a burgundy leather chair was Council-man Larry Wu. He was one of my favorite people. In a world that could no longer define gentleman, Larry personified the definition. He was a man of moral courage, integrity, and simple speech. The difficulty with Larry was reconciling his round Chinese face with his mild Texas accent. Larry had spent his childhood years in Texas, moving to Santa Rita when his father's firm transferred him. He's been here ever since, building a well-respected accounting firm and serving the city as one of its representatives. Larry was one of my opponents when I ran for mayor. He came in third but has never uttered a disparaging word in my presence. He gives politicians a good name.

Seated with him was the best-dressed man in city hall, Titus Overstreet. I couldn't call Titus a friend—we never saw each other outside the office—but I admired him. He was the kind of man who showed strength through quiet words and concrete resolve. He was six foot two, trim and fit. I knew the last part because I saw him play basketball at a fund-raiser for the family of one of our firemen who died on duty. Titus loved basketball and had been a high school star. Good as he was, he wasn't good enough for the major universities and he knew it. He traded his dream of pounding the boards with the Lakers to get an MBA in marketing. He ran a public relations business when not handling city business. This day, he was dressed in a dark blue blazer, gray pants, ivory dress shirt with a red power tie. He also wore his trademark bright smile that beamed from his ebony face.

Both men had come to the office to ask about the police action out front. I asked them to stay for a few minutes for no other reason than to keep others from poking their heads in the door. Perhaps if we looked like we were in a meeting I might not have to answer the same questions.

"You want me to prepare something?" Titus asked.

"Something?"

"A press release. The man did die on city property."

"And not just any city property," Larry added, "city hall property."

"I suppose you're right, Titus," I said. "I'd appreciate you writing something up for the media. I assume you'll do the usual, 'We have every confidence in the police . . .'"

"We don't know that it's a crime yet," Larry observed. "It could be a death by natural causes. Still, you're right, we should be prepared."

"What's going on out front?" A new voice added to the mix. Jon Adler hovered at my door. He looked at Larry and Titus. "I didn't know we were having a meeting. Why wasn't I invited?"

A thousand responses began to buzz in my brain. I have a smart mouth. It's been my burden for as long as I can remember. For most of my life, I didn't care. I considered it just quick wit, but lately I've been trying to rein in my tongue and failing more times than not.

"Because it's hard to talk behind your back when you're in our face," Titus snipped.

Councilman Jon Adler was a pain. He caused his mother pain in childbirth and apparently found he had a gift for it. He was never happy unless he was unhappy and could find a reason for disagreeing with anyone about anything. He was as welcome as the flu. A thin, pinched-face man, he wore his emotions like a threadbare coat. An attorney, he too had run for mayor and almost won the seat. The thought chilled me. He had outspent me two-to-one but paid little attention to the only woman in the race. He attacked the other candidates with flourish and gusto. He was pit bull on the outside but easily backed down with a decent slap on the nose with a rolled-up newspaper.

"We're not meeting, Jon," I said, stuffing away the more cutting remarks that came to mind. "People have been trailing through my office for the last twenty minutes. Larry and Titus are serving as buffers."

"I'm not sure I believe that," Adler said.

Titus's wide smile tightened like a guitar string. There was no love lost between those two. "I suppose we should tell him. We're planning to overthrow the city and make Mayor Glenn queen. You get to be the court jester."

"Still trying to be funny, Titus," Adler shot back. "Keep trying. You'll manage to crack a joke someday."

"I know something I'd like to crack—"

"All right, gentlemen," I said. "As much as I'm enjoying this, I think I'd better get back to work."

"I'm sorry, Mayor . . . I'm sorry . . . Excuse me, please." I squashed a smile as Floyd Grecian, my aide for the last six months, finally arrived with his usual dramatic flare. "I was reading this morning and lost track of the time. I know I'm late. It won't happen again."

Floyd is a mixed bag of nuts. One moment he's brilliant and insightful, the next he's as lost as a puppy in the woods. Just twenty-two, he had graduated from California Baptist University in Riverside with a degree in business. A conflicted young man, he was trying to find himself and his place in the world. Right now, he was somewhere between entering the real estate market or being an actor in dinner theater. I hired him after I lost Randi Portman, something still too painful to dwell on. Floyd wasn't that interested in politics, but his father insisted that he get a job until he could figure out who he was going to be and what he was going to do. His father is the senior pastor of the church I started attending a few months ago. Hiring his son was a favor I was glad to do. Most of the time.

He pushed past Jon Adler who frowned so deeply I thought the corners of his mouth would touch his shoes. "Did you know that the police are out front and there's an ambulance and—" Floyd caught his foot on the leg of Titus's chair as he approached my desk. "Ouch! Sorry."

"Easy, kid," Titus said.

Floyd is a klutz. A lovable, efficient, and loyal klutz.

"Yes, I know," I said. "I found a dead man in his car."

"Wow," Floyd said. "Did you know he was in your parking spot?"

I looked past Floyd and saw Larry bite his lip in order to stifle the explosion of laughter that bubbled just behind his teeth.

"Yes, Floyd. I noticed that, too." I turned to the others. "Okay, you deadbeats. I enjoy a party as much as the next girl, but we've just started a new year and I have work to do. Come to think of it, so do you."

Titus and Larry rose, smiled, and exited. Jon hung around a little longer.

"Is there something I can do for you, Jon?"

"What are you not telling me?"

He didn't want to know. "You know, Jon, if paranoia was gold you'd be a wealthy man."

I didn't think it was possible but he frowned even more. Since he seldom left anyplace without the final word, he turned to Floyd. "If you were my aide, I'd fire you before you could take a new breath."

"He's not your aide, Jon, he's mine. Now stop fouling my air." The power of the tongue won out over the discipline of the mind. I wished I could feel sorry about the comment but I couldn't see the advantage of adding hypocrisy to my sins.

He left without a word but not before making a dismissive sigh like a parent too frustrated for words. I do my best to get along with him and his council buddy, Tess Lawrence, but I take two steps back for every one I advance. I just wish I didn't enjoy it so much.

"Thanks," Floyd said. "Sometimes I think I cause you more problems than I solve."

"What? Jon Adler. No need to apologize for that. You're not responsible for his attitude."

"I was referring to my being late—again. You're so punctilious, and I'm so oblivious to time."

Punctilious. I love that word. It rolls off the tongue. It also describes me pretty well. I hate being late, I don't like disorder on my desk, and I'm happiest when I can check things off my to-do list. "Maybe *you* need an assistant to assist you."

"Maybe I just need to grow up a little more." His shoulders drooped.

"Cheer up, Floyd. You've already done one good deed today. You annoyed Jon Adler."

"I don't think he likes me."

"He doesn't," I said, "but take that as a compliment."

"The guy that parked in your parking spot was really dead?" he asked.

"I'm afraid so."

"Then why the ambulance? A dead guy doesn't need an ambulance, right?"

I had forgotten that he mentioned an ambulance was at the scene. "That's true." Why was there an ambulance out front? Had someone gotten hurt? I immediately thought of West. My curiosity revved up. "I don't know, Floyd. Maybe . . ." Maybe what? "I think I'll go see." I stood and rounded the desk. Floyd reluctantly stepped to the side. He looked like he wanted to ask something but was weighing all the possible answers. "Sure, you can come with me."

"Really?"

"Yeah, really."

chapter

Most days I love being mayor. It adds order and purpose to my life. Other days, I would sell the whole thing to the first person who walked into my office with a dime in his hand. Fortunately, those days are rare. Most mornings my job compels me out of bed, draws me to the office where I deal with matters that would cure most insomniacs. Zoning laws, budgets, taxes, ten-minute meetings that last hours, documents written by state lawyers, county lawyers, and even federal lawyers pile up every week. In all the tedium, despite the infighting, I find a sense of purpose. And purpose is more than a luxury in my life.

I live alone. Not by choice. Well, partly by choice. Nine years ago, Peter Glenn, businessman, sales executive for his father's commercial flooring company, kissed me good-bye in the morning and drove to his death in Los Angeles. The city of Angeles was a familiar place to Peter. He was a principle in his father's firm, a company that manufactured flooring for large commercial buildings. Much of what they made ended up adorning the concrete floors of high-rise office buildings. It sounds boring, but it was the wind in

Peter's sails. He loved the business, the travel, the sales, and the interaction with clients.

It was after a meeting with one of those clients that two men decided they deserved Peter's yellow BMW Z3 Roadster more than he did. In LA they call it carjacking. Peter was not inclined to give things away, especially his car. He was not brave to the point of stupidity, but intimidation was not a natural response for him. His hesitancy cost him his life.

The call came at 10:12 that evening. To this day, I tense if the phone rings after dark.

Glenn Structural Materials carried a large life insurance policy on Peter. It paid off the house and gave me investment money to live on. Peter's father still pays his son's salary. He has for the last nine years. Twice a month an executive-size check arrives in the mail and no matter how much I protest, Peter's father continues to send them. "Twice a month," he once told me, "I can pretend that my son is still alive."

Murder kills more than one life.

We married young, Peter and I. I was still in my senior year of college at San Diego State University. San Diego was home for Peter. I majored in political science and he in business. He was movie-poster handsome, with eyes that seemed to give more light than they received. Our years together were good, but too few. People tell me that someday, I'll get over his murder.

No one gets over a murder.

So I live alone, in a three-thousand-square-foot house on the beach. It's a beautiful place, but even places of beauty have dark corners.

Peter was on my mind as I exited my office with Floyd following closer than my shadow. Almost a decade had passed and I'd adjusted to the solo life and to the fact that two hoods with a handgun widowed me, but certain things launched the old memories. Seeing a dead body in a car added to the list. But, like Floyd, I was eager to know what else was going on in the front parking lot. Less than half an hour had passed since I walked into the office and less than an hour since I had called Chief Webb, but my curiosity had reached the outer limits of its patience.

We walked down the corridor and into a larger area filled with a half-dozen desks, most empty. At one time, all the secretarial work was done by employees seated at these ugly gray desks. We remodeled the office wing of city hall a few years ago, expanding the council members' offices to include an additional office for one primary staff member. It increased privacy and made communications easier. Part-time and temp help used these desks. One of my greatest challenges was keeping down the cost of doing city business. It won me no awards and made a few enemies, but such things came with this job.

The open area bordered the lobby and was separated by a short pony wall. The wall was the demarcation line between the public world and the realm of civil servants. To one side of the large lobby was the city clerk's office; on the other side was the building department. These offices need direct public access. Council members' offices were off limits to the public unless they had appointments. Politics brings out the anger in some people. It is good to have at least a symbolic barrier between them and us.

A wide desk sat just inside the pony wall and seated behind it like a sentry in a castle tower was Fritzy, a gray-haired woman who had left middle age in her wake. Her real name was Judith Fritz and a sweeter woman never walked the earth. Her smile was wide, as were her hips and everything connected to them. In a world where magazine covers and movie screens dictated beauty, Fritzy was comfortable with who she was and how she appeared. A little dye from a box would have matched her hair to her dark eyebrows, but such things never seemed to cross her mind. Her beauty was self-generated and poured out of her like light streaming from a lighthouse. Two or three years ago, Jon Adler had the audacity to suggest that the city "might benefit from a younger, more attractive receptionist." The silence that filled the conference room was as cold as arctic water. No one spoke but a message was delivered so clearly that Jon never brought it up again. I hope Fritzy never changes.

"Good morning, Madam Mayor," Fritzy said as we approached the lobby. "Did I miss you when you came in?"

"Good morning, Fritzy. I came in the back way. Had to park in the back lot this morning." Members of the council and key staff can enter the building through a private entrance, allowing us to avoid whoever might be sitting in the lobby.

"There's a dead guy in the front lot," Floyd said with enthusiasm.

Fritz cringed, then looked at me. I rolled my eyes. Floyd's mouth often worked without the encumbrance of premeditation.

"A man passed away in his car last night," I said. "The police are investigating."

"Yeah, he parked in the mayor's spot, too," Floyd added.

"I didn't know," Fritzy admitted. "I thought I heard a lot of whispering around here."

Fritzy lives in an older part of the city and the shortest route to city hall brings her in over the back streets. She wouldn't have seen the front lot.

"I'm going out for a few moments, and I'm taking Floyd with me. Will you take messages for me?" It was an unneeded question—that was part of her job—but courtesy never hurts, or so my mother has told me many times.

"Of course. Be careful."

I smiled. I wasn't sure what I should be careful of, but it was always good to know someone cared.

The sun had climbed a few more degrees along its course when we pushed through the large golden oak doors and into the outdoors. The air smelled of ocean salt, and a gentle breeze was picking up from the west. It would have been another picture-postcard day in Santa Rita had it not been for the blight of death parked in my space.

We moved from the front of city hall along the meandering concrete walk that split the carpet of lawn that lay between the black asphalt of the parking lot and the arched mission-style building that served as our local seat of government. The lot was more crowded than when I had left. Just as Floyd had said, an ambulance had been allowed into the lot. A white van was parked to one side. Two men, both smoking, leaned against the Ford and looked bored. The county emblem was on the side of the van as was the word CORONER.

"Wow," Floyd said. "This is amazing."

"I want you to mind your p's and q's," I said. "Let's try and remember that someone has died."

"Yes, ma'am," Floyd said. His eyes were wide. It never ceases to amaze me what people find interesting.

I glanced over the scene. The Gremlin was still where I found it and even from twenty feet away I could see the lifeless driver.

"This is so cool," Floyd said. "Maybe I should be a cop."

"Is there anything you don't want to be?"

"Yeah, a butcher. I don't want to be a butcher. Too much blood and guts."

"But you think being a police officer ... never mind. I'm sure you'll settle on a career someday—maybe several careers."

"You're back," a familiar voice said. My stomach went soft. I ignored it and smiled.

"Detective West, this is Floyd Grecian, my new aide. Floyd, this is Detective Judson West."

"It's a pleasure to meet you." Floyd extended his hand. West took it.

"Mr. Grecian," West said with a nod. He turned to me. "I didn't expect to see you back so soon."

"Floyd's curiosity was swelling. What's with the ambulance?"

"Routine. We need someone to pronounce our victim dead, even if it's obvious."

"Ah. I hadn't thought of that," I said.

"Couldn't the coroner have done that?" Floyd asked.

West shook his head. "The position of coroner is an elected office in this county. He's an administrator, not a medical professional. The coroner's office hires medical examiners to do autopsies. Sometimes they come to the scene and declare the deceased ... well, deceased. In this case it was quicker to call in the paramedics."

"Oh," Floyd said. "So the guys by the van aren't coroners?"

"No, they work for the coroner. When we tell them it's okay, they'll take the body and turn it over to a medical examiner for autopsy. Then we'll have the car towed to the county forensics lab."

"Forensics?" I said. There was something he wasn't saying.

West looked at me, his expression set like concrete. "I was going to come and see you as soon as we had the body moved. You should know—our victim was murdered."

That chilled me. It was unsettling enough to find someone dead, but to find a murder victim. Old emotions that I kept chained in the dungeon of my mind broke free. "How—"

"The only details I can give you must stay with you. This is an active investigation. I want to control how information is released. Understood?" I said I understood. West shifted his eyes from me to Floyd.

"What?" He looked at West, then me, then West again.

I sighed. "He wants to know if you can keep your mouth shut, Floyd. No talking to the media, no talking to friends, no talking to anyone until Detective West says it's okay. Got it?"

"Yeah sure. I understand."

"I'll release a statement this morning. The media can do what they want with it." He looked back at the car. "I found bruising on his jaw. The bruises are consistent with fingers. It looks like someone broke the man's neck."

"Wow!" Floyd said again.

"You can tell that from some bruises on his jaw?"

"I can't be dogmatic about it. That's for the medical examiner, but a closer look at the head and neck has convinced me."

I didn't ask what he meant by that. I was afraid he'd tell me. "So this guy—"

"His name is Jose Lopez. He lives in Camarillo. I ran a wants and warrants on him but it came back clean. No real trouble with the law, one DUI about three years ago." I must have looked confused because West explained, "We found his driver's license in his wallet. The name matches the car's registration."

Of course. I chastised myself. "So this guy pulls into this lot, parks in my space, shuts off the engine, but leaves the key turned so he can listen to the radio, then someone attacks and kills him."

"That's what we have so far, but there are a dozen permutations and lots of questions."

"Like what?" I asked.

"The car for one. It's a two door."

"So?"

"It's hard to break a man's neck when you're seated next to him." West turned back to the car. "I'm not saying it's impossible, but it is unlikely. Usually such things are done from behind and since there's no sign of a struggle, it appears that the deed was done quickly, professionally."

"What radio station?" Floyd asked.

"What?" West furrowed his brow.

"The mayor said the dead man was sitting in his car listening to the radio. What station was he listening to?"

"I think the dial was set around 640, but I'd have to double-check. The car only has an AM radio. Why?"

Floyd shrugged. His mind often seemed to orbit a different star than most of us, and at times that had been useful to me. "Just curious. Maybe it was 620, that's close to 640. What time was he listening?"

"We think he died sometime after two this morning."

"Robby Hood," Floyd said. "Probably Robby Hood."

West shook his head. "Who is Robby Hood?"

"You're kidding, right?" Floyd said. "You know who he is, don't you, Mayor?"

Just what I love, a direct question certain to embarrass me. "I've heard of him. He does late-night talk radio, right?"

Floyd nodded. "Robby Hood is an institution in late-night radio, and he's right here in Santa Rita."

"Wait a minute," West said. "Is he the guy that does all the UFO and Bigfoot stuff?"

"He does a whole lot more than that. He explores remote viewing, government conspiracies, transdimensional beings, Mars fossils ... His show starts at eleven at night and goes to three in the morning. I listen to him a lot."

"Which explains why you're late to work so often," I added.

He blushed. "Robby Hood rivals Art Bell, George Noory, Whitley Strieber, Jeff Rense—"

"We get the idea, Floyd," West said. "What bearing would this have on the murder?"

He shrugged. "I don't know."

West shrugged. "I'll check the station, but I don't think it really matters if he was listening to country-western music or some guy talking about leprechauns." He walked away.

"I think I upset him," Floyd said. "I didn't mean to, I was just trying to be helpful."

"You didn't upset him. Detective West is a man of singular thought. While most of the world goes around with flashlight thinking, he's a laser beam. Most of the time, that's a good thing."

"Most of the time?"

"Forget it. I'm just mumbling. Let's get back to work." I started up the gentle grade and back to my office. I left the murder scene behind, but I had a feeling it wasn't going to leave me.

chapter 4

Returning to work after New Year's is always a challenge. This was the second week of January, and most of the employees were still weary from the joy of Christmas shopping and the fun of having distant families in their homes. Little work gets done. People in other agencies are difficult to contact, mail service slows to a crawl, and the minds of city employees are elsewhere. Coming back to reality is always a bit of a shock, one from which I am not immune.

I had spent the morning reviewing year-end reports from city agencies, memos complaining about the final changes in the budget, new regulations and laws that affected Santa Rita, and a dozen phone calls from people determined to be more efficient this year than last. Other people's New Year resolutions can be annoying. I know, I've pressed enough of mine on others to see the effects.

I had expected a call from the *Register* about the murder in the parking lot, but it never came. Maybe Doug Turner was still recovering from his holidays. Doug covers politics and crime for the *Register*. Big-city papers had different reporters assigned to such things, but the *Register* was too small for such luxuries. Doug, as the senior reporter, got to choose most of his assignments. If it involved city hall, he was sure to be the reporter on the scene. Today, he was missing in action. That was fine with me. I had nothing to offer anyway, although I had silently practiced my line: "We at city hall have every confidence in Chief Webb and his professional staff of officers. We are all wounded when such a horrible crime has been committed in our city and we are certain that justice will prevail." It was a good line. I was almost sad I hadn't been able to use it. But then the day was still young.

I left my office at twelve forty-five and wriggled my way north through traffic and the inevitable bottleneck just south of Santa Barbara and finally pulled into the parking lot of the White Gull restaurant. My meeting was set for one fifteen, and I was going to make it just in time. The White Gull is a trendy place nestled between two low-lying hills and facing a wide ribbon of sand that hemmed this edge of the ocean. Natalie and I were to dine outside, and the day was cooperating. The breeze was light and perfumed with salt from the ocean and juniper from the hillsides. A white medallion sun hovered in a cerulean sky, now free of the marbled layer of clouds that crept in almost every night and slinked away every morning by ten. The temperature was perfect for outdoor dining.

The White Gull boasts the best sushi bar in the area, but that means nothing to me. Sushi is just another word for bait. I have friends who have tried to correct my misguided conclusion, but I just can't get by the word "raw." I entered the lobby and was greeted by Victoria. I didn't know her last name—the name tag she wore revealed only a first name. I had seen her almost every Monday for the last two months.

"Good afternoon, Mayor," Victoria said. She was a short black woman with dark eyes and an infectious smile. "She's already here."

"Usual spot, I assume?"

"Yes. Allow me to seat you." Victoria was as efficient as they come. Bright, articulate, and the heart of a servant, she led me through the crowded dining room, weaving between tables and chairs with the grace of a ballerina. I was convinced she could do this blindfolded. Like many restaurants on the beachfront, the dining area was used to its fullest, with artificially distressed wood tables popping up from the tile floor like toadstools on a spring lawn. Only the minimum of space necessary was left for walking. More than once I had to turn sideways to scoot past diners. It was one reason we met outside. That, and our conversation could be kept private.

"There she is." Victoria strolled to a table in the corner farthest away from the noisy restaurant. "Shall I bring your usual drink?"

"If you're still making raspberry tea, then I'm still drinking it."

"We're still making it."

I said thank you and sat at what had become "our" table. I noticed that the other tables around us were empty. Victoria was conscientious—she was seating her other outdoor patrons at the far end of the concrete patio.

"For a moment I thought you were going to be late," Natalie said. "I was getting ready to call the papers."

"I'm never late. Well, almost never late."

Across the table from me sat a woman of stunning beauty: blond, brilliant blue eyes, round lips lightly touched with lipstick, and skin the color of cream. She wore a butterscotch Shaker sweater and simple pendant necklace that dangled down a single pearl. Her hair reached to her shoulders, covering ears that had not sported earrings for several years. I knew this because I knew Natalie Sanders well. We met last year under unusual circumstances and have become fast friends.

I shifted my chair in place which caused me to think of Natalie's chair. Her seat was different from mine. Hers had wheels and a powerful electric motor. While Natalie could maneuver her chair better than I could walk, the interior of the White Gull was not wheelchair friendly. Although it was legal, meeting all the California laws regarding handicapped access, it was nonetheless awkward. There was more open space on the patio so Natalie preferred it.

My tea arrived and Victoria—who always insisted on serving us herself—took our orders. I chose a shrimp salad and Natalie opted for New England clam chowder served in a bowl made of sourdough bread.

As soon as Victoria trotted off, Nat asked, "So, you getting back into the humdrum of civic life?" She raised a glass of Boston tea— tea and cranberry juice—to her lips. She used her right hand. Her left hand hadn't held anything for seven years.

"Not so humdrum today. A little more excitement than I care for."

"Really?" Her arched eyebrows elevated an inch. "Dish it, sister. You know I live vicariously through you."

I laughed at the last remark. People who didn't know Nat looked at her with pity. "Such a beautiful woman stuck in a wheelchair," they thought. I thought the same thing. But Nat was as smart as she was beautiful. She possessed the keen kind of thinking that intimidates we lesser mortals. A former television news anchor, she had garnered ratings that made news directors weak in the knees. And she was more than a talking head. She knew her stuff and stored it all away in a computerlike memory. The auto accident that left her legs little more than vestigial appendages and her left arm a badge of tragedy had done nothing to her mind. She left the news business to found a research company—a company of one employee—that services writers and the news media. Need a fact, call Nat. She was doing well for herself.

Nat had been a help to me last year. In fact, several people owe her their lives—me included. She had become my friend, my confidante, and my campaign manager. It was the last reason we had been meeting every Monday and talking on the phone several times a day. Over the next few months, that would increase.

"I'm waiting," she said.

"I found a dead man at city hall today." I said it as if it happened every week. "He was in my parking place."

"He was dead *before* you found him, right?"

"Of course, Nat. I wouldn't kill a man over a parking place." I sipped my tea.

"I guess not. It's not like it was a chocolate brownie."

"Now that, I might kill over." I filled her in on what details I had. It was a short description of events.

"What is it with you? Trouble seems to follow you like a fog."

"All I did was show up at work."

"Did the media come after you?" Now she was getting down to business. Anchorwoman with years of political reporting turned researcher turned campaign manager percolated to the top. She didn't ask directly, but she wanted to know what I said and to whom.

"I haven't heard a thing so far," I said. "I thought Doug Turner would be on my doorstep, but he's yet to show."

"His mother died last week. He's up in Oregon taking care of her final affairs."

"I didn't know that," I said, embarrassed. "Was it in the paper?"

"The obits. Even that's unusual since she lived out of state. I think they ran it as a way of honoring Doug. He's been with the paper for a lot of years."

"I'm sorry to hear about his loss." I thought of my own mother and of the heartache I'd feel at her passing. "I'll send a card or something."

"But no other media has come snooping around?" Nat pressed.

"No. I'm not too surprised . . ." I trailed off as Victoria appeared and set our lunch before us. We thanked her and she left. "I'm not surprised. There's no need to interview me. I know very little."

"But if they catch wind that it was the mayor of Santa Rita who found the deceased, they'll want more. It's a great hook: 'Mayor finds dead body.' I'd use it myself if I were still in the business. No, wait." She paused in thought. "'Congressional candidate finds body.' Yeah, that'd be the angle."

"You're ruining my appetite."

"You can take it. You're tough." She picked up the wide spoon in her right hand and shoveled some chowder into her mouth. I attacked my salad. Gentle music—some New Age strain—trickled out of nearby speakers, struggling to be heard above the music of the ocean waves. It was no competition. The sea had been playing its songs since creation, and it would be playing the same tune long after some developer tore the Gull down.

"Now that the holidays are over, I assume we're in for the big push," I said between bites of shrimp.

"Your life is about to get more complex. Running for mayor will look easy compared to this. So far, we've got the lead, or at least we think we do. Polls are iffy at this stage. Your name ID has gone up, but there are still too many people who don't know the name of Madison Glenn."

"Martin Roth is still on board," I said. Roth was the sitting congressman for our district, but he leaked his retirement early last year. Last November, he made it official. He was going home to stay, devoting his time to fishing and grandchildren. He carried a lot of political weight. If I was going to win, I needed his endorsement. He had implied that it was mine but implication was all I had. Politics is like white-water rafting: What you see on the surface is only part of the danger. It is the current and rocks below that are the real dangers.

"Roth will endorse you, unless Robert Till pulls some kind of coup." Robert Till was the county supervisor whose district covered much of the same ground as the congressional district. He frightened me. He was well entrenched with the Republican machinery, a good communicator with natural charm and a chin worthy of Kirk Douglas. In his last run for supervisor, he took 58 percent of the vote in the primary. That was an enormous number considering there were four other candidates. He also had money, and money was the lifeblood of a campaign.

"It's Till that scares me," I admitted. "The guy is a juggernaut. There are some in the party already touting him as the next congressman. I'm not going to get very far if I can't win my own party."

"You will. We've been doing the groundwork. Don't sell yourself short. You're the darling of the party. They'll back whomever they think will win. Besides, I've been studying Till. He has an exploitable weakness."

"You know my rules, Nat. Nothing underhanded or dirty. I agreed to run as long as I can do it in the cleanest fashion possible. No mudslinging, no name-calling, no investigations to find skeletons in the other candidates' closets."

"I know and what's more, I agree. My point is he's not a perfect candidate. There are no perfect candidates."

"I'm waiting for you to say, 'Present company excluded.'"

"I wish I could, but you know as well as I do that you have obstacles to overcome. The March primary is just a couple of months off. After that, the real work begins."

"If I win the primary."

"You'll win."

I loved her confidence but had a ton of doubts. "How can you be so certain?"

She shrugged. Just her right shoulder moved. "Being a pessimist doesn't help." She paused, played with her chowder, then added, "You have to stay out of trouble. The news reports last year may have helped you, but they could come back and bite us on the girdle. You were both victim and hero. That works once. Twice, and it looks contrived."

Last year two of my former campaign volunteers were abducted. One died. It's a long story and one filled with too many pains to relive. Each time I think of it and the friends it cost me, my stomach feels as if I had swallowed a handful of thumbtacks. "I can't change what has happened, Nat. It is what it is. I've learned to live with it, and my campaign is going to have to learn to get past it. I sure don't want to go through anything like it again."

"I understand. I'm talking about perceptions, not reality. They are not always the same. There's truth and perceived truth. Take your new interest in church things."

"What about it?" I was getting uncomfortable. Nat is a good enough friend that she doesn't sugarcoat things for me. She cares enough to speak the truth.

"After last year's crisis you started going church. I know it brings you comfort, but some are going to suggest it's just a ploy to get the Christian vote."

"It's not," I said, stronger than I intended. "I've tried to explain it to you."

"You have explained it. You've told me about your husband's conversion before his death, and you've told me all about Paul Shedd and his influence on you. That's all well and good. For one, I've seen you change over the months, and all of the changes are good. My point is that the next two months are going to be crucial. You are a contender in this, and that means you now have a target on your back. I've been studying Till's last two campaigns. He's a nice guy until he gets cornered, then he starts throwing wild punches. I think that's going to happen soon."

"I'll be ready for him." I looked down at my lunch. The shrimp was firm and tasty, the lettuce crisp, the dressing tangy. So why was I losing my appetite?

"I think you're ready for any attack on the issues, but are you ready for a personal attack? Are you ready for innuendos?"

"I just can't see Till doing that."

"It won't come from Till; it will come from some so-called citizens' group who pretend to speak for thousands. You know how this works. You've seen it."

I had seen it and Nat was right. Till could let others attack me while he stood on the sidelines looking shocked at such behavior. The third-party candidates could raise questions. One didn't have to be evil to lose votes; they just had to appear evil or stupid. Campaigns have been sunk on misspoken phrases, doctored photos, and rumors.

Nat continued. "All I'm saying is, get ready. I think you are good enough to frighten Till and the others. You know the first rule of campaigning: If you can't run fast enough to be lead dog, then shoot the lead dog."

"How poetic. I'll be ready."

"You also need to be careful. Take this dead man in the parking lot thing. It wouldn't take much more than a question like, 'Why is it violent crime follows Madison Glenn?' Or maybe, 'Can we expect law and order from a person who constantly finds crime on her doorstep?' You get the idea."

"I don't find crime on my doorstep. Just because—" Nat was looking at me and smiling. "I know, I know, perception and reality are not the same things. You don't suppose—no, that's too extreme, even for politics."

"What? That someone killed this man in your parking place to rob you of some votes? Doubtful, but not impossible. It would take one sick puppy to go that far."

"I seem to attract those kinds of puppies."

We finished our meal and sat looking at the waves tumble on the shore. An elderly couple walked through the sand while their cocker spaniel barked at the waves. They held hands as they walked. We were close enough to the beach for me to see that they were well into their sixties. They walked in silence, like only old couples could, confident that more was communicated in the touch of their hands than in any words that could be spoken.

I thought of Peter. Of our love. Of his violent death and how much I missed him. Something began to twist in me as the Kodak moment became a reminder that I would never walk along the beach with Peter again. Not as a young couple. Not as an old one.

I had become a person of faith. Nat had mentioned Paul Shedd and the image of him floated to the surface of my thoughts. He was a former banker who went through a midlife crisis, but instead of buying a fast sports car or trading his adorable wife in for a younger model, he bought the Fish Kettle, a restaurant on the Santa Rita pier. It was one of my favorite places.

Paul Shedd had kept a secret from me for years, uncertain how to handle it. Peter, always on the lookout for new business clients, had been invited to go fishing with a group of businessmen. They would rent a half-day boat, a charter that would take them deep-sea fishing and bring them back. He soon learned that more than fishing went on there. On the way out and on the way back, the men held a Bible study. I don't know how Peter felt about it. For some reason, we never discussed it. He went out several times with them and seemed to enjoy their company. Each month he went out with them and each time he returned, he seemed a little different. I was never able to put my finger on it, but it was noticeable.

At some point, he decided to entrust his life to Christ. Last year, I didn't even know what that meant. On his way out of town, he stopped by the Fish Kettle to let Paul Shedd know. Paul gave him a Bible, one he had been reading and writing notes in. It was something Paul did. Each year, he would buy a new Bible, make notes in it as he read, then give it away to someone. That year, he gave it to Peter. Peter left the restaurant and drove to LA. Within hours he would be dead.

The police returned his possessions to me in a cardboard box that I left unopened for eight years. Inside the box was the Bible Paul had given him. I now keep it in a drawer in my desk at home. When I have the courage, I remove it from the drawer, trying to ignore the bloodstains on the cover, and read a few of the notes Peter had read shortly before he died.

It was through that Bible and several long conversations with Paul Shedd that my life, my eternity, changed. Faith has strengthened me, enabled me, empowered me, but I still hurt for the love I lost.

"So how's your love life?" Nat asked.

She asked just as I raised my glass to my lips. I almost choked. "Excuse me?"

"Your love life, how is it?" She gave another one shoulder shrug. "I saw you gazing at that old couple out there."

"I wasn't gazing—"

"Yes, you were. It's my legs that are bad, not my eyes. You were getting misty."

"I don't get misty." I put my glass down and directed my eyes to the horizon. No couples out there.

"Yeah, you're a statue, all right. Granite, baby, that's you." Her words were playful, but like a pillow fight that gets out of hand, there was a little unintentional pain involved. "Is the good doctor still coming around?"

"Jerry?" I snickered. Dr. Jerry Thomas always made me feel good. He was kind, funny, attentive, and patient—most of the time.

A pediatrician, he had an office on Castillo Avenue. We dated in high school, but at that age I wasn't looking for love; I was looking for magic. We drifted apart. He married but his wife left him. She wanted more time than his physician schedule allowed. It left wounds. After Peter was killed, Jerry became more attentive, but never pushy. Over the years, he has tried to rekindle our high school love, but the flame has yet to take. Maybe my kindling isn't dry enough. I'm an optimist but Jerry is Olympic class in that department. "Yes, I see Jerry from time to time. We're old friends."

"Uh-huh." Nat grunted. "Friends are good, I guess. What about that handsome detective? I know you've got a thing for him. I can hear it when you speak his name."

"Oh, stop!" I had to laugh. "First, college kids have 'things' for one another. I'm far from old, but I'm well beyond those years. Second, we've never dated. He hasn't asked, and I'd probably turn him down if he did." *Probably. Perhaps. Maybe.* "I'm not sure a mayor should date a detective on her police department. You just gave me a lecture about how things appear to voters."

"Some things are more important than politics. Besides, after you're in congress, none of that will matter."

"That's what I like about you, Nat, you can direct my political and personal life all at the same time. You're starting to sound like my mother."

"I've met your mother. You'd be wise to listen to her."

I started to launch another quip her way when her face clouded over. I noticed her staring at the elderly couple as they and their dog meandered down the shore. I wasn't the only one wondering who would hold my hand when I was old.

chapter

The front parking lot was empty of police cars, and the green Gremlin was gone, towed to the county forensics lab I assumed. The yellow tape with the emblazoned words "Crime Scene—Do Not Cross" was still in place, a reminder that something inhuman had happened in the wee hours of the morning.

I wondered about Mr. Jose Lopez, the dead man in my parking stall. Did he have family? Were their children waiting for a father who hadn't come home the night before? For most, violence on television and in the movies was entertainment; it is something far different when it leaves the idiot box and camps on your doorstep. Jose Lopez was somebody's son, perhaps somebody's brother, and maybe someone's husband and father. The world had lost one more of its six billion people but went on as if nothing had happened.

After Peter was killed, I was amazed how little changed. My life was different, of course, as was his side of the family, but the rest of the world chugged on. Stoplights did their job, surgeries went on, baseball games were played, marriages took place, meals were served, and naps were taken. Except for those of us stitched to his existence, the rest of the world paid no attention.

When I was a kid and still living at home, I looked out our front window one Saturday afternoon. The house across the way was bustling with quiet activity. Cars I had never seen before were parked along the curb; people with faces I didn't recognize stood on the front lawn; people came and went. Of all the folks I saw, I noticed that I didn't see the woman who lived in the house. I assumed they were having a party, but it was unlike any party I had seen. My mother is a sensitive soul, looking worried when I mentioned what was going on out our window. She said, "Oh no," then told me to stay put. She exchanged a look with Dad, who looked puzzled but said nothing. Mom left the house and returned fifteen minutes later, pale and shaken. "It's Nick Gentry, Jennifer's husband. He was killed at work on Monday. The funeral was today. I didn't know. I didn't know." Mom shed silent tears.

None of us knew. Later I would learn Nick had fallen under his bulldozer in a freak accident. It was a horrible thought that kept me awake for several nights. When Monday came, I went to school just like the Monday Mr. Gentry died. It was the same school, the same teacher, the same classes, and the same lunchtime. Nothing was any different because Nick Gentry had died. Nothing for me anyway. That has always bothered me, so when I drove by the lot, I wondered whose life had been changed because of someone's cruelty twelve or fourteen hours before.

I parked in the rear lot and glanced at the police station, which shared parking with us. A sea of asphalt separated city hall from "crime central," as a friend of mine used to call it. I wondered if Judson West was seated at his desk, working on the case. I entered the office through the back door and worked my way down the hall and slipped into my office. Floyd was waiting for me.

"There's a man in the lobby waiting for you," he said.

I waited for more but nothing was forthcoming. "What kind of man?"

"What kind of . . . I don't get it."

"Who is he and what does he want, Floyd?"

"Oh, I see what you mean." He smiled. "I mean, there's only one kind of man, right? Your question confused me."

"Trust me, Floyd, there are many different kinds of men. What is he? Constituent? Salesman? What?"

"He said he was a reporter."

"From where?" I pressed.

"I . . . I didn't ask. Sorry."

I sighed. "Don't worry about it, Floyd. In the future, take his name, his business, and what he wants to see me about. Write it down so I can have it in front of me if I need it."

"I'll go ask him now."

"Wait. You said he was a reporter, right? Show him in but tell him I have only ten minutes."

Floyd was out the door a second later. He was a good kid with lots of promise, if I could only get him to focus. Pastor Lenny was going to owe me big time for hiring his kid. I walked into my office and found six phone messages written on pink While You Were Out forms. The notes were lined up in a neat little row, straight enough to please the most demanding obsessive-compulsive. I rifled through them quickly, putting each one aside for later. There was nothing pressing and for that I was thankful. Today already had enough stress.

I had just dropped my purse in the desk drawer when Floyd reappeared with a thick, tall man with cropped light brown hair. He wore a white T-shirt and faded jeans. He also wore a khaki photographer's vest, lined with pockets. I know most of the media reporters in the county, and I was sure I had never met this man.

"Madam Mayor," Floyd said, "this is Barry Harper, the reporter I mentioned."

"Come in, Mr. Harper." I stood and waved them in. "Can I get you anything? Water? Coffee? Soda?"

"No, thanks." His voice had an uncomfortable rasp that made me want to clear my throat. I judged him to be in his early thirties. He eyed me. I don't like to be eyed. He strode in like it was his office and took a seat before I had a chance to offer it. So much for courtesy. I continued to stand to see if he'd catch the hint. He didn't. I'm not formal by nature, but I think that certain social protocols should be observed when in a business or social setting. Inviting a guest to sit might be outdated, but it was something I valued. Much can be determined about a person's character by the manners they show. So far, I hadn't seen any manners.

"If you'll sit down we can start," he said.

My blood temperature rose. I sat. Slowly. "Floyd, I want you to join us."

"Really?"

I stuffed a sigh. "Yes, really."

"That's okay," Harper said. He pulled a small notepad from his rear pocket. "I won't need him."

I began to wonder how many votes I'd lose if I strangled him right where he sat. My patience thinned. "I wasn't asking for your benefit, Mr. Harper. What media did you say you were with?" Floyd started in, stopped, returned to his desk, and reappeared with a notepad of his own.

"I didn't." He shifted his weight. "This morning a dead body was found on your property. Do you have any comment?"

"The tape recorder," I said softly.

He shifted his weight again. "What?"

"Take the tape recorder out of your vest pocket and turn it off."

"Can't you see that I'm using a notepad—"

"Floyd, call security."

Floyd was on his feet before I could finish the sentence. At times, Floyd had concentration problems, but he was paying attention now. He reached for my phone.

"Okay, okay, ooookaaay," Harper said. "No need to get nasty about it." He reached into one of the front pockets of the vest and removed a small tape recorder. He turned it off. "I don't know why you're so touchy about a little thing like that. Reporters use them all the time."

"Not covertly. You're being deceptive. I don't like deception." He started to return the recorder to his pocket. "Let's just leave that on the desk for a while, shall we?" He frowned then set the device down.

"You're being unreasonable. Can we get started now?"

"Who do you represent?"

"I told you, I'm a reporter."

I held my words and waited.

"I'm with the *Register.*"

I almost laughed out loud. The *Register* wasn't always my friend, but it was always professional. I had never known them to play games when it came to the news they reported. "You're with the *Register*? The Santa Rita *Register*?"

He blinked, and there was a hitch in his answer. "Yeah."

"How long have you been with them?"

"I'm . . . I'm new."

"So if Floyd calls over there, they'll know who you are?" I pressed.

"They should . . . they might. I'm a stringer."

That explained it. He wasn't an employee but a freelancer trying to find a scoop. "Let me guess, you've been monitoring police transmissions on a scanner and thought you might beat everyone to the punch."

"Something like that." He squirmed. I shouldn't, but I get a small thrill watching reporters fidget. They had put me in that position often enough.

"Okay, Mr. Harper. I'm all for the entrepreneurial spirit so I'll let you stay, but know this: If you ever want to interview me again, you will do it as a professional, and you will be aboveboard with me at all times. Understood?"

He didn't answer. His expression told me he was not used to being on the receiving end of such conversations. Maybe he didn't like being told off by a woman.

"Don't press me, Mr. Harper. I am a woman of patience but the meter is reading close to empty. Do you want to continue or not?"

Just as I thought he was about to blow his second chance, his face softened. "Yes, please."

Please! There was courtesy hidden in the young man after all. "You had a question for me."

"A body was found on your property today. Do you have a comment?"

I sighed for dramatic effect but refrained from shaking my head in disgust. "You're asking about the dead man in the car?"

"Of course."

"First, Mr. Harper, he was found on city property, not *my* property. The citizens of Santa Rita own city hall and every other piece of city property including parks, the pier, police station, fire stations, and much more. So no, I didn't find a body on my property, I discovered a body in a car parked in the front lot of city hall."

"But you are the one who found it?"

"I discovered *him,* Mr. Harper, when I came to work this morning. I came in a little early and was the first in the lot. Most of our employees park in the rear lot."

"What can you tell me about the man?" He wrote a note in his book.

"Nothing."

"You won't tell me anything about the deceased?"

This had just moved beyond the ridiculous. "I can tell you that I didn't know him, had never seen him to my recollection, and I have no idea how he came to be parked in the front lot."

"What about his name?"

"I think you're confused, Mr. Harper. Maybe it's just your inexperience showing. I'm the mayor of Santa Rita, not a detective. Those questions should be asked of the detective in charge, not of me. Go ask them."

"I did. They kicked me out."

"Really. Imagine that."

"All right then, maybe you could tell me what you plan to do about the spike in crime we're seeing in Santa Rita."

"To what spike do you refer?" The crime rate in our city had been the same for the last ten years. Considering what other cities were going through, that was a remarkable thing.

"Murder for one. Here is yet another murder, and it happens right on your doorstep."

"How do you know it was murder?"

"Detective West told me."

"Before he threw you out?" He nodded. "How many murders have there been in our city over the last twelve months, Mr. Harper?" He said nothing. This time I did shake my head. "Santa Rita is one of the safest cities in California. On average there are two murders per year within city limits. That's two murders in a city of 125,000. Escondido had five murders last year, Corona eight, Lancaster eighteen. All cities of roughly the same size as ours. The number of violent crimes in Santa Rita was just 160 for the last twelve months. Other cities our size number seven or eight times that. So I ask again, what spike in crime?"

"You seem to know your numbers, Ms. Glenn—"

"That's Mayor Glenn, pal." A new voice spoke, one with an edge to it.

I looked up to see Doug Turner standing in the doorway. He was dressed in black slacks and a striped dress shirt punctuated with a gold tie. Every time I had seen the *Register*'s star reporter he was dressed nicely but always seemed as if he had just stepped off a grueling transcontinental flight. There was always something amiss with his attire. Today, his tie hung to the right of midline.

"She's the mayor; it's her job to know facts about the city."

Harper jumped at Turner's words.

"I don't appreciate you horning in on my job."

"I'm ... I'm freelance. I can interview anyone I like."

"Yes, you can," Turner said, turning up the heat in his voice, "but you need a place to publish it, and I can make sure the door to the *Register* stays locked to you." He looked at me. "Is that his?" He pointed at the tape recorder. I nodded. Turner picked it up and tossed it at Harper. "Take a hike. And don't use the name *Register* again unless you are on the payroll."

Harper rose. "You're just jealous that I got here first."

"Jealousy is the fear of losing what you have. Trust me, there's nothing about you that makes me jealous."

Harper started to speak, but thought better of it. Turner was a gentleman—most of the time. He did have his limits. Apparently he and Harper had some previous tension between them. Harper walked from the room and Turner turned to me. "I apologize, Mayor. Guys like him crawl out of the woodwork every now and again."

"You don't know him?"

"Never met him before, but the paper occasionally uses stringers."

"Just how long have you been listening?" I asked.

He looked chagrined. "Just a few minutes. Long enough to pick up on his attitude. I know I've been a pain in your side a few times, but I like to think I've been a professional pain."

"You have always been that," I said. "You know Floyd, right?"

"We've talked a couple of times over the last few months." He did the male head-nod thing, and Floyd returned it. Unlike Harper, Turner remained on his feet until I offered him a seat.

"I just heard about your mother. I'm sorry," I said.

His eyes softened, and he pressed his lips. "She was a good woman. Gave me a love for the printed word."

"Was she a reporter, too?"

"No, a simple housewife and mother in the days when that was considered a noble career. I guess that's changed. We buried her last Thursday."

"I would have sent flowers had I known." I was feeling guilty.

"No need. I wanted to keep things simple. Death happens to one hundred out of every one hundred people. Her time came, and some-day my turn will come."

"'It is appointed for men to die once, and after this comes judg-ment,'" I mumbled to myself.

"That sounds familiar," he said. "Shakespeare?"

I looked up, surprised that I had spoken loud enough to be heard. "It's from the Bible. Book of Hebrews, I think. I heard it in church the other day."

"Reading the Bible these days? I didn't know you were a reli-gious person."

"Neither did I."

The conversation fell silent for a few moments. "When did you get back?"

"This morning. I went into the office late and heard about . . . your find."

I looked at Floyd. "Thanks for staying, Floyd, but you can get back to work now. I think I can handle Mr. Turner." I smiled. Floyd left and I turned my attention to Turner. "I don't have anything to add. I really don't know much."

"I was talking to Detective West. He gave me what he could. He also told me Harper had been by and made a nuisance of himself. I hustled over here."

"I appreciate it. He was getting on my nerves."

"I could tell." He pulled a notebook from his shirt pocket. I didn't ask if he had a tape recorder. He usually did but didn't always use it. "I just need to verify a few things, if you don't mind, and then see if you have a statement to make." He recited what West told him and I acknowledged its accuracy, then I gave a line or two about the city's confidence in the police department and its highly trained professionals to bring the matter to a speedy resolution. It wasn't poetry but it was succinct. The more succinct a statement, the less chance of it being misquoted or edited.

He wrote everything down, then closed the notebook. "How's the campaign going?"

"Great. We're on target, the organization is working like clockwork, the polls are good."

"Wish it was over?"

"Off the record?"

"Of course."

"Yes. I've always enjoyed campaigning, but this is far more laborious than I anticipated." I was more open with Turner than I would be with other reporters. In some ways, I owed my campaign to him—or at least my decision to run. Months ago he had asked me if I was considering a run for congress. I had become evasive. Finally, Turner said, "Why is it that every time a politician is thinking of running for higher office they deny it? It's like they're ashamed of wanting to do more for the community." I didn't let him know it at the time, but his words stuck with me, haunted me.

"Glad to hear it," he said, then stood. "Again, I apologize for Harper. With his attitude, he'll never make it in the business. Watch out for him. I don't think he has both oars in the water, if you know what I mean."

I did know.

chapter 6

There are only a handful of people I allow to have my phone number. Home is sacrosanct; a place removed from every other place. While I often work from my home, it is not a place of business, and I work hard to make sure it never becomes one. Someone once said that he refused to have a phone in his home because he never "saw the sense in having a bell in the house that any idiot could ring at any hour of the day." There are times when I agree with that. So the number of people who can dial me direct is as limited as I can make it. My parents, my brother and sister, a few friends like Dr. Jerry Thomas, each member of the council—that was a needed concession—the city attorney, the city manager, the chief of police, and that's about it. Detective West also has the number, something he needed last year when he was investigating a painful event in my life. Those people also have my cell number.

One other person can ring me at home: Fritzy.

When my husband was killed, the call came at 10:12 in the evening. I've always hated late-night calls, but now I was paranoid. This call came at 2:23 a.m. No call at that hour could be good. The ring was shrill and sharp as if it had edges. It coursed through me like an electrical shock. I bolted upright in bed, still too groggy to know if I heard right or dreamed the disruption.

It rang again, and my heart thumped in double time. I began to hope it was a wrong number. At that hour, I'd be happy if it were a drunk too bleary-eyed to punch the keys of his cell phone in the right order.

I tossed back the covers and swung my bare legs over the edge of the bed. The phone rested on a nightstand just to my right. All the emotions of the night Peter died flooded my mind. That was many years ago; that was just yesterday. I blinked hard several times, reached for the light on the stand, and pulled the chain. I didn't need the light, and upon retrospect, I was stalling. The third ring had started when I snapped up the receiver.

"Yes," I croaked. It was impossible to sound professional and ladylike when yanked out of a deep sleep. There was no answer. In the background I heard someone sniff. "Who is it?"

"Mayor?" A soft, tiny, bruised voice.

"Who is this?"

A few feet from my bed stands a French-style oak vanity with a full-length mirror. It was a wedding gift from Peter's parents. The mirror bounced my image back. Lit by only the forty-watt bulb in my bedside lamp, I struck a ghostly reflection. My face seemed pale as if patted with pancake batter and the individual hairs on my head had decided to chart their own courses.

"Mayor ... I'm sorry ... I ... it's Judith."

Judith? My memory tumbled in my brain like rocks in a dryer. "Judith who—Fritzy?" Yes, it had to be her, but I couldn't recall the last time she referred to herself by her given name. She had always been Fritzy.

"Yes, Mayor. It's me. It's ... horrible. I don't know who to call ... what to do ... I shouldn't have bothered you ... not at this hour ..."

She trailed off in tears. I have known Fritzy for over a decade, and I had never seen her cry or ever heard her complain. Her optimism made Pollyanna seem mired in a PMS funk. She brightened a room when she entered. Not even chronic malcontents like Jon Adler and Tess Lawrence could rock her boat.

The room chilled. "What is it, Fritzy? What's happened?"

"I . . . It's . . ." Sobbing swallowed her words.

"Is Jim there? Let me talk to Jim." Fritzy had been married to the same man for nearly forty years. They had tied the knot right after high school and right before he went into the navy.

"He . . . he . . ."

An arctic wind swept through my soul, and I clenched the phone so hard I feared it or my fingers would break. My stomach turned, roiling with bitter acid. "Oh, Fritzy. I don't . . . Where are you? Are you at home?"

"Yes, but—"

"I'm on my way."

"You don't have to . . . I didn't mean to be a bother, I just . . ."

"Make some coffee, Fritzy, I'll be there in a few minutes."

"Okay."

I hung up. The coffee was a stupid thing to say, but I know where it came from. The night I learned of Peter's murder, I walked into the kitchen, made coffee, then dissolved into tears. I spent the rest of the night sitting at the dining room table sipping coffee I didn't want and couldn't taste. Sometimes a woman just needs something to do, even if it doesn't need to be done.

I dressed in the closest thing at hand—a blue jogging suit. I don't jog; I walk on a treadmill and most days I hate it, but I do it anyway. Usually, I work out in a pair of shorts and a cotton T, but it was the wee hours of the morning and although our temperatures are mild, it would still be cool at this hour. I was already cold, but that had nothing to do with the weather.

Less than five minutes after I hung up, I was backing my SUV out of the garage onto the street at the front of my house. The night was still. Even the typical sea breeze was missing, as if it had stopped to bow its head. The moon hovered high, reflecting an ivory glow. I had left my window down when I pulled into the garage, and the sound of gentle surf stroking the shore just a few yards from my back door wafted in on salt air. I rolled up the window, shutting out nature's lullaby, and crammed my emotions into the mental lockbox where I keep things too disturbing to face.

I gunned the engine.

Fritzy lives "on the hill" as we say around here. Santa Rita begins with the beach on the west, a wide expanse of sandy shore, a wide strip of land that runs from the south and through our city limits in the north. Large, expensive houses occupy most of that property. There, people live what most assume is the ideal California life: sun, sea, and sunburn. Thanks to great financial planning on Peter's part and his ability to sell ice to Eskimos, I lived in one of those homes. It was far too big for a single woman to occupy, but I refuse to give it up. It was Peter's place, and I plan to live my days out there.

The rest of Santa Rita is on and around the low coastal hills. US Highway 101 bifurcates the city. The expensive homes dot the coastline; the affordable homes are in subdivisions on the slopes overlooking the ocean or tucked away in one of many narrow valleys. Fritzy's home was nestled in one of the valleys, one of 120 or so homes built in the 1970s. The subdivision was called Equine Park. It was a dumb name, because the lots were too tiny to stable anything larger than a beagle. Fritzy's home was on the south side of the street. In the moonlight I could see blue-gray trim, the white shutters, and the beige walls. Rosebushes lined the driveway. A single light shone from the living room window.

I pulled up the drive, flashed my bright lights in the window, and hopped from the car as if I were eager to do the job before me. I wasn't. By the time I stepped up to the front stoop, Fritzy had already opened the door. She was draped in a flower print robe, and fuzzy, pink slippers adorned her feet. Protruding from the bottom of the robe was a pair of thin legs that looked like twigs ready to snap. A pair of yellow pajama bottoms covered the legs to the middle of her calf. She held her robe closed with her left hand, an act that had less to do with modesty than with needing something to hang on to. With her other hand she covered her mouth. That hand was shaking. I felt ill.

I moved quickly, as if haste could lessen the pain or change the circumstances. Words formed in my mind but I wasted them, letting them dissolve back into nothing. I took Fritzy in my arms and pulled her to my chest. I laid my head on her mat of gray hair and determined to be strong for my friend.

Judith "Fritzy" Fritz convulsed into waves of weeping. She was a geyser belching out shock and sorrow. I still didn't know what happened, and at the moment it didn't matter. I had to be there for her. I had to be strong, sturdy, and resolute. I had to be the rock she could depend on.

A second later I dissolved into tears.

chapter 7

We sat at a round oak dining table, each ignoring the coffee cups before us. There was enough bitterness in our bellies. It had taken a full five minutes before we could move from the doorway and into the house. The weeping had stopped, not because the situation had changed but because the tank was empty—at least for now. Once inside the small home, I closed and locked the door behind us, poured the coffee that Fritzy had dutifully made, and then led us to the dining room table.

The house had that wonderful lived-in look, the look that can only be achieved by a family who had spent years within the walls. I had been to Fritzy's house on several occasions, usually to celebrate a birthday. She liked to celebrate her birthdays at home. The furnishings were nice but well worn. Inexpensive paintings gathered from decades of marriage and flea market sales hung on the walls. An old china hutch held its place in the dining room, proudly displaying teacups, antique plates, and knickknacks.

"He called first, then came by." Fritzy wiped her nose with a tissue.

"Who?" I sipped my coffee. It had been made in a percolator, which I assumed had followed the family for decades. Do they still make percolators?

"That nice detective," she said. "The one who is so interested in you."

Fritzy had been trying to play matchmaker for me for years. It had become second nature to her. I doubt she realized what she said. "Detective West?"

"Yes. He was very kind. Very supportive. Very . . ." I reached across the table and touched her hand. It was the only thing I could think of to do. "I called you as soon as he left."

I waited, mustering the courage to ask. "Can you tell me what happened? If not, I understand and—"

"It's okay. I called you, remember?" She smiled. There was no joy or humor in it. "Jim was working late. He does that sometimes when people need their airplanes in the morning. You know how some of the big business types are."

I nodded. Jim Fritz was an aircraft mechanic. Fritzy had told me he had enlisted in the navy a few weeks before they had wed. It was a rough way to begin a marriage, but he hadn't wanted to go off to basic training without first committing to her. He was one of those men who understood nobility. The navy trained him to fix airplanes and jets. Twenty-two years later, he retired and started his own company. It was a small company, just him and one other mechanic, but that was the way Jim wanted it. He had his retirement pay, his home was paid for, and he just wanted to keep his skills up. He set up shop at Willis Jackson airport, the private airport at the south end of the city. It was named after a local fighter pilot killed in Korea.

"Yeah, I know," I said. "They want their planes, and they want them right away."

She gave a weak nod. "He called from the shop and said not to wait dinner for him, that he was going to be real late, that he had a rush job come up." She shook her head. "I've seen him spend the whole night down there." A tear fell to the table.

"He always struck me as diligent."

"He was." She choked on *was*. I knew what that was like. Past-tense verbs taste bad. "Security found him ... he was sitting in the plane, and he was ..."

There was no need to finish the sentence. "Take your time, sweetheart. Quit anytime you like. I understand."

"I know you do. Maybe that's why I called you. I didn't know who else to call."

"You did the right thing." Fritzy and Jim never had children. I never asked why. Maybe because I didn't want to answer the same question.

"You've been through this. You know what it's like."

"It's hard to lose a husband," I said. It was stating the obvious, but sometimes the obvious needs to be stated.

"Not just lose, Mayor." She cut her eyes away to see what only she could see. "To have a husband murdered."

The words were a punch to the stomach. My spine stiffened. "What are you saying, Fritzy?" I had assumed that Jim had had a heart attack or stroke.

"Detective West said ..." Tears now streamed down her wrinkled cheeks and fell on her robe as if watering the flower print. "He said my Jim had been murdered."

The natural inclination is to ask how. How was he murdered? Why was he murdered? What are the details? But I knew enough from my own experience not to raise the question. That would come at the right time.

"I'm sorry," I said. "I was assuming that his heart ... or something."

She shook her head slowly and kept shaking it as if her neck had lost control. "They found marks. His neck was broken."

Again she melted into tears.

I sat frozen to my chair.

chapter

I wandered into my office at nine thirty, a full ninety minutes after I normally do. I was late and for once, I didn't care. I had called the office from my cell phone and left a message for Floyd. I spent the early-morning hours sitting with Fritzy and making a few calls once eight rolled around. Fritzy was as truly alone as a woman her age could be. Jim was her only family. She did have a few friends. I called one named Betty, who agreed to come over and take my place for a while. She brought sleeping pills, but I made her promise to put them away and not to play doctor. Fritzy was in the early part of her sixth decade. I judged her friend to be about the same age except, unlike Fritzy who was as sharp today as she ever was, her friend seemed to have dropped too many mental bread crumbs along the road of life. Nonetheless, she appeared to have a good heart. So I left Fritzy in the care of the overly perfumed next-door neighbor, Betty.

I parked in the rear lot and came in the private entrance. I told myself no lies. I did so because I didn't want to look at Fritzy's empty desk. I was sleepy, worn, and edgy. I was not at my best. I strolled down the corridor, my eyes fixed on the terrazzo tile and my mind ricocheting around in my skull. Just before I stepped through the door into the outer office, I heard, "Well, where is she? When will she be here? Don't you know anything?"

It was *the* voice—the discordant, piercing, prickly voice of Councilwoman Tess Lawrence—the female version of Jon Adler. To be fair, Jon may have been the lawyer, but Tess had twice the brains and half the soul. Given a choice between listening to her and dragging my knuckles on a cheese grater, I would gladly choose the latter. I walked through the door.

"I asked you a straightforward question, Mr. Grecian—"

"You asked him three questions, Tess," I snapped. "If you want answers, you should speak to me."

"Well, you did decide to show up for work," the weasel said. I glared at her. Tess was a stately woman with short white hair held in place with some kind of industrial-strength gel. She was a couple of years older than me, an inch or two taller depending on the shoes she wore. I felt like a teenage girl in the shadow of a glamorous older sister. She was wearing a coral jacket and skirt with a white blouse. As usual, she looked like she had stepped out of a Nordstrom catalog. "And you're late, you who insist that every meeting start the precise moment the second hand sweeps by the appointed time." She paused and drank in my appearance. "What did you do? Sleep under the pier? You look like death warmed over."

"Go away, Tess," I grumbled. "I have a pain in my head, I don't need one in my—" I stopped, once again trying to tame my tongue. It remained a battle. My mouth has been my greatest asset and a constant liability. Some days I'm more successful than others. I had a feeling this was going to be the one of my less successful days.

"No wonder city hall is falling into disarray. Its leader is as slipshod as some of its employees."

I walked past the iceberg in panty hose and plopped down behind my desk. Tess followed. "What do you want, Tess?"

She folded her arms across her narrow chest and gave me a hard don't-you-take-that-tone-with-me look. "It's about tonight's council meeting. As you know, we still elect the deputy mayor from the council. Since this is the first meeting since the new year began, we should address that issue straightaway."

"Straightaway, eh?" I wrestled down a smirk. Tess must be watching the BBC again.

"Yes, straightaway. Councilman Wu served last year. Councilman Adler thinks I should have the position—"

"I wonder where he got that idea," I mumbled.

"What?"

"Nothing. You want me to cast my vote for you, too. Is that it?"

"I imagine Wu will nominate Titus Overstreet."

I already knew that for a fact. "So your fear is that Jon will nominate you, Titus will nominate Larry, and the vote will be split, leaving me to cast the deciding vote. Have I got it right?"

"Well, yes. Put succinctly, that's it."

"I doubt you have anything to worry about." The thought of Tess as deputy mayor made me feel funny inside—like the early stages of the flu.

She seemed stunned. "You're going to vote for me? I mean it makes sense and it would send a strong message having two women at the helm."

"You wouldn't be at the helm, Tess, and you know that. The role of deputy mayor is ceremonial and only has policy implications in my absence. And no, I plan on voting for Titus."

"You said I didn't have anything to worry about."

"I said I doubted that you have anything to worry about. Titus is too much of a gentleman to vote for himself. It is his most endearing attribute but also one of his weaknesses. I imagine he'll abstain."

"That would leave the vote split. You and Larry on one side; Jon and myself on the other. What happens then?"

"Then the council is hung, and we don't have a deputy mayor."

"Our rules of order demand that we have one," she retorted.

"Yes, they do. I suggest you go make nice with Titus and Larry. Mend a few fences—mend a lot of fences."

"There's no chance you'd vote for me?" For the briefest of seconds, I thought I detected a touch of hurt in the statement, but then it was gone.

"Not today, Tess. Not after I caught you harassing my aide."

A frown scarred her face. I could see her jaw clench. "You need help to run this city, Mayor. You need someone who isn't afraid to speak their mind, someone who is willing to call people on the carpet for neglecting their duties."

"This city doesn't need Big Brother–Big Sister peering over everyone's shoulders. We have good staff and employees."

"Really? You mean like Ms. Fritz? You know she hasn't shown up for work today—"

"Tess—"

"The front desk is vacant. The public has a right to expect a proper greeting—"

"Tess—"

"Instead they get an empty desk." She bared her teeth. I had never seen Tess so angry, and I knew it had nothing to do with Fritzy. "I'm going to speak to her the moment she arrives. We should have forced her to retire years ago. A woman her age—"

"Shut up." Heat rose up my neck and cheeks. It must have been visible. Tess's tirade stumbled.

"What did you say to me?"

"I told you to shut up. You know, close your yap. Zip it. Stop talking."

"You can't talk to me that way."

"I just did and trust me, there's a whole lot more I'm not saying." I stood and leaned over my desk. Tess took a step back. "The city employees answer to the city manager, not to you. Clear? You will not speak to Fritzy. You try and scold her, and I'll be there the first second after your first word, and you won't like it."

She opened her mouth, but nothing came out. My lack of sleep and my raw nerves had stripped away some of my control. I was a half second away from bounding over the desk and dribbling the woman around the office like a basketball. The feeling was out of character for me, but my emotional engine was running hot. I was beginning to frighten myself. I looked past Tess and saw Floyd standing just outside the door. His face was white.

I swallowed hard and forced myself to sit down. "Fritzy won't be in today. She won't be in for several days." Tears were percolating to the top again. I couldn't tell if I was feeling sorry for Fritzy or myself or was just crying mad. "Her husband died last night. He was murdered. She called me early this morning."

Tess worked her mouth again, but nothing was forthcoming. Her gaping maw made me think of a bass.

"I'll make sure that we get someone to cover the desk this morning."

"I . . . I didn't know." She lowered her gaze.

"Tess, you need to learn to find out the facts before you start working your mouth. Now go away."

"Mayor—"

I raised a hand. "Just go away."

Tess left without another word. I considered it a miracle. I leaned back in my chair and closed my eyes. My neck was tightening like a watch spring and my body felt like rigor mortis was setting in.

"You okay?"

I opened my eyes. Floyd, still white faced, stood in the doorway. "I've been better."

"Poor Fritzy. Murdered?" He shook his head.

"Yes. That's what she told me."

"What can I do?"

I leaned forward. "I'm spent, Floyd." I looked at my watch. I was ninety minutes late to work and had only been on the scene fifteen minutes, yet I felt like I had put in double overtime. "Make a tour of the office. Tell everyone, council members, city staff, city hall employees, that I want to meet with them in council chambers in thirty minutes. I have to announce this, and I want to do it just once."

"Will do." He started to turn.

"But first, see if you can get your father on the phone. I need his professional help."

chapter

I stood, not behind the raised, curved council bench but before it. I wanted to be on the same level as those who gathered at my request. The council chamber was home to me. Every Tuesday, we held public meetings here. Today, however, the meeting was private.

A few arrived looking shell-shocked. The word had spread before I could make the formal announcement. I had Tess Lawrence to thank for that, I'm sure.

I wasted no time in delivering the news about Jim Fritz. Everyone—with the exception of Jon and Tess—loved Fritzy. It was best to pour out the news quickly and let each person deal with it in his own manner. On the first row sat the council members, the city attorney, city manager, city clerk, and other executives of Santa Rita. The seats of the council chamber were filled with various receptionists from other departments, secretaries, inspectors who were still in the building, and others. They took the news as well as anyone could in that environment, but I saw tears in the eyes of some. Others crossed themselves, some sat rock still as if I had been Medusa and turned them to stone.

I watched as what had started as a chattering group of employees shuffled back to work with the shocking news still simmering in their brains. As the others left, Titus and Larry tried to comfort me. They were good men. Floyd stood nearby looking every bit the broken reed.

"What else can we do?" Titus asked. I looked into his dark face and saw sincerity and concern.

"We should do something for Fritzy. Flowers and . . . and . . . I don't know."

"I'll take care of that," Titus said. "If she needs any help with . . . you know . . . costs, just let me know."

"That goes for me, too," Larry added, his Oriental face revealing his sorrow.

"I promised to help her make arrangements," I said. "The next few days are going to be especially hard."

"I assume she has leave on the books," Larry interjected. "If not, I'd be happy to make a motion in tonight's council meeting that we extend some time with pay for her."

"It's a good thought," I agreed. "I'll check with Fred and see if that's legal. If not, we'll find another way of getting it done." Fred Markham was our city attorney.

A chipper tune filled the air: a tinny Mozart piece. I glanced at Floyd who fumbled for his cell phone. He said a few things, then directed his attention to me. "My dad's here."

chapter 10

My first inclination was to ask Floyd to find his father and show him to my office, but I changed my mind. The council chambers were empty now and I didn't want to go back to my office. I kept seeing Fritzy's empty desk.

"Madam Mayor." A booming voice echoed in the empty assembly room. I turned to see a deeply tanned man with stark white hair enter through the private corridor reserved for city staff. He had broad shoulders, dancing blue eyes, and a dimple in his chin. He wore a light gray knit turtleneck and a blue blazer. His pants were the same shade of gray as his shirt. His smile dimmed the lights.

"Pastor Lenny, thank you for coming on such short notice."

"No problem." He approached and shook my hand. "You know we ministers only work on Sundays. The rest of the time is spent on the golf course."

"I haven't been in church life very long, Pastor, but I'm pretty sure that's not true." Actually, I knew it wasn't true. I have a habit of learning as much about the people I spend time with as possible. I had been going to Ocean Hills Community Church for less than a year. It had been Pastor Lenny who baptized me. Pastor Lenny Grecian—what a name.

"Let's have a seat." I took the few steps necessary to reach the front row of the gallery.

"I have a confession to make," he said.

"Isn't that my line?" It was a lighthearted comment mired in heavyhearted emotion. I was compensating.

A polite laugh burbled from the man. "I'm not a priest," he said. "I confess, I've never been in this room before. I suppose I should take a greater interest in city life." Small talk meant to put me at ease. He was good.

"Most people find it boring. The chamber seats two-hundred-fifty people, but I've seen it full only two or three times. Usually, we have a handful of people and the occasional senior citizen who finds this more interesting than television. Unless you have a love for civic matters, this is the dullest place on a Tuesday night. I've seen a lot of people nod off." I wrung my hands.

"I'll bet I've seen more," he said with a smile. There was a soft kindness in his eyes.

"I doubt it."

Pastor Lenny was not dynamic. He did not pound the pulpit or wave his Bible, but he could fix the attention of his listeners faster than anyone I have ever seen. He was more teacher than preacher but his communication skills were phenomenal. If you fell asleep in one of his sermons it was because you weren't listening or were on medication. "Where's Floyd?"

"My son said you might want to talk to me alone, so he bowed out and went back to the office. By the way, how's he doing?"

"He's doing well. Adjusting." Floyd and his father could not be more different. Pastor Lenny was an outdoor man, as his tan testified. A surfer, he spent his high school days on the beaches of California looking for that perfect ride. After graduation, he learned that surfing doesn't pay well, and he took to driving trucks. "To be outside," he once told me. Someplace along the line his thoughts shifted from the waves to the Maker of the waves. At the age of twenty-five, he went to college then on to seminary. He started Ocean Hills Church the week after they handed him his master of divinity degree. That was twenty years ago.

"I appreciate you giving him the job, Maddy. He still lacks focus. I was hoping some consistent oversight by someone like you might help him settle on a track."

"Would it have helped you at his age?"

He erupted into laughter. "No, it most certainly wouldn't. I needed time to be me before I could become what I was intended to be. That's why I'm so patient with Floyd. He's battling genetics."

"That may be his greatest asset."

Pastor Lenny shook his head. "His greatest asset is the Lord. At least he has that settled."

"He'll find his direction. He told me yesterday morning that he might enjoy being a police officer."

Lenny made a sour face. "Officer Floyd Grecian," he mumbled. "I just don't see it. Still, I think he can be great at whatever he chooses. I just wish he'd choose it." He paused and looked up at the council bench. "Do you like it up there?"

I admitted that I did. "It's hard to describe. The job is hard, frustrating, carries less glamour than most think, and gives more bruises than caresses. Still, I love it. The position makes me feel . . ."

"Complete?"

"That's a good word for it. Complete. I feel like I belong."

"Do you feel like you'll belong in congress?" Somehow the good pastor had changed the subject from himself and his son to me, and I hadn't seen it coming.

"That's an unknown. I think so. To be honest, I feel a little guilty. The people elected me to this position. I'm the first full-time mayor, and now I'm running for a higher office."

"I have a question. Why do you call congress a higher office?"

I shrugged. "That's just the way it's done. Everyone speaks of politicians running for higher office."

"Are you saying that being a congresswoman is more important than being mayor?"

"I wouldn't put it that way. It's probably more prestigious."

"Is that important?" he asked.

I looked at him and weighed my answer. "I'm not sure. Are you saying that I'm running for the wrong reasons?"

"Not at all. I don't know what your reasons are. I'm just curious. As mayor you serve a group of people within city boundaries. As a congresswoman you'll be doing the same thing. Some of the issues will certainly affect those outside the district and maybe even the whole country, but in the end, you're a person serving other people. There's no higher or lower in that."

That started my brain churning, and I appreciated it. A few moments thinking of something else was a welcome break. "I'm not sure the distinction would make a difference in the campaign."

"It wouldn't, but it might make a difference in you. Don't sell yourself or this office you hold short. Anything done for God, anything done for others, is important, which, if I understand my son correctly, is why I'm here. I was very sorry to hear about your friend's tragedy. How can I help?"

The heaviness that had been threatening to squeeze the breath out of me returned. I filled him in on Fritzy, the phone call, my visit, and the reason I wanted to meet with him. "I promised Fritzy that I would help with the arrangements. Would you be willing to do the funeral?"

"Yes," he said immediately.

"I don't know her spiritual state or that of her husband. I feel guilty admitting that."

"Guilt is a useless emotion. It's good for alerting us to a problem but nothing more. It's like a fire alarm that goes off. Once we know of the danger, the alarm is doing nothing more than making noise. I'll be happy to do the service. Give me her phone number and address. I'll make an appointment to visit her. Has she chosen a funeral home to work with?"

"I doubt it," I said.

"There are several good ones in the city. I'll make a recommendation. You'll need to call her before I do. Tell her who I am, and that I'll be calling. Lawyers have a reputation for chasing ambulances. I don't want to be accused of chasing hearses."

I chortled and told him I'd make the call.

"Now, how are you doing?"

"Me? I'm fine. Why?" I squirmed in my seat.

"Why? Let's see. Floyd told me you discovered a murder victim yesterday, and this morning you get a call about the murder of a friend's husband. Considering the experiences you've endured in the past, well, I just want to make sure you're doing okay."

"I'm fine, Pastor," I said. "Some old hurts have been reopened but that's to be expected. Right now, I'm hurting more for Fritzy than for myself."

He smiled. "That's what I like about you, Maddy—your heart. If you need to talk, just give me a call. We'll have coffee or something. Of course, you'll have to pay."

"I'd be happy to pay."

He studied me for a second and then, apparently convinced that I wasn't going to melt into a blob of broken woman, he said, "Let's have a word of prayer."

He took my hand and bowed his head. I closed my eyes and did the same. It still felt strange to me. The prayer was short and to the point.

When I raised my head, I said, "Thank you." I noticed his eyes shift from me to something behind me. I turned.

Tess Lawrence and Jon Adler were standing just inside the chamber at the same door Pastor Lenny passed through a few minutes before.

"Do they always look that unhappy?" Pastor Lenny asked.

"You don't know the half of it."

chapter 11

That was sweet," Tess said. Sarcasm is sarcasm no matter how pleasantly it is said. I chose not to respond. I brushed past the two and entered the corridor that led from the council chambers to my office. To my dismay, they followed.

"Some might think the council chamber is an inappropriate place to have prayer." It was Jon.

"Don't be ridiculous, Jon. Anyone who has attended council meetings knows that we often begin the meeting with a guest minister leading in prayer. It's a very old tradition. You've seen it scores of times. It began with Ben Franklin."

"Still the issue of separation of church and state—"

"Don't go there, Jon. If I want to hear talk like that, I'll join the ACLU." I stepped up my pace. The air in the hall was getting thick. "All I did was have a brief, *personal* prayer with my pastor. If you have a problem with that, then . . . you have a problem—period." I stopped outside the outer door to my office. "What did you want?"

"The police are asking a lot of questions about your murder victim," Tess said. "We should talk about how to control the press on the matter."

"He was not *my* murder victim, Tess. He is the responsibility of the police. All I did was drive to work and make a phone call."

"Still, everyone knows you're the one who found him," Tess persisted.

"If one of the maintenance crew found the body, would you be dogging his heels?"

"If you haven't noticed," Jon piped in, "you're not on the maintenance crew. You're the mayor."

"Yeah, Jon, that occurred to me. As far as controlling the media, it can't be done. The media does what the media does. I've already spoken to Doug Turner—"

"You called Doug Turner?" Tess was aghast.

"No, I didn't call him; he came to me."

"What did you tell him?"

"The truth. Read the paper when it comes out." I crossed the threshold into my office and stopped short. Tess and John almost collided with me. I turned on them. "I have work to do. I'm sure you understand." I turned again, nodded at Floyd as he stood behind his desk—he always stood when I entered the room—and marched into my private office. I hoped Jon and Tess would retreat to their underground boroughs.

"Mayor . . ." Floyd began.

I longed for a few moments alone, but I was destined to keep on longing. Judson West sat in front of my desk reading the *Register*.

"Detective West is here to see you," Floyd said.

"I see that, Floyd." I said thanks and closed the door behind me.

Unlike Floyd, West didn't rise. He just folded the paper and set it on the empty seat to his right. I plopped down in my chair and rubbed my eyes. I should have felt some apprehension at seeing West, but instead I felt a measure of comfort. I always felt good in his presence. He was a comfortable man; comfortable with himself and with his surroundings.

People act strangely around me. As mayor, they either voted for me, against me, or not at all; in some cases, as with city employees, I'm their boss; in other cases, I'm the city scapegoat. With West, I always felt that I was just me.

"I don't know how you put up with those two," West said.

"You heard?"

He nodded. "I admire your control. Strength under pressure. It suits you."

"It's not a very comfortable fit today," I admitted. "Do you get people like that in the police department? What do you do with them?"

"We shoot them and drop their bodies just beyond territorial waters." He kept a straight face.

"Is that just for sworn officers of the law or does it extend to elected officials?"

"We're always looking for ways to branch out." He smiled and straight white teeth became visible. He looked good. His dark hair was just the right length, and his eyes shone with rested confidence. "I've been interviewing everyone in city hall as part of the investigation. I saved you for last."

"You're personally interviewing everyone in the building?"

"I have a couple of senior officers helping. I get to interview the big, important people. I've talked to everyone on the council, and now I'm down to you."

"I told you everything I know yesterday. There's nothing more I can add."

"I know, but I want to cover all the bases." He paused. "I also wanted to see how you were holding up. I understand Mrs. Fritz and you are close."

"We don't pal around. She mothered me, and I returned the favor. It's a good relationship. My heart breaks for her." It was my turn to pause. "She said you were very kind to her. Thank you."

"Some people deserve an extra measure of kindness. She struck me as one of those. How's she holding up?"

"Better than I would have guessed, but she has her moments. The emotional roller-coaster ride has started. After the funeral the ups and downs will even out some."

He shifted in his seat. "Do they ever go away—the ups and downs, I mean?"

"No." The answer came quickly. "Most days the peaks and valleys are not as extreme. Other days, they're as bad as they can get. You just learn to deal with them."

His eyes softened, and he drew his lips into a line. "I'm always on the other side. I used to think I had the hard job making the call, visiting the family to ask questions they don't want to answer. While it's no picnic, close friends and family do the real work. They shoulder the real burden."

I was starting to feel the rising pressure of sadness again. It was time to change the subject. "Have you learned anything?"

"I had the medical examiner do a preliminary evaluation on Mr. Lopez. He confirmed that someone broke Lopez's neck, and that it was most likely the cause of death. I say most likely because the ME hasn't done the full autopsy."

"It seems a horrible way to die."

"I don't know of many good ways," West said. "The thing about breaking someone's neck is that it is an intimate act. If it's premeditated, the murderer has to plan on laying his hands on the victim and committing an act of violence. A gun allows distance. Most stabbings are done in the heat of the moment. Poisoning allows for distance in space and time. One has to be really angry or really nuts to kill with his bare hands."

"Are you sure it's a he?"

"As sure as I can be without the autopsy reports. The bruising on Lopez's jaw indicates a large hand and wide fingers. It also takes a good bit of strength to snap a neck. Even the way this one was done."

"How do you mean?"

"It looks professional. It doesn't look like something done in rage."

"Professional? There are professional neck breakers?"

"Some military personnel learn how to kill with their bare hands." He paused as if considering that thought. "I visited with the Lopez family. They're estranged. His wife, Julia, hasn't seen her former husband for two years. The address on the license was from when they were still married. She kicked him out. Said he was getting too weird for her and the children."

I was interested in the details, but other questions were insisting on being voiced. "Fritzy told me that you thought her husband had been murdered."

"That's one reason I'm telling you all this, Mayor. Mr. Fritz was murdered in the same fashion as Mr. Lopez. We found him sitting in the pilot's seat—a Cessna Caravan. Apparently he had been working on the plane when he was killed."

I didn't know what a Cessna Caravan was, but my mind still created a picture of a lifeless Jim Fritz sitting behind the controls of a plane. "It's horrible; horrible and ironic."

"How is it ironic?"

"Just yesterday I told a reporter that we average only two murders a year in Santa Rita, and now we have two in a row."

"Two in a row and probably done by the same man." He worked his lips a little, then added, "The connections bother me. One murder takes place in front of city hall; the other happens to the husband of a city hall employee."

That had occurred to me but I had pressed it to the back of my mind—too many things competing for my brain cells. "You're saying that I should be careful."

"Yes, and that you should be observant. For all we know, it may be a city employee."

I started to object, but caught myself. Madness could strike anyone in any profession; just because they worked for my city didn't make them saints. "I assume you're doing some kind of background checks."

"I've asked the city manager to review employee files. We're looking for someone who might have received specialized military training."

"But a nonmilitary person could have done this."

"That's true, but we look where we can and take whatever clues we find. You know me, I like to be thorough."

I did know him. I had been on the receiving end of his thoroughness last year. "You'll keep me posted?"

"As much as I can." He stood. I joined him.

"I'm helping Fritzy with the arrangements. When will . . . I mean, will the . . ." So much for being the great communicator.

"I've asked the coroner to light a fire under his medical examiners. Since this may be a serial killing, I want things pushed to the forefront. Mr. Fritz's body should be available for burial by the end of the week. I don't think you can pull together a funeral much sooner than that."

I walked him to the door and opened it. To my relief, Tess and Jon were gone. Floyd, however, was still standing behind his desk. He held the business end of the phone in his hand. I shot him a quizzical glance.

"It's a Betty somebody, and she wants to talk to you. She said it's urgent."

"I need a few minutes to myself, Floyd. Take a message and . . . Who did you say it was?"

"All I got was the first name."

"Betty." I said the name out loud. It hit me—the perfume lady. Fritzy's neighbor. I stepped to Floyd's desk and reached for the phone. "This is Mayor Glenn."

"Oh, Mayor, I'm so glad I reached you. It's Judith." She stopped and took a couple of deep breaths.

"What about Fritzy, Betty?"

"I just went in the bathroom. I had to . . . you know—"

"What has happened?"

"She's gone. I came out of the bathroom and she was gone. And she took her purse . . . and I looked for her car and it's gone, too."

chapter 12

Where would she go?" West asked. We were in his city-issued Ford sedan. It was four years old, and if it were Chief Webb sitting behind the wheel instead of West, I'd be hearing about unreasonable budget constraints. It was a small thing but worthy of note.

"How should I know?" I snapped. I took a deep breath. "Sorry. It's been a rough couple of days. I don't know where she would go."

"Family nearby? Friends?"

"She has no family. I'm sure she has friends, but I don't know who they are any more than I know who your friends are."

"Okay," he said, his eyes fixed ahead. "For now I'm headed to her house. Maybe she just took a drive around the block. How well do you know this Betty person?"

"I don't. She lives next door to Fritzy. Fritzy seemed comfortable with her. Why?"

"Did she strike you as someone who might panic over nothing? I mean, if Mrs. Fritz is watering her tomatoes in the backyard, would Betty think to look?"

"I don't know her, but my first impression was that she is a sweet little old lady who isn't fully aware of all that goes on around her."

"So this could be nothing."

"We still have to check it out."

"That's what we're doing."

The police radio in West's car came to life. The first thing West did before leaving my office was to call dispatch and ask that a patrol car be sent to Fritzy's house. The officer was already there, and the news wasn't good. He had searched the property and drove around the neighborhood but there was no sign of Fritzy. West radioed his thanks.

"No news there. Since her car is missing we have to assume she drove off, but where? Where would you go?"

"Excuse me?"

"You lost a husband to murder. If you were Mrs. Fritz, where would you go?"

I had to think about that. "I remember being very confused the first few days. My emotions were all over the place, and it was hard for me to focus. Thankfully, I had help from my family. Peter's parents were great, too. But that doesn't help." I didn't want to think of those days. I spent too many months and years trying to focus on the good times before *that day*. Instinctively, I resisted anything that forced me to relive the worst days of my life. But I did it anyway. I recalled the phone call, the searing pain of the news, the fog that filled my brain, the calls I made that night, the place in the kitchen where I collapsed under the irresistible weight of grief.

I once read an article by a psychologist who said the human mind cannot distinguish between reality and fiction. It's the reason we jump in a scary movie. We know the scenes on the screen aren't real; we even know that they're two-dimensional representations of actors and events, but when the gun goes off, or the monster charges, we jump anyway. I told myself that Peter's death was many years ago, and I was just trying to recall an interesting detail. My guts still twisted into a knot.

"I'm sorry," West said. Apparently I was more transparent than I realized. "I shouldn't put you through this. I just thought you might have an idea."

"I do," I said a moment later. "The day after I heard about Peter's murder, I had an almost overwhelming desire to drive to LA and stand at the scene where he died. It made no sense, but the desire was there, and it kept growing. My mother talked me out of it, but I doubt she would have been able to if Peter had been killed outside of town instead of LA."

I looked at West and could tell that his mind had just found fourth gear. "It makes sense. It's like those people who lose a son or daughter in an auto accident and cover the site with flowers, pictures, and toys." His head gave a little nod. "She's gone to the airport."

"I think so," I said.

"Then that's where we're going."

We had been on the surface streets, working our way toward Fritzy's house, but West made a command decision. He pressed the accelerator and steered toward the freeway. Five minutes later we were scooting down the wide ribbon of the 101.

Ten minutes later I saw the signs to the Willis Jackson airport. I doubted West needed any signs. Minutes chugged by, and I spent the time praying I was right. Most people work through their grief in a normal pattern; some lose their minds. I was praying for the former and fearing the latter. Back on the surface streets, West pushed through traffic, passing when it was safe and tailgating when he couldn't pass. He was making me nervous.

He pulled up behind a Chevy pickup with what looked like a good ol' boy behind the wheel. Bright spots appeared then disappeared on the tailgate of the truck. West was flashing his lights. The driver gave a wave that lacked some fingers. West mumbled something, reached down to a red plastic globe just under his police radio, and set it on the dashboard. A moment later, red light poured through the windshield. A half second after that, West reached for a switch on the radio, and I heard the blare of the police siren.

The truck shot to the curb and began to slow. I caught a glimpse of the driver. His eyes were wide and his face seemed to have drained of color.

"You enjoyed that, didn't you?"

"I don't know what you're talking about. I'm just trying to get to the airport." He glanced at me and grinned.

Jim Fritz's shop was on the north side of the small airport. This was a municipal airport, owned by the city and used by recreational and business fliers. Unlike a large commercial airport Willis Jackson Field has only two short runways, a single tower, and a small terminal. No airlines landed here, nothing larger than a business jet. West steered the car through the parking lot toward a metal building a hundred yards north of the terminal. FRITZ AIRCRAFT SERVICES was painted in fading red letters on one side. That was our goal.

West switched off the red light and pulled to the curb in front of the building, stopping in a no-parking zone. As I began to open my door, I heard him give our location over the radio. He slipped from his seat and started for the entrance door. By the time I made my exit, he was already trying the doorknob.

"Locked. This way." He pushed by me, rounded the building, and opened the chain-link gate that was meant to keep outsiders out. I saw an open silver hasp lock dangling on the gate. I followed West, who was moving faster than my pump-clad feet would allow. I saw him disappear around the runway side of the building. I rounded the same corner four steps behind him.

She was there. Standing in front of one of two open bays, Fritzy was a frail statue. She wore the same dress I had seen her wear on Monday. Her hands clasped before her, just below the waist. A small beige purse hung from those hands like a frozen pendulum. West approached slowly. So did I. As I drew near I could see what was in the open bay. A white, single engine plane stood as if waiting for someone to call it back to life. It was one of those planes with the wings over the fuselage. Its cowling was open, revealing the engine—the same engine Jim Fritz had been working on the night he was killed. A yellow ribbon barricade ran from the doorjambs and across the open bay door.

"Mrs. Fritz?" West said. "Are you all right?"

Fritzy said nothing. I expected to see tears coursing down her checks but her eyes were dry. They were also empty.

"Mrs. Fritz, you shouldn't be here," West said. He spoke with authority cushioned with kindness.

I brushed past him and stood next to Fritzy. I looked into the bay. When the aircraft was towed in the day before, or whenever it arrived, it was just a simple plane. That's all that most would see, but I knew Fritzy saw something different. It was the place her husband of decades had died—had been killed. I put my arm around her.

"He was alone," Fritzy said. "I was at home asleep when he died. He was here, by himself, no one to talk to, no one to hold his hand."

"Mrs. Fritz," West began. "It wouldn't matter—"

I cut him off with a wave of my hand. He was still thinking with facts, Fritzy had moved beyond that.

"Did you know that we still held hands? When we went shopping, or even when we were just walking down the street, he'd reach for my hand."

The tears were building. I wanted to do the stupid thing and say, "There, there, it's all right," but I caught myself. I knew better.

She continued. "Jim used to say that when a couple stopped holding hands there was trouble brewing."

I gave her shoulder a squeeze. "He was a wise man, that husband of yours."

"I wish I could have been here for him. I know it wouldn't have made any difference, but I still wish it. I wish it with all my heart. This hurts so much." A sob escaped.

I bit my lip.

"I know," I whispered. The whisper was unintentional. I wanted to sound strong, to show that life continues on after tragedy. I wanted her to see me, Madison Glenn, mayor of Santa Rita, widowed by violence but still a whole, strong, resolute person. What a sham. I was a papier-mâché battleship pretending to sail the high seas. At the moment I was nothing more than a paper cup in a hurricane.

She looked at me. There was understanding in her eyes. She unclasped her hands and put an arm around my waist. Together we stared at the Cessna, the open engine that had been the last thing Jim had touched, and the cockpit where his body had been found. Fritzy made no attempt to cross the flimsy barricade. She was close enough.

I heard footfalls and saw a uniformed officer round the same corner West and I had a few moments before. West saw him too. "Secure the front of the building."

The officer looked puzzled. "Sir? There's nothing to secure."

West turned to face the man fully. "I said, secure the front of the building."

The officer looked at West, then at us, and the light went on. "Of course." West retreated to the corner of the building and pretended to watch airplanes land.

Fritzy and I continued to stare at the Cessna. Something about it bothered me.

chapter 13

I drove Fritzy home in her car and used the time to tell her of my conversation with Pastor Lenny. She was grateful and said that if I trusted him, then she would do the same. West followed and then gave me a ride back to city hall. There was little conversation. I was as wrung out as a dishrag. I leaned my head back and closed my eyes. West gave me the gift of silence while I tried to calm my nerves and quiet my brain.

Once back in my office I spent the rest of the evening preparing for the city council meeting. A few minutes before seven, I entered the council chamber, then gaveled the meeting open precisely on time. The agenda was clean and simple, not unusual for the first meeting of the year. We followed our usual routine of roll call, the pledge of allegiance, the reading of the minutes, and report from the city manager. We waved the closed-session report since we had not met in closed session since before the holidays. We dealt with one zoning change, agreeing to allow a piece of residential property to be rezoned commercial.

The only issue that was close to contentious was the election of one of the four sitting council members to the position of deputy mayor. To my surprise, Jon made a motion that a decision be put off until council had had time to discuss the matter in closed session. I was sure Tess had put him up to it, but nonetheless it came as a breath of fresh air. Tess seconded the motion. No surprise there. I waited for Titus or Larry to argue the point, but neither rose to the challenge. In the face of two murders, one the husband of a beloved employee, little that we did that night seemed to matter.

We dismissed at 8:10. That night was a slow one, but there were storm clouds on the horizon. There were always storm clouds. I returned to my office, filed a few papers, and then drove home.

Home sounded good. Before I pulled from the parking lot, I was already dreaming of a massive dose of hot chocolate and bed. It hadn't occurred to me that I had skipped dinner until I turned on my street. Maybe a grilled cheese sandwich would precede the hot chocolate. I saw a large car at the curb. Someone was behind the wheel. A second later, I recognized the vehicle. It was a Ford Excursion—Jerry's SUV. I pulled onto my drive and activated the garage door opener. Moments later, I was parked inside. I exited the car and saw Dr. Jerry Thomas standing on the driveway.

"Chinese food?" He held up two white paper bags.

"What are you doing here? And how do you know I haven't eaten?"

"It doesn't matter." He smiled and held up the bag in his left hand. "Brownies. Warm brownies with macadamia nuts."

"For a physician, you sure are devious. Come in."

Jerry followed me through the garage and into the house. I closed the door with the press of a button, walked to my security system, and entered my code.

I have known Jerry since high school, where we were sweethearts. Like many high school romances, nothing worked out. We each married someone else and lost that someone. My husband was dead; his wife was living somewhere with a man who had more money and didn't keep doctor's hours. Jerry is fairly trim, but over the last few months a little paunch had been testing his belt. Middle age catches up to everyone sooner or later.

"So you haven't eaten, right?" he said, making his way straight for my kitchen. The floor plan is simple. The first floor holds a large living room, which adjoins the dining room, which in turn is open to the kitchen. The rest of the lower floor is taken up by the laundry, walk-in pantry, and a large bathroom. Since I rattle around in this house alone, three of the four bedrooms are guest rooms. All the bedrooms are upstairs as is the game room, which I've converted to my home office.

"No." I set my purse down on one of the wrought-iron end tables that bracketed my white leather sofa. I walked to the dining room. "I was just thinking of a grilled cheese sandwich and some hot chocolate."

"Belay that grilled cheese, Matey. I's brung you a bounty of Hunan shrimp, lo mein noodles, and kung pao chicken."

As he removed the small boxes of food from the bag, I pulled two plates from the cabinet. "What was that? An imitation of a pirate?"

"Not just any pirate, a Chinese pirate. Nothing but the best for you."

"Were there Chinese pirates?" Sometimes Jerry was a nutcase.

"Ask your dad, he's the historian. I'm just a lowly pediatrician trying to do a good deed by feeding the mayor. It's my civic duty."

"And Chinese food shouldn't be eaten alone. Right?"

"Absolutely. What say we eat out on the deck, then we can have brownies and hot chocolate."

"Both? That's a little overkill, don't you think?" I helped dish the food.

"It will give our pancreases something to do, sort of insulin push-ups."

I was starting to feel good. The smell of the food made my stomach rumble, and Jerry's off-the-wall humor made me smile. With plates filled with steaming chow, we went out the sliding glass door that separates my dining room from the outside and sat in the pair of loungers I kept for sunning.

The night was cool but not cold, and the ocean breeze made the food smell even better, something I didn't think was possible. "Sorry, I don't have chopsticks. Forks will have to do."

"It's a shame. You'd be impressed with my skill and dexterity. I've thought of teaching classes."

That made me laugh. "Last time I saw you wielding chopsticks, you dropped a shrimp in your shirt pocket."

"I was saving it."

The moon stood guard overhead and dribbled its light on the ocean. A lullaby of waves kissing the shore massaged my ears and mind. Tension began to drain from me. I was thankful Jerry had shown up. It was late, I was tired, but having a friend nearby was the best therapy.

"You've had a rough couple of days," Jerry said.

"Is that why you're here? To cheer me up?" The soft noodles were wonderful. Food was such wonderful therapy.

"Partly. Partly because I like being with you. We haven't talked in two weeks."

"It's just been a week, Jerry." In the distance tiny white lights danced on the water; fishing boats plying their trade.

"Yeah, well, it seemed longer."

Jerry is a good friend, and there are times when we come close to being more. His gentle spirit, keen intelligence, and caring heart make him irresistible—at least they should. For some reason, I can't move beyond friendship. I know if I winked at him twice he'd propose, but I've held off on winking. My mother thinks we're ideal for each other. She's probably right. So what's the problem? I don't know. I do know that when I am with Jerry, I keep comparing him to Judson West. It's a stupid thing to do, but it comes from my unconscious, and that's where I store all my stupidity. When I'm with West, I compare him to Jerry. Sometimes I feel like a boat with propellers fore and aft: I churn up a lot of water but don't make much headway.

"Thanks, Jerry, I needed this."

"What you need, young lady, is me, and you know it."

"Young lady," I guffawed. "I haven't been called young lady in a long time."

"Well, you're not old."

"I feel old. I walked into a fast-food place the other day and I could see the counterperson eyeing me. I know she was wondering whether or not to offer me a senior discount."

"When you're sixteen, everyone looks old." He put his plate down. "I'll be back. It's time to rescue the brownies from the sack prison."

"I can do that." I started to get up.

"I know you can, but you're not. Sit back down."

I did as I was told. He walked back into the house. I shouted, "There's whipped cream in the fridge!" I paused then added, "It's not mine. I'm keeping it for my mother."

There was a laugh and a muted, "Yeah, right."

I leaned back in the lounge chair and let the cool night air wash over me. It was January, and the night was cool enough to raise the occasional goose bump but not enough to be uncomfortable. I love Southern California.

Minutes later Jerry reappeared with brownies and hot chocolate on a tray. He set it down on the short redwood table between the lounge chairs and retook his seat. I took a brownie and studied it. Guilt covered me like the night air. I thought of the calories, the sugars, the refined flour. I chomped down. Wonderful! The second bite was better.

We listened to the gentle surf and for a few moments I was able to forget about Jim Fritz, the dead man in the Gremlin, Tess and Jon, and life in general. A brownie on the shoreline is magic. I was in a thin glass bubble of comfort, but there's a problem with thin glass bubbles.

"You want to talk about it?"

Crash. Tinkle.

Not really. Still, I told him what I knew and what I had seen.

"So Detective West is handling the case?"

"He's the head of robbery-homicide and the only homicide detective we have."

"I don't have a problem with it. I was just asking."

"That's good."

He broke off a piece of brownie and nibbled it. That was Jerry: Do one thing at a time, do it slowly, do it well, and then move on. I was doing my best not to press the whole thing in my mouth and swallow it whole. "It's odd. Both men had their necks broken. Both are indirectly tied to city hall; one by location of the murder, one by marriage."

"West made the same connection," I said. "He also said they were intimate murders. By that, he meant that the murderer required a close proximity to the victim and had to make physical contact. That's almost too obvious to state."

"Makes you wonder." He broke off another piece of brownie and held it between his fingers as if it helped him think. "Are there other similarities?"

"You're not going private eye on me, are you?"

"I'm a reasonably intelligent man, and I enjoy a challenge. I'm just thinking out loud."

"I see more differences than similarities," I said. "Different location. Lopez drove a beat-up AMC Gremlin, is Hispanic, and younger than Jim Fritz by a couple of decades. Lopez was estranged from his family; Jim was a candidate for perfect husband."

Jerry didn't speak at first. He stared out at the moon-painted waves. "It's good to look at things that way, but it's also good to look for other connections. Everything is connected. Take the ocean. It's easy to see the connection between it and wind and the shore, but it's not so easy to see its connection to the moon. Every grade-school kid knows the sun and moon influence the tides. The moon is 240,000 miles away but it will have an impact on all the oceans of the world, including that little strip we're watching now."

"So you're saying that there may be other connections we're not seeing?"

"Yes, and I know it's not our job to see the connections. That's up to Detective West and his pals. Still, it is intriguing."

I chewed on that like I was chewing on the brownie. "Give me an example."

"Okay." He repositioned himself in the chair as if he expected it to take off and fly around for a while. "When I was in med school and doing my rotations, I spent some time in the emergency room. I worked with a Dr. Mendelssohn. The guy was a genius at emergency medicine. The paramedics would roll in and say, 'Auto accident, adult male, thirty-nine years of age, head trauma,' then spout off a list of vitals. Mendelssohn sucked the information in like a sponge but also asked questions. 'Was he alone in the car? Drugs and alcohol involved? Did the car have air bags? What type of collision was it?' It all meant something to him. Air bags indicated one type of injury. No air bags made him think of chest problems. He would examine for these things anyway, but the more information he had the better he liked it, the better judgments he made." Jerry chortled. "He used to say, 'The problem with the obvious is that it is obvious.' It took me awhile to figure that out. What he meant was—"

"The obvious keeps us from seeing everything," I said.

"Yeah, that's it. If a man walks into the hospital with an arrow sticking out of his forehead, I'm pretty sure I know why he's there. Of course, I would treat the problem, but I wouldn't be a very good doctor if I didn't start asking questions. How does a man get an arrow in the forehead? Accident? Foolishness? Maybe he has other wounds. Did he fall when struck? You get the idea."

"So you're saying I should be looking for other connections?"

"This is only a mental exercise. You should stay out of the investigation. My point is this: When you started listing differences I kept hearing similarities. That's the way I'm trained to think."

"Like what?" I reached for the hot chocolate. Jerry had my interest.

"You noted that they were men of different age, my brain heard that they were both men. You said that one drove a beat-up car and the other was found dead in an airplane; my brain heard that both were in vehicles of transportation—both parked, I might add—"

"And when I said that one was estranged from his family while the other was a perfect husband?"

"I heard both have wives."

"I still don't see any meaningful connections," I admitted.

"There may not be, but it would be a mistake not to look. Was there anything else unusual about the guy in the Gremlin?"

I thought for a moment. "He was listening to the radio. Floyd figured out from the estimated time of death and the radio station that Lopez was listening to . . . that UFO, parapsychology guy."

"Robby Hood? Interesting."

"I didn't know you went in for that kind of thing."

He smiled. "I don't. Occasionally, I get called into the hospital late at night. I've heard his program while driving. He's provocative. I don't suppose Jim Fritz was listening to the show."

"I don't know. I think you're stretching."

"That, my dear, is how you reach things. Want some more hot chocolate?"

"No, I ate too much and too fast. I feel a food coma coming on."

He rose, picked up the plates, and took them to the kitchen. I gathered up the cups and followed. "I'll get these in the morning," I said, then kissed him on the check. "Thanks for dinner and conversation." I was saying good night.

He knew it. "Next time, I'll make waffles."

"For dinner?"

"You need to learn to live on the edge." He kissed me on the forehead and left.

chapter 14

It was Jerry's fault. I lay in bed staring at the red numerals of my alarm clock, watching 12:15 become 12:16. Normally, I fall asleep quickly—the benefit of a clear conscience. Tonight was different. For the last hour I told myself I was teetering on the edge of sleep. If I would just remain still, nature would take its course and wing me to the land of slumber. I could lie to myself for only so long. I teetered as long as I was going to teeter. I wanted to blame the chocolate for keeping me awake, but I knew the truth. Jerry had kick-started my brain. Were there other similarities between Jose Lopez and Jim Fritz? I had been focusing on the differences: different age, ethnicity, social class, family relations, but there were some commonalities. Certainly dying by broken neck was the foremost.

I thought of the radio station that had still been playing when the police opened Lopez's car. Why not? I was losing sleep already; a few more minutes wouldn't matter. I reached for the clock radio and punched the sleep button. I set it for thirty minutes and hoped that the quiet conversation would lull me to sleep. Then I flipped a switch from FM to AM and dialed in ... It took a moment for my sleep-deprived mind to recall Floyd's words. They came to me. I set the dial at 620.

The radio immediately came to life, and I was met with a commercial. Another spot followed, then another, and I was beginning to wonder if I had remembered the wrong dial position. Perhaps I had stumbled onto the only all-commercial-all-the-time radio. Then came the voice—deep, smooth, like distant thunder. "The darkness has fallen, but the light of truth shines in each of us. You're listening to Robby Hood, and we'll be back to stretch your minds after this." Another set of commercials oozed from the speakers. I considered switching off the radio and picking up a book. I was good at falling asleep with a book in my hand, but I persisted.

After a series of thirty-second pitches for gold investments, human-growth hormones, solar-powered radios, and vitamins from the sea, Robby Hood returned to the air on the heels of a New Age–sounding instrumental.

"Welcome back, this is Robby Hood, your guide into the night and into the places the timid dare not go. This is open-call night so get on the phone and make your opinion known, share an experience, ask a question." He gave an 800 number. "Tomorrow we will have mind-control expert Daniel Pat with us and you will be amazed at what the government—*your government*—has been up to now. It has to do with the coffee you drink. So be careful the next time you order a double latte. More about that tomorrow. Now let's hear from you."

At least he didn't pick on hot chocolate. There was the briefest pause, then "You are on the air with Robby Hood, who's this?"

"Um, Robby?"

"Yes, who's this?"

"Are we on the air?"

I was bone tired, but I laughed. Maybe this was the entertainment value of the show, listening to confused people call in.

"Yeah," Robby said, "that's what I meant when I said, 'You're on the air with Robby Hood.'"

"Oh . . . good . . . I've . . . I've been trying to get on for a long . . . time—"

"Turn off your radio, friend," Robby said.

He sounded tired. I imagine he said that a lot.

"What?"

"Turn-your-radio-off. There's a ten-second delay."

"Oh, okay."

I heard the caller set the phone down. The book I was contemplating was looking better.

"Okay, folks," Robby said. "Let's cover the ground rules again. When you call, turn your radio down—better yet, just turn it off. I know it's fun to hear yourself, but you'll go nuts trying to talk and then hearing the same words coming at you ten seconds later. So please, squelch them radios."

Squelch?

"I'm back. Sorry." The caller was male, sounded under thirty and a little confused.

"You're not the first. You won't be the last. Tell me your first name—no last name."

"My name is Bob Rec—"

The radio went silent for a few seconds, then Robby was back on. "That's it for him. I tried folks, I tried. We'll let him consider the sins of his ways off the air. Let's try this again." Pause. "Hi, welcome to the Robby Hood show."

"Let's talk chemtrails, Robby. This is Ted in Santa Barbara."

"You mean those *contrails* we see in the sky every few days." Robby stressed *contrail* and followed it with a laugh. Apparently it was an inside joke. That was last night's topic, pal."

"I know. I tried to get through but the lines were all jammed. Gimme a break."

"Okay, Ted, never let it be said that Robby Hood doesn't love his listeners. What about them?"

"Well, I used to be a pilot. Flew for the navy in Nam in the late sixties, so I've logged a lot of airtime. I know contrails. I've left a few in my day, but what I saw out my window this morning weren't no contrail. Contrails disappear soon after they're laid down, but these babies hung around for hours."

"That's what they do. The question is, what are they?"

"Well, there are lots of theories," Ted in Santa Barbara said. "You had a guest—"

"Edward T. Hart," Robby interjected. He was nothing if not enthusiastic. "He was on last month. We may have him on again."

"Yeah, that's the guy. He said that the chemtrails is the government's way of inoculating the population against biological terrorist, but I think it's something else."

"Really? Like what?"

"You know the planes lay them down in a pattern, right? I think they're used to calibrate spy satellites or maybe some kinda Star Wars weapon satellites like Reagan wanted when he was president."

"Calibration?"

"Yeah, calibration. I mean, wouldn't the optics or radar or whatever they use up there in space have to be calibrated from time to time? If a plane flies at a certain altitude, a known altitude, say 35,000 feet or something, and that information is fed into the satellite's computer, then maybe it could compare an image of the ground with an image of the chemtrail and somehow adjust its cameras."

"Hmm," Robby said. "Are you sure you're not some government operative pushing a little disinformation on ol' Robby?"

"Hey, I wouldn't do that. I'm just a truck driver these days."

"Yeah, but I bet you have some history or some secrets you could share."

The caller laughed. "Not me, Robby, I'm just an ordinary guy."

"Yeah, well, it's the ordinary people who scare me. Thanks for the call. Now remember, my merry men and women, you can visit my Web site and see some of the latest pictures of chemtrails, UFOs, and more. You can also order my latest book, *To the Brink of Sanity: How to Remain Sane in an Insane World.* Robby Hood's mother will thank you. Now this."

Music rose and ten seconds later another string of commercials rolled out of my radio. I wondered how many sponsors the man had. I rose from bed, walked downstairs, and poured myself a glass of milk. I looked out the window. The moon had moved along its path but it still bejeweled the rolling ocean. I stared at the sky. Chemtrails, eh? I chastised myself, then dragged my body and the glass of milk back to the bedroom. I arrived in time to hear the end of a conversation about what *really* went on in Iraq, followed by a woman who was certain JFK was still alive and living in the Florida everglades.

I sipped my milk and listened with greater fascination than I would have guessed. Some of the callers were whacky, but others seemed intelligent, educated, and well spoken. One thing was certain: the program wasn't dull. Thirty minutes after I turned on the radio, the timer turned it off. I finished the last sip of my milk, lay down, pulled up the covers, then set the radio to play another half hour.

Finally, I drifted off. Sleep closed my ears.

chapter 15

Regardless of what hour I go to bed I like to rise at the same time. Routine is my best friend. This morning, however, I didn't crawl out of bed until six. I went into the bathroom and did what needed to be done, which included dousing my face with cold water. The interrupted night's sleep Monday and the late bedtime last night—or maybe I should say, early this morning—made my eyes feel like sandpits. I slipped into some cotton shorts and a light T-shirt and embraced my weekday torture of forty-five minutes on the treadmill. Some days are easier than others. Today wasn't one of them. I'm new to the Christian faith, so I'm filled with questions. Most are doctrinal or questions about things I read in the Bible; others are frivolous, such as why isn't ice cream health food, and why doesn't exercise get easier with age?

Fifteen minutes into my walk I had my speed up to three-point-five miles per hour, and it felt like thirty, but I was awake. The blood was flowing, my lungs were working like bellows, and my heart had fallen into its rhythmic thumping. My mind began to clear.

I finished the walk, took a quick shower, chose a pantsuit over shaving my legs, and went into my home office. There I spent the next thirty minutes in Bible study. This was a new discipline, but one I had stuck to for the last six months. The day never felt complete without some study time. My Bible had a previous owner. Paul Shedd, owner of the Fish Kettle on the Santa Rita pier, gave me his just like he had given one to my husband.

When finished, I slipped downstairs, poured a cup of coffee in a travel mug, grabbed a banana, and headed for work. My mind tossed ideas around like balls in a bingo machine. Today was going to be busy, and I needed to hit it running. I would follow my plan: be in my office before eight, read the paper, check my calendar, then immerse myself in the work I love.

I marched into the building as if I had the best night's rest ever. I wasn't ready for the surprise that awaited me. I had come in through the front door and aimed myself for the reception area. Fritzy was sitting behind her desk.

"What are you doing here?" My tone was a little sharper than I meant. "You don't need to be at work today."

"I know, I know." She raised her hands. She seemed frailer than yesterday. "I'm not staying. I just wanted to get a few letters together, and a few things organized for the temp girl. You are hiring a temp girl, right?"

I smiled. "Why, you chauvinist. What makes you think it will be a woman?" I stepped to her and gave her a hug. "You okay?"

"I'm fine." She was lying, but it was a polite lie.

"Really? Did you sleep?"

"Some."

I knew what that meant. "I've decided to call Celeste Truccoli to fill in for the rest of this week and next. The week after, too, if you want."

"Celeste will be good. She's a smart girl."

Celeste Truccoli was the daughter of a former campaign worker. She lived with me for a short time when her mother was missing. It was a difficult time for both of us, but the furnace of anxiety forged a friendship. Our ages were far apart but sometimes that doesn't matter.

"What about her schooling?" Fritzy asked. Celeste was a sophomore at the University of Santa Barbara.

"Her school starts their semester classes later than most. She still has a couple of weeks of winter break." My dad, who teaches at USB, was gearing up for classes.

"I feel like I'm leaving you in the lurch."

"Nonsense. You have this place so organized that it can run itself for a week or two. Celeste can fill in the gaps. Besides, it will give Floyd a thrill." Floyd was enamored with Celeste, and to my surprise, she seemed smitten with him.

She looked down at her desk. I knew what she was doing. She was looking for another anchor to see her through the storm. This place was a second home to her, the staff another family. "Reverend Grecian called last night. He came over and sat with me for a while. He was very nice, very kind." Her voice trailed off.

"Everyone calls him Pastor Lenny. He's a good man. Did he help with the arrangements?"

"Some. I have to go to the funeral home today and select a casket and . . . the other things."

There was a stroll through the shadowy land of heartache. I had been forced to do the same with Peter. I'd just as soon not have to repeat the process. "You're not going alone, are you? You should have someone with you."

"Pastor Lenny is going to meet me there at nine. That's why I came in. I get fidgety when I have to wait, and I woke up early so—"

Woke up early? I doubt she slept. "Listen to Pastor Lenny. He's helped a lot of people through difficult times, and you can trust him. Is he going to perform the service?"

She nodded. "Thank you for sending him to me. I wasn't sure what to do. We never were much on church. Jim worked six days a week. Sunday was his only time off."

"I understand." I put a hand on her shoulder. "You know to call me if you need anything."

"I'm sorry about running off yesterday. I just needed to get out of the house. I needed . . ." Tears were percolating again.

"No apology needed." The office was starting to get busy. Secretaries, aides, other department employees were showing up for work. Each looked our way, casting sorrowful glances, eyes filled with genuine pity.

"Pastor Lenny said he would ask the funeral home to inquire about when Jim's . . . body might be released. I . . . I can't imagine him on that cold autopsy table—"

"You don't need to, Fritzy. It doesn't do any good." I tried to watch an autopsy once. I pushed my mayoral weight around to get in. A friend of mine had died suspiciously and I wanted to know why. I was trying to be helpful. I didn't last long. The image of my friend on the autopsy table lasted much longer. "There are happier memories. They will surface in time."

"I know," she whispered. "I suppose I should be going. I don't like to drive on the freeway anymore, so I take the surface streets. It's slower, but I get there. Besides, I need the time to pull myself together."

"Do you want me to go with you?"

"No, then I'd feel guilty about taking you from your work. I'll be fine."

"Okay, but I'm going to walk you to your car, and I don't want any argument. Come on, we'll go out the back way." As we moved down the rear corridor that led to the employee parking lot, I saw Tess enter. Her face was drawn into that stern constipated look I had come to expect. She saw Fritzy, looked puzzled, then for the briefest of moments I saw a crack in the concrete facade. I saw the look of shared sorrow.

Fritzy opened the door to her red Volvo sedan. During the short walk from the office to her car she had gathered the pieces of crumbling composure. "I appreciate you very much," she said. I felt a little embarrassed.

"Thank you. You'll get through this. The only advice I can give is take one day at a time, and if that's too much then take life one hour, even one minute, at a time. Give yourself time to heal."

"I know you understand what this is like. Before, I just felt sorry for you, now I understand." She sat in the car.

"May I ask a dumb question?" I said before she closed the door.

"Of course. You may ask me anything." She looked up at me, and I almost changed my mind.

"This is going to sound strange, but did Jim listen to someone on the radio named Robby Hood?"

"Oh, him," she said with a look of disgust. "Jim used to listen to him almost every night. If he worked late, he had that man on the radio. When we went to bed, he would fall asleep listening to all that nonsense about flying saucers and Bigfoot and conspiracies, and whatever you can think of. He even called in a couple of times. I complained, but Jim said he couldn't sleep without some noise in the background." She faded off. "I shouldn't have complained."

"Sure you should. You're his wife. It's your job. Check the fine print in the marriage license. Nagging is a privilege."

She smiled without humor, said good-bye, and closed the door.

chapter 18

I spent the morning trying to find my desk. I can measure the success of any day by the amount of paper and files that I move across its surface. I had finished massaging my schedule, something that qualified as a complete workout in some books, then digested a report from the planning commission on a requested variance for a new restaurant on the north end of town. It was a chain restaurant, family style, lots of seating, and another good source of tax income and job opportunities. The problem rested with a citizen's group that opposed any franchise restaurants setting up shop in our borders. I hated to admit it, but many of our citizens were snobs, preferring that Santa Rita not become a haven for Denny's, Bob's Big Boy, Applebee's, and all the other family restaurants that spring up in California like toadstools. Truth be told, I tended to agree with such dissidents. On the other side, however, are the businesses, chamber of commerce, and others who see such additions as ways of strengthening the local economy.

It is one of those "stuck between a rock and a hard place" issues. If the city simply said no, the restaurant chain could bring legal pressure to bear, which was costly for the city. It would also compel us to fight back just for the principle of the thing. Not long ago our board of supervisors caved under the pressure of the People for Civil Liberties to remove a concrete cross that had stood on county property for sixty years. The board's logic was pitiful: "We'll lose money if the county gets embroiled in a lawsuit." They caved like an egg under an anvil. Leading the retreat was none other than my opponent for congress, Robert Till. I had attended the meeting and spoke on record that such a response was beneath elected officials. It didn't matter; they chose the path of least pain. They took the cross down. Erected in its place was my resolve not to let someone as weak in the knees as Till win the congressional district.

Now the shoe was on my spectator-pump–clad foot. Bennie's was a large chain with, according to the report, 1,600 restaurants in forty-eight states, 1,200 owned by franchisees. A charismatic CEO who had made a name for himself by turning around the failing company in less than five years led them. He knew what he was doing. The Wall Street Journal had done a profile on him about four months ago calling him "The Juggernaut of Restaurant Row."

I called for Floyd and handed him the report. "I want you to do some detective work. Find out as much as you can about Rutger Howard. He's the CEO of the Bennie's restaurant chain. Pull together a report."

"What should I look for?"

"Anything of interest."

"Are we getting a Bennie's in town? They're great. They make nachos to die for."

"I don't know. Is Celeste here yet?"

"Um, no, not yet, but I think traffic is bad and—"

I raised a hand and gave the young man a smile. "No need to defend her, Floyd. I only called her an hour ago. I was just wondering. Let me know when she arrives."

He said he would. I picked up the phone and called our city attorney, Fred Markham. "I assume you're calling about the planning commission report," he said. Fred is a favorite of mine. A UCLA Law School graduate, he represented the city in all its legal matters. He had a keen, hungry mind and he read widely. Santa Rita was lucky to have him. I know other cities have approached him offering more money, but so far he has stayed put.

"That I am. I think we need to do a little research on the company and the man behind it. I have Floyd doing the basic Internet work. Could you do the legal searches? See what kind of lawsuits his firm has brought against cities and counties, that sort of thing."

"I've already started. When should we meet?"

I heard keystrokes over the phone. Fred was a computer guy. Everything he did sooner or later involved a computer. I love computers, but I still love the feel of pen and paper. I have a computer on a credenza in my office and on my desk at home. I even carry a handheld computer, but I leave it off more than on. "It's a busy day. How about tomorrow?"

"That's right, you have the big hoopla, fund-raiser thingy tonight?"

"Thingy? They taught you to say 'thingy' at UCLA?"

"The word communicates, that's all that matters. How about ten? I assume you'll be sleeping in after tonight's grand party."

I love politics; I hate fund-raising. I always feel like a beggar. Fred was speaking about a fund-raising barbecue on the pier tonight. I had successfully kept any thought of it at arm's distance, but now it was upon me. At least I had other people to plan and run it. I just had to show up, press the flesh, pose for pictures, and make a short speech. I was hoping for an early night, but I've been known to hope for snow in July. "I'll be at my desk by eight. Let's make it ten thirty." Just because I was going to be at my desk didn't mean I was going to be awake.

The meeting was set. No sooner had I set the receiver down than my phone buzzed, and Floyd's voice drifted upward from the speaker. "Councilman Wu is on the line."

chapter 17

Larry Wu and Titus Overstreet were waiting for me when I entered the conference room. The room was designed to hold the five members of the council, the city staff, and an administrative aide for each. When everyone was present, the room was confining, but with just three of us present, it seemed spacious, almost overkill. Larry had called and asked if I had a few minutes for him this morning. When I assured him that I would make time, he asked to meet in the conference room. That was unusual. Normally we met in one of our offices.

When I pushed through the doors I saw Larry sitting in his usual spot to the right of the table's head. Titus sat opposite him. Both men remained seated when I entered, but I had worked with them enough to know that had anyone else been present, they would have stood.

Larry looked good. Today he wore a gray blazer, black pants, and collarless black shirt. The usual smile that decorated his face was missing.

Only the mayor's seat was full time. Council members were part-time city servants. The city was not large enough to pay full-time salaries to all its elected officials. I was certain that was going to change over the next ten years. Larry and Titus were seldom in on Wednesdays. The only other person on the council who worked full-time was Tess. She didn't work for money, she had more than enough. She worked for, well, for whatever motivated her. On most days, I assumed it was for attention.

Yes, Larry looked good, but Titus didn't. His black face seemed a shade lighter and was drawn and slack as if his muscles were on strike. As usual, he wore a suit and tie. I took a seat at the head of the table, which put Titus on my left and Larry on my right.

I studied both men for a second. That's all the time it took. "All right, guys, what's wrong?"

"I have bad news and worse news," Titus said. "Which do you want first?"

"Does it matter?" I asked.

Titus shook his head and looked at the table. "I've been going through my annual physical. After a certain age, they want men to undergo additional, routine tests. I'm over that age." I didn't like how this was beginning. "Yesterday I had a colonoscopy. You know, the steel eel, they used to call it."

"I know what you're talking about."

"They found something." He paused. "I have a growth that looks like colon cancer. They rushed the biopsy. I have it."

"No. Titus . . ." I ran out of words.

"It's not bad," he said. "At least they don't think it is. It's a small growth, and it's in a good spot—if there is such a thing. I won't have to wear the bag."

I blinked and glanced at Larry. I wanted to make sure I was getting it right. Larry didn't look back. His attention was on Titus. I returned my attention to Councilman Overstreet. "You're talking surgery, right? Surgery for colon cancer?"

"That's right. The doctors are very confident that they caught it in the early stages. Surgery should do the trick."

"When?"

"In two days. I'll use the time to tidy up some business, then check in early Friday morning. Surgery is scheduled for eight o'clock."

"What can I do to help?" I asked.

"Thank you, but there's nothing for you to do. You need to know that I'll be out for some time. I'm a pretty quick healer, but I won't be keeping office hours for several weeks, maybe a couple of months. It will take longer than that for me to get back to 100 percent. That's assuming chemo isn't needed."

"Oh, Titus, I'm so, so sorry. How's Cindy holding up?"

"She's doing well. I'm sure she's stuffing down some emotion for my sake, but she's a strong woman. She'll be running my accounting firm while I'm enjoying the life of luxury in the hospital."

"Some luxury," I said. "Is it going to be done at PHH?" Pacific Horizon Hospital is our local, private hospital. Those in the know consider it one of the best in Southern California.

"Yes. I'll be there for a week or so, then I go home to recoup." He nodded across the table. "I've asked Larry to join us for a couple of reasons. First, he's a friend, and I needed the moral support. Second has to do with the other news. Since I'm going to be out of commission for a while, there will be an even number of members on the council. I won't be here to offset some of the silliness of Tess and Jon."

"Don't worry about that, Titus. Larry and I can handle them."

He paused and licked his lips. "I think we should meet in private session and make Tess deputy mayor. Actually, we don't have much of a choice. I may be out for several months."

Larry spoke up. "The problem is this: the deputy mayor is chosen each year from sitting council members and no one can serve two consecutive terms. I served last year so I'm ineligible. If Titus is out, then that only leaves Jon and Tess. Tess is annoying but not nearly as self-serving as Jon."

The flu-feeling came back. "There's nothing in the bylaws to keep Titus out. Let's say he doesn't return for three, even four months, which still leaves eight months of service."

"I understand your reluctance, Mayor," Titus said. "Tess has opposed you on just about everything, but we have to be realistic. Besides, I have a hidden agenda."

I raised an eyebrow. "Really?"

He smiled and raised his own eyebrow. "I believe you're going to win the seat for congress. I want to run for mayor after that."

I looked at Larry. Larry had run against me in the last election and came in third. He had been a gentleman all the way. I assumed he would take another crack at it.

"Not this time, Maddy. I had my shot, and I didn't fare all that well. My business is becoming more demanding. I can still do the city work but I can't do that, run my business, and take another shot at mayor. I plan to help Titus any way I can."

"And . . . ?" I prompted.

"And in March, you win the primary, then face off with whomever the Democrats put up. That election happens in November. You win there and move on to congress in January of next year. Tess's time as deputy mayor will be up—"

"And, Lord willing, you'll be on your feet ready to run for mayor."

"Not only that, there's a good chance that I will be elected deputy mayor, which will make me acting mayor. The council will select someone to fill the fifth seat."

"And you'll be able to run as the acting mayor's seat which might give you an edge. Is that it?"

Titus nodded. "Let's be fair. Tess is a burr under our saddle, but she has never done anything to hurt the city. Jon is clearly out for himself, Tess is at worst a self-centered annoyance."

My mind was shuffling like a deck of cards. I tried to slow it and put everything in perspective. All they said was true. I needed to see things from Titus's perspective. I admired his confidence in the face of bone-rattling news about his cancer. There were many ramifications to consider, but the one that stuck in my throat the most was Tess. The tension between us had grown over the years until it was a wonder that we could work together at all—but we did. Since my spiritual experience, I had tried to change my attitude and tame my tongue, but it was tough going. At thirty-nine, it's hard to change one's spots.

"I know I'm asking a lot," Titus said.

"No, you're not," I said. "You're right. Tess and I need to get beyond our differences. But I have a question: What if I don't win the congressional seat?"

"You'll run for mayor again and win in a landslide," Titus said. "I won't run against you. I promise you that. Tess will, of course, but I won't. I'll support you."

I studied Titus. We had been friends for several years. I had grown to admire his determination and intelligence. Once he had even put himself in harm's way to protect me and sported the bruises for weeks to prove it.

"Okay," I said. "On one condition." Titus gave his head a tilt. "You get well as fast as you can. I'm gonna need backup."

He laughed. "I promise."

chapter 10

The rest of my day tumbled by. Celeste Truccoli was waiting for me when I returned to my office. Floyd had been entertaining her. Celeste laughed freely, which did my heart good. We exchanged pleasantries, and I asked about her mother and learned that she was doing well. I put her to work at Fritzy's desk.

I then placed a call to Tess's office and left a message for her. I skipped lunch and spent the afternoon working on my speech for the evening. The campaign was gearing up and I was thankful that I had trustworthy volunteers. Without them much of the work would fall on my shoulders, and I didn't need any more to think about.

At four I left the office, went home, and took a nap. I needed it and I slept soundly. One hour later, I fixed a thin, lunch-meat sandwich, which I washed down with milk. There would be plenty of food on the pier tonight, but it wouldn't do for the candidate to be shoveling chow down the hatch two fistfuls at a time. I would nibble my way through the evening.

The Santa Rita pier is a source of pride for our citizens. It is a quarter-mile long with heavy timber construction that projects out over the rolling ocean. White sand beaches stretch to either side. It's open every day and only in the worst weather is it ever empty of fishermen or couples strolling over its planks. It was built in the early sixties and had tolerated abuse from patrons and Mother Nature with dignity. About once every decade a storm comes along that proves too much for the pier—taking a pylon or two from its support structure or gobbling down a hunk of railing. Twice in its history it had to be rebuilt. This evening it looked radiant as I pulled onto the wide, black parking lot. I found a space marked off for me. It had no name, just two orange safety cones placed at the mouth of the stall. I knew it was my spot because Floyd was pacing up and down in the stall. He saw me and waved, motioning to the cones.

I pulled close and stopped. He looked puzzled. Lowering my window I leaned my head out. "The cones, Floyd." He snatched them up.

"Sorry."

I smiled. There is a lot of potential in Floyd. He just has yet to piece it all together. I parked and exited my SUV.

"I was getting worried," he said. "People are arriving, and you're not here ... weren't here."

"I'm still fifteen minutes early, Floyd. Have you ever known me to be late?"

"No, but ..."

"But what?" We moved from the parking lot to a concrete walk that led to the pier. I was glad I didn't have to walk across the sand in my bone-colored pumps. I was wearing a light blue, double-breasted jacket, matching trousers, and an ivory blouse, hoping to strike the balance between professional executive and I'm-still-a-woman look. Simple gold and pearl earrings dangled from my lobes, and a gold rose-shaped broach—a gift from my mother—clung to my left lapel.

"You're the guest of honor. I thought you might be here earlier."

"It's a fund-raising gig, Floyd, and I'm the candidate. I'm not supposed to be here early. Most people expect me to arrive late."

"I'm just nervous. I've never been to one of these things before."

We crossed from concrete to the creosote-soaked planks. I looked down and through the spaces in the planks. I could see the sandy shore. Now the hard part began: Walking with dignity without plunging one of my heels between planks and breaking an ankle. It's hard to walk with poise while contemplating every step. I was glad I went with the midheel pumps. Anything taller in this situation and people would wonder if I had enough smarts to be a congresswoman.

"There's nothing to worry about, Floyd. It will be what it will be. Worry is like having one foot on the brake and the other pressing the gas pedal. You get lots of noise but you don't travel very far. I'm sure everything is going fine. I assume Nat has everything under control."

"Yeah," Floyd said. "It's amazing. She just sits there and directs people."

"She's in a wheelchair, Floyd. Of course she just sits there."

"That's not what I meant. I meant . . ." He caught my wink and replied with a nervous smile.

Situated in the middle of the pier is the Fish Kettle, Paul Shedd's restaurant. He was catering the fund-raiser, and I was glad for it. The former banker was great in the kitchen. I don't know what kind of banker he had been, but everyone who crossed his threshold was glad he had made the career change. I looked down again, trying my best not to appear like a teenage girl learning to dance and watching her feet so as not to step on her father's shoes. The sand had given way to churning ocean. The surf was small and rolled through the pier's columns in a gentle, leisurely pace. Beyond the pier the ocean was a dark blue and turning darker as the sun's disk crept toward the horizon; beneath me, however, the water was green with frothy white foam.

I took in the surroundings. It was a beautiful night with a gentle salt breeze, a clear sky decorated with white gulls, mottled terns, and the occasional brown pelican. A section of the pier had been cordoned off with a red, white, and blue cord in the center and extending to the guardrail at the end of the pier. The pier was public property, and my campaign had to rent it for the few hours that we would be here. It wasn't cheap, and as mayor I couldn't ask for a break. As a public venue, we couldn't close it off completely, not without accusations of favoritism. We took the end portion, which was plenty large enough. Others not associated with the fund-raiser could come and go as they pleased.

In the south corner, a small band was setting up and tuning instruments. Nat had told me that she hired a band that played all the "great pop tunes." Knowing Nat, she had reviewed their playlist and edited it. I judged the band members, a woman and three men, to be in their late twenties, early thirties. One of them stepped to a microphone and said, "Check, check." His voice boomed from speakers in front of the stage area. He made an adjustment on the mixer board with what looked like a thousand switches and knobs. He repeated his "check, check, check." It sounded the same to me but apparently he could tell a difference.

"This place looks great." I stepped through the break in the rope barricade that marked the transition from plain ol' pier to the Maddy-for-Congress fund-raiser area. Nat Sanders had pulled her wheelchair up to one of the many folding tables that would serve as the dining area. She had several folders before her, one was open. She looked up at my words.

"She's here," Floyd said.

"I can see that," Nat said. To me she added, "I didn't expect to see you for another half hour. It's fashionable for the candidate to be late."

"We've done, what, five of these fund-raisers?" I bent over and gave her a quick hug. "I haven't been late yet."

"Six," she corrected me. "You should try it sometime. Being late affords a better entrance."

"It's a phobia with me."

She laughed. "No kidding." She looked around. "What do you think?"

Balloons hovered in the air, anchored to the ends of tables and the rough wood guardrail. Each balloon had my picture and the words, "Elect Maddy." It embarrassed me. This was the part of campaigning I hated. I've always believed that ideals should be enough to garner votes, but campaigning has a long history of tradition. Fanfare remained the pattern. To the north side were three wide barbecues. Only in California does one barbecue in January. Waves of heat rose from the grills. Paul was well under way.

"The count looks good," Nat said. "We had a few people drop out because of illness but we also had some late RSVPs come in. Every spot is filled. The others will have to stand while they eat. I have get-well cards for you to sign."

"That was thoughtful."

Nat had arranged for a limited number of tables and chairs and had designated them for those who had bought the hundred-dollar-a-plate tickets. Volunteer waiters would serve those people, and I would spend most of my evening schmoozing with them. Others were welcome but had no assigned place to sit. In an innovative flash of brilliance, Nat had made campaign buttons for place markers. Instead of my name in big print there was the name of the supporter, and instead the traditional "Vote Maddy" or similar, in bright red letters it said, "Elected by Joe Contributor." An ingenious piece of marketing, I thought. Not only would the badges tell the people where to sit but it gave them a souvenir to remember the event and loss of at least one hundred dollars.

"You never cease to amaze me, Nat," I said. "This is wonderful." It was especially wonderful since I had done none of the work. Nat was brilliant and possessed a memory that was almost frightening. Not only were facts and faces logged away in her mind, but she seemed able to access them like some people access computer files. But she was far more than a repository of research; her journalism experience had taught her to think outside the box. She was brilliant, creative, and driven.

When we first met I had assumed her zeal and unending work were overcompensation for her paralysis, but I soon learned that she was that way from childhood. All the auto accident did was put her in a chair; it changed nothing else about personality or drive.

"Yeah, I am pretty incredible." She closed the folder, but not before I saw that it was the expected guest list. She opened another file that rested on the table. By the wheel of her chair was a black-leather briefcase. "I went over your speech again. For a politician, you write pretty well. I can't find anything to change."

"That's good. I hate last-minute alterations."

"I do want you to do something, though. I figured you'd be here early so I spoke to Paul. He said you can hide out in the restaurant."

"I don't want to hide out," I protested.

"Sure you do. I want you to make an appearance. If you stand around here as people arrive you'll look too eager, maybe even desperate."

"Nonsense, I'll just greet people and be my usual captivating self."

"Don't make me recite our agreement again." She narrowed her eyes so deliberately, I knew she was acting. The agreement was the only thing I regretted about our relationship. I have always been self-motivated and very involved in my campaigns. Of course, those were much smaller efforts. Running for congress was a good light-year beyond my experience. As a former political reporter and later news anchor for a major LA television station, Nat had seen more campaigns than I. It had been she who finally pushed me into candidacy. I had thought of running for congress but had put the idea off. When the sitting congressman Martin Roth leaked his retirement plans, it put me in a tight spot. Defeating an incumbent is always tough. Running for an open seat is preferable. It was now or maybe never. Nat pushed and I let her. My agreement to run came with a stipulation: Nat would be my campaign manager. She objected at first but only mildly. Not to be outdone, she had her own stipulation. I heard it then, and I've heard it several times since: "I'll run your campaign, but I run everything. On matters of policy and ethics you can overrule me, but not on anything else." I agreed, and now she was reminding me of it.

"How often are you going to remind me of that?" I said it with a smile.

"Every day if necessary. Now mosey into the Fish Kettle, or I'll have young Mr. Grecian toss you over his shoulder."

I looked at Floyd and watched the color slip from his face. "That's all right, Floyd. I'll save you the indignity of carting my carcass across the pier."

"Paul has a booth set aside for you. Sip a soda or something, but go light on any food. You have to eat with your guests. I'll send Floyd to get you when it's time."

"Aye, aye, Captain."

"That's better. And don't spill anything on yourself."

I went, but I took my time. I said hello to several of the volunteers and thanked them for their fine work. I'd send thank-you cards later. Nat would make sure of that. Two minutes later I took a seat in a corner booth that had apparently been saved just for me. Paul Shedd's wife, a round woman with blue eyes, greeted and seated me.

Like her husband, she was a deeply spiritual person and had become a role model for me. I was sure I'd never grow in my faith like she had. Every time I saw her I expected to see a halo. This evening she looked a tad tired, and I said so.

"Ain't nothing but age, Mayor. I don't know what's wrong, but I seem to get older with every passing year."

"Maybe you should see a doctor, Martha. I'm sure they have some magic elixir to make you grow younger." Paul and Martha were only in their early fifties, but I've noticed that people who cross the fifty barrier love to banter about their age. Maybe it was a way of accepting the inevitable fact that no one gets to stay young forever.

"I've learned to be content with whatever circumstances I'm in."

"Wait, I know that one," I said as I took my seat. "Don't tell me. It's John, right?"

She smiled and shook her head. "The apostle Paul. Philippians 4:11."

"Rats! I thought I had it this time."

"Give yourself time. The Word has a lot in it. It takes time to get some of it down."

I had been reading the Bible daily for almost a year. I had been taught the basics at a new believer's class at church, but I was having trouble retaining it all. "I have a good memory, but sometimes the Bible just seems beyond me."

"It's beyond all of us, Mayor. The thing to remember is that it is a process, not an event. Just keep reading, and more and more of it will take root. You'll see. Can I get you anything?"

I looked around the room. The restaurant could only seat about 125 people and it was doing so now. There was a buzz in the air and waiters and waitresses moved with precision between the tables. I didn't have to be a prophet to know that Martha and Paul were busy and that my fund-raiser just added to the day's challenge. "Just tea.

I'll be eating later." I felt guilty for taking up an entire booth that could hold four paying customers.

"I'll bring you an assortment. What about you, young man?"

Floyd looked at me, then back at Martha. "I need to get back out there and see what Nat wants me to do."

A second later, I was alone gazing through tinted glass as volunteers scurried around. I drummed my fingers on the table. I removed a folded copy of my speech from my black purse. I would be speaking from memory and it was my job to make it all sound spontaneous. My eyes traced the words but my mind took a detour.

Suddenly, I felt cold.

chapter 10

ost people move their eyes when reading."
The words yanked me up from a dark place. Standing by my table was Paul Shedd, a smile creasing his deeply tanned face. He had an empty cup in one hand and small plate with one of those restaurant-sized metal teapots in the other. On the saucer were several types of tea bags. He set it all down. "Hey, Paul. I'm sorry. I didn't see you walk up. I was just going over my speech."

He raised an eyebrow. "May I join you?"

"Sure, if you have the time."

"I have a few minutes, then I have to help my crew toss down some meat on the grill." He sat. "It looked to me like you were glancing through your notes, not reading them."

"I may have been daydreaming."

He nodded. Paul is one of those intuitive people who know if something is wrong with you by the way you blink your eyes or move your lips. He studied me for a second. "Are you okay?"

"Sure, why wouldn't I be?" Ants began to crawl inside me.

He worked his mouth a little before speaking. "I know it's hard for you to come to the pier."

Last year, during some of the worst days of my life, a friend of mine was found strapped to one of the mussel-laden pylons. Her body wasn't discovered until low tide the next day. "Facing hard things is part of life. I can't avoid this place."

"No, I don't suppose you can. I, for one, am glad for it. We're always glad to see you at the Fish Kettle." He paused and looked out the window. "You ready for all of this?"

"I was born ready." I was overstating things, something I did when I felt uncomfortable. I was never ill at ease around Paul. It had to be something else.

"So how's the walk?"

The walk. It was Paul's shorthand for my newfound faith, a faith he was instrumental in bringing into my life. "Forever forward," I said, "but . . ." I didn't know where the "but" came from.

"But what?"

I ripped open a tea packet, Apple Orchard, and dropped the bag in the hot water. "I don't know why I said that. Really, I'm fine."

"Let me guess," he leaned back and studied me as if I had my anxieties tattooed on my face. "You're having trouble adjusting to the Christian life."

"I wouldn't put it that way."

"How would you put it?"

I played with the tea bag, lifting it from the water and dropping it again, as if I were torturing it for some crime it had committed. "I'm excited by my faith, and I'm learning new things every week . . ."

"But you're struggling with something."

I released the tortured tea bag and closed the lid on the tiny metal pot. "I'm not having trouble believing, although I have a great many questions. I'm struggling with myself."

"Well, after you've been a Christian as long as I have you'll . . . still have a great many questions. It goes with the territory."

"I've always been such a quick study; I just thought that I'd have a better handle on the spiritual things by now." I poured tea into my cup. It looked weak. Apparently I was feeling impatient.

"By spiritual things, do you mean Bible knowledge or the daily stuff?"

"Stuff? Is that a theological term?" He smiled but the little joke wasn't going to derail his thoughts. "It's me. Do you remember that verse you asked me to memorize after I gave myself to Christ? The one about being a new creation?"

"'Therefore if any man is in Christ, he is a new creature; the old things passed away; behold, new things have come,'" he quoted. "That one?"

"That's it. I don't feel like a new creation. I feel like the old creation with a new coat of paint. The structure is all the same."

"What brings all this on?"

"Life brings it on. Business brings it on. When I'm around people who annoy me or who I think are doing things for selfish motives, I turn back into the old Maddy. I've always had a quick tongue and tend to speak my mind. That's not always good."

He considered what I said, then, "Is it always bad?"

"I don't understand."

"Someone at work is annoying you and you let them know what you think. Is that it?"

"Pretty much."

"Do you curse at them? Run them down? Degrade them?"

"No, of course not."

"Was there a time when you would have?" He leaned forward.

It was my turn to mull things over. "Yes. I've been known to take head shots at my detractors and a couple of people on the council."

"Do you still do that?"

"I've had a few terse conversations, Paul. Some of them pretty blunt."

"It sounds to me like you need to give yourself a break. How's Floyd working out?"

Paul attended the same church as I did and knew Floyd was Pastor Lenny's son. "He's catching on but has a long way to go. I think he has potential. He just doesn't know it."

"Sounds like you're pretty patient with him, Mayor."

"Well, of course I am. This is all new to him. It's going to take time for him to find himself."

"Why not fire him and get someone more competent?"

I sipped my tea. I had the feeling I was being taken for a ride. "I don't fire people for not having had the time to learn what they need to."

He gave me a gotcha smile. "I have to scoot out and start throwing things on the grill so let me do this quickly. You are far more patient with others than you are with yourself. Of course you're going to struggle with old patterns and habits. Every believer does. The apostle Paul called it the old man and said he struggled with it every day. You can look this up later, but Romans 7 tells of Paul's inward struggle. He said, 'For I know that nothing good dwells in me, that is, in my flesh; for the wishing is present in me, but the doing of the good is not. For the good that I wish, I do not do, but I practice the very evil that I do not wish.'"

It still amazed me that Paul had so much Scripture at his mental fingertips.

He went on. "If he was in a daily wrestling match, who are we to think that we'll fare better than he?" He reached across the table and laid his hand on mine. "You are a new creature in Christ, but the Christian life is a process of becoming. We're not one thing one day then, *boom,* something else the next day. Victories in the Christian life come one day at a time. Give yourself a chance to change. By the way, speaking your mind is not a sin if done in love. Okay?"

I took a deep breath and let it out.

"You're under a great deal of stress. You've faced several tragedies in your life, you're mayor and now running for congress. Add to that a death on the doorstep of city hall and the loss of a friend's husband." I must have looked puzzled because he added, "Floyd filled me in. I imagine you feel all sorts of things in the course of a day."

"That's true enough."

"You're doing fine, Mayor. You really are. My advice: It is better to know things with your head than with your heart. The fact that you're thinking about these things is proof of your faith in Christ. Enjoy the process of becoming."

He stood. "Knock them dead tonight. Oh, and one last piece of advice: Be sure and try the au gratin potatoes. I outdid myself this time."

"Thanks, Paul. I will. And thanks for everything else you're doing tonight."

"It's my pleasure. Besides, it's great advertising."

He walked away. Friends, I decided, are God's way of saying, "I'm thinking of you."

chapter 20

The fund-raiser went well. Nat sent Floyd to retrieve me fifteen minutes after the official start. I exited the Fish Kettle, made one careful step after another, and walked to the staging area. People stood and applauded. I did the meet-and-greet thing—shaking hands, touching shoulders, passing out compliments like flowers, and listening to the flattering words of my supporters. No matter how many times such things are done, I'm left with the feeling that I'm a pretender, an actor playing a part hidden behind costume and props.

The meal was a mile or two beyond good. Paul had served up barbecued Ahi tuna steaks, Southwestern chicken breasts for those who didn't like fish, and hot dogs for those who brought their children or anyone passing by who showed an interest. My volunteers waited tables, handed out brochures, and collected contributions. I made the rounds to every table, shared jokes, talked politics, and schmoozed with extra flair. The band had performed a set before the meal, then played CDs while everyone ate.

Following the meal I thanked everyone, then delivered my twenty-minute speech in seventeen minutes. The rest of the evening the band was center stage. Songs ranged from the Beatles to REO

Speedwagon. A few people danced to the music but most chatted, exchanged jokes, and enjoyed an evening that was better than could be expected.

Titus and Larry provided some support from the council with their presence. They said nice things about the speech and wished me well. Then each of them worked the crowd and several times I overheard, "Maddy is the one I plan to support." It was especially kind of Titus who was facing surgery in a couple of days. I don't know if I would have shown if I were in his place. Neither Tess nor Jon made an appearance. I didn't expect them to do so. They opposed me on almost everything.

The crowd began to thin around eight, and I discovered some time to myself. I sipped pineapple punch, meandered over to the band, and extended my thanks. Nat had been right, they had been good. They seemed to sense the desires of the crowd and put forth a mix of contemporary music. I heard songs I hadn't heard since high school. It was refreshing.

Volunteers busied themselves with cleanup. I saw Paul Shedd cleaning his grills and a few of his employees bussing the tables. There was little for me to do. I continued past the band to the rail at the end of the pier. It had been a while since I walked out this far. My schedule was twice as busy with the campaign, and there were some deep hurts here. It was here that Paul had told me about my husband's spiritual decision, something of which I was unaware. He died—was murdered—the same day. I look back upon that revelation with mixed emotions. I now held the same belief, and because of that, I believed Peter to be in heaven. Still, it was just one more place that reminded me that I was a widow who lived alone.

I leaned over the rail and watched the waves lit by ivory moonlight and harsh white light from lamps on the pier. They rolled in, one upon another in rhythmic progression, unperturbed by the hubbub of the fund-raiser. The tide came in and went out no matter what happened in human history, or in my history. In a few months I might stand here as the new congresswoman for my district, or I might be here having lost in a landslide. I decided it didn't matter. I would do my best. The rest I'd leave in the hands of the voters—better yet, in the hands of God.

"I thought things went well enough that you wouldn't need to consider jumping."

The words jarred me out of my thoughts, and I jumped with a start. I snapped my head around to see a man of maybe forty years, sandy hair, and bit of a Robert Redford look. Not quite as good looking, but I imagined he turned a few heads in his day.

"I apologize. I didn't mean to frighten you." His voice was smooth and his words came with the ease of confidence. He smiled, showing teeth too perfect to have arrived naturally, and his eyes were a comfortable hazel.

"I didn't hear you coming."

"My fault. I'll try to be noisier next time."

I gave a practiced, polite laugh. "Don't do so on my account. I'm a little tired. I probably wouldn't have heard you if you drove up in a tank."

"I left my tank in the garage." He held out his hand, I shook it. "My name is H. Dean Wentworth. I enjoyed your speech. You might have a future in the politics game."

"It's not a game. I can tell you that." I studied him for a moment. I recalled that I had seen him standing to one side during my speech. He was not seated at one of the tables, meaning that he had not been on the select list. "H. Dean?"

"Everyone calls me Dean. The *H* stands for Horace. I dropped that sometime around first grade."

"I can understand. I'm named after a dead president." He tilted his head to one side. I explained. "My father teaches history at the university in Santa Barbara. He has a thing for biographies."

"Madison Glenn . . . Madison . . . James Madison?"

I nodded. "I'm just glad he wasn't reading a bio of Ulysses S. Grant. At least Madison is a girl's name."

"Oh, I don't know. If he had been he could have called you Uly . . . never mind. I see your point." He turned and faced the ocean. "It's a beautiful evening."

"We specialize in beautiful evenings. It's in the city charter." I also turned to the ocean. *Who was this guy? He wasn't tipping his hand.* For some reason, I was feeling uneasy.

"You do a great job. I live in Atlanta. Don't get to watch the sun set over the ocean much there."

"I guess not. Excuse me for saying so, but you don't sound like you're from Atlanta."

"That's because I was born and reared in Oregon. I settled in Atlanta after grad school."

My back was beginning to hurt. Standing, walking, bending, and stress had settled in my lumbar muscles. I stretched and turned. I saw Nat looking my way. She made no motions, but her expression set off alarm bells.

"I don't believe we've met before," I said.

"We haven't. I work for Rutger Howard and the Bennie's restaurant chain. I'm Mr. Howard's personal aide."

"I see." I said the words softly and stripped of any emotion.

"No need to be nervous. I'm sure you already know that we're considering putting a company store here. My job is to test the waters, see what kind of hoops we have to jump through, that sorta thing. But that's only one reason I'm here."

Uh-oh.

"We at Howard Enterprises—that's the parent company over our other business interests—believe in the political system. We often make contributions to campaigns we believe in."

I heard a soft thumping and a tiny whine. It was getting louder.

"Whoa, let me stop you right there, Mr. Wentworth."

"Please, call me Dean."

"No thanks, Mr. Wentworth. You know it would be inappropriate for me to take a contribution from someone who has business before the council."

"Don't get me wrong, Mayor. We're not wanting to make a contribution for a run for mayor. Of course that would be wrong. You're running for congress. That's different. And before you say no, I'm under orders from Mr. Howard to be as generous as the law and loopholes allow."

"Laws and loopholes, eh." That didn't sit well. The whirring and thumping was closer. "Perhaps you're unaware that the Federal Election Commission limits contributions from individuals and Political Action Committees."

"As a matter of fact, I am aware of that. Individuals may give up to one thousand dollars to a candidate and PACs can give five thousand dollars. Of course, we can also give to your party with the understanding that the money would go to you. I'm sure that can be arranged. You may not be aware that we have a great many employees who trust our judgment and offer to contribute to campaigns like yours. We tend to attract patriotic, civic-minded folk."

"That's called bundling, and I'm well aware of it. You collect money from one hundred employees at a grand a piece, and all of a sudden you've passed on a hundred thousand dollars."

The whine and thumping stopped. Nat had made a beeline to us and stopped her wheelchair a foot from my leg. "How we doing?" she asked.

"Just fine, Nat. Let me make introductions. Mr. H. Dean Wentworth, meet my campaign manager Natalie Sanders. Nat, this is—"

"One of Howard's boys. I know." She smiled but in a way that made me think the pier was going to cave in.

He nodded at Nat. "Ms. Sanders. I don't believe we met."

"Not officially. You came across my desk a couple of times."

"I'm sensing some hostility here," Wentworth said. "I think I'm being misunderstood. We're not trying to buy you, Mayor. We don't need to do that. We have sixteen hundred restaurants in company stores or franchises. People love us. We're welcomed into every city we go."

"That's not what I've heard," I said.

He shrugged. "There have been a few isolated cases in which certain civic leaders lacked foresight, but the courts have always held up our cause."

"It's not for me to say whether or not you should be allowed to build. There's a process for all of that."

"I'm well aware of that, and our planners and lawyers are good at dotting the i's and crossing the t's. That's not why I'm here. The campaign contribution offer is genuine, but I also wanted to give you a heads-up on something. It's only fair."

I didn't like this. I encouraged him to go on.

"As you know, retail property is scarce in your city and getting water rights can be a challenge. Santa Barbara is the same way. We feel the best way to go is building on an existing business site."

"I don't see what that has to do with me."

"The owner doesn't want to sell. We think he should. We've offered more than the land is worth. We think eminent domain is the way to go."

"You're not serious," I said.

"I'm always serious, Mayor." He smiled and turned his back to the sea. "It's an older building, built in the fifties. I'm sure that it's not up to code on several counts, so you and the council should have no problem declaring it blighted and thereby justify an eminent-domain ruling. You'd be doing your city a favor." He gave me another Hollywood smile.

"It doesn't work that way."

"Of course it does, Mayor. You know that. Or at least you should. It's done all the time. A major newspaper in New York followed the same process to acquire the property it needed to build its new office building. We're not thinking that large."

I could feel heat radiating from my face. It had been a long time since I had completely lost my temper, but I was close, and the fuse was burning fast. "We're not New York, and our council members are close to their people. You won't get past the first meeting."

"Not all of the council. I've already spoken to one who is in agreement with me and I'm pretty sure I can get more."

"Who? Who did you talk to?"

He cut his eyes to the side. "Oh, look. Smile." He stepped close and put his arm around my shoulders before I could react.

I turned my head. The flash of a camera strobe stung my eyes. A half second later my eyes cleared, and I could see the cameraman. It was Barry Harper, the self-styled reporter who tried to interview me earlier.

He smiled and gave a little wave.

"Thank you, Mayor. Please reconsider my offer of a contribution. You'd make a stellar congresswoman—and a beautiful one." Wentworth started away.

"Don't underestimate me—Horace." I had to force the words through my teeth. He stopped midstep. I could see his shoulders tense. He didn't turn; he just resumed his path, stopping for a second to say something under his breath to Harper. The weasel nodded and walked away, distancing himself by several paces from the man who hired him.

Blood surged through my veins. If I had an aneurism anywhere I'd know in moments. I had just been worked over by an expert. I wondered how the papers would handle it if I tossed Horace Dean Wentworth on one of Paul's still-hot barbecues. For a few moments I considered risking it.

I looked at Nat. She had turned her wheelchair so she could watch Wentworth walk down the pier. She was mumbling. At first, I thought she was speaking in a different language. She was. Twentieth-century longshoreman.

chapter 21

Nat and I conferred in the Fish Kettle until nearly midnight. Paul and his wife could tell that something had gone wrong and that we needed privacy. They gave us a wide berth as they and two employees finished cleaning up and closing down the restaurant. We sat at one of the tables to accommodate Nat's wheels. Her language had cleared up but she was still strung tighter than a banjo string. She drummed the table with her one good hand.

"We need to think damage control," she said. "We need to take the lead, the initiative."

"Okay, let's not make this worse than it is." I wanted to sound calm and self-assured. "All that has happened is that he's asked for something he's not going to get, offered something we're not going to take, and took a picture that will do him no good."

Nat looked at me as if my brains had begun leaking out my ears. "Do I need to lay this out for you?"

"No. I'm just trying to be optimistic. I'll say one thing: he's slick, and I don't mean that in an admirable way." I took a sip of coffee. I didn't want it, but I had a lot of nervous energy to burn.

"So is an eel." Nat pulled a small package of crackers from a holder on the table. Paul kept them there for folks who like crackers in their chowder. She began breaking them in their plastic wrapper. I don't think she knew she was doing it. "Okay, let's break this down. You gave a good summary. Let's look at each one. What did you say?"

It took me a second to realize that she was referring to my attempt to soften what happened. "He asked for something he isn't going to get, offered something we won't take, and took a picture that will do him no good. It was something like that."

"Right. He offered a contribution to the campaign. Not unusual in and of itself. He was smart to do it here. After all, this was a fund-raiser."

"But he didn't offer the legal limit or under, he offered to bundle the contribution."

Nat crushed the crackers some more. "It's a way to work around the law, a way to give large sums of money to a candidate. It's done but frowned upon."

"We shouldn't have any problem with that. We refuse to take a dime from him or his organization. Of course, he could have people send money in individually, then later reveal that they worked for him. He might be able to twist that to make it look like we organized it all."

"I'll check into all the contributions we've received and see how many come from outside the district, then track them down to make sure they're valid." She set the crushed crackers on the table. The squares were now just bits of their former shape. She took a spoon and began smashing those to dust. I was pretty sure who she was crushing. "What was this about blight?"

"It has to do with eminent domain." I pushed the coffee cup away. Paul made the best coffee in town, but it was going down like acid. "Eminent domain is the power of government to appropriate private property for public use. For example, let's say the state needs to add a new off-ramp from one of its highways, so they need to build a curving ramp from the highway to a surface street so people can exit sooner and thereby lighten the traffic load on the freeway. Most likely they'll have to build on or over someone's property. Two things can happen. One, the state can purchase the property at fair market value, which is often less than the owner thinks it's worth, or they can declare eminent domain, removing the choice from the owner."

"I understand that part. What did he mean by 'blight'?"

"Governments can't seize property willy-nilly. They need some legal ground to proceed. In the case of the off-ramp it can be argued that the community benefits by allowing cars to exit sooner, decreasing traffic and traffic-related injury and death. But in the case of a single piece of property or several contiguous pieces like a city block it is more difficult to show the benefit. In Ohio a few years ago, a city wanted to replace some older homes with new condominiums. Their logic was that the city would benefit in permit fees and increased taxes. Naturally, the home owners who had worked decades to obtain and pay off the older homes were furious. To get what they wanted, the city council, led by the mayor, declared the neighborhood blighted and thereby created the legal ground to proceed."

"The homes were old and decrepit?"

"Not at all. The neighborhood was lovely. Even the mayor went on record calling the community 'cute.' That came back to haunt her."

"If the homes were well maintained then how could anyone call them blighted?"

I reached across the table and pulled the cracker packet from beneath Nat's vindictive spoon. "Paul has enough to clean up." Nat blushed but said nothing. "The city council defined what the word *blight* meant in that context. They said any house that didn't have three bedrooms, two baths, and an attached garage was substandard and therefore a blight."

"That's ridiculous." She started drumming her fingers again.

"It gets worse. The majority of the homes in the city fell into that category, not just the neighborhood in question. Now get this, every member of the council including the mayor lived in a house that would have been declared blighted if it were in the subject neighborhood. In other words, the mayor's home had only one bath, two bedrooms, and a detached garage. Blight was in the eye of the beholder."

"Or in the wallet. Tell me there's good news in this story."

"In this case, yes. The neighborhood fought back and the mayor and some council members were voted out of office."

"Good."

"I think so, but there have been other cases that didn't go so well. No happy ending in those."

Nat chewed her lower lip. "If I have this right, Wentworth wants the council to declare a single piece of property blighted so the city can claim eminent domain. Pass it off to Rutger Howard's organization so they can build their restaurant."

"Yes. That's my take on it. He said he already has a supporter on the council. I've got that narrowed down to two people."

"Jon Adler and Tess Lawrence."

"Exactly."

"Well, the good news is two people don't make a majority on the council. Assuming he has both. If he doesn't, he will."

Someone turned up the heat in my belly.

"Uh-oh. I don't like that look." She stopped drumming her fingers and gave me a long stare.

"Titus Overstreet has cancer. He has surgery in a few days." I could see two emotions fighting in Nat. As someone who had spent more hours in a hospital than most, she could empathize with Titus. The no-nonsense, steel trap mind of Nat also did the simple math.

"He'll be out for a couple of months leaving just four on the council. Still, at worse, that's a tie vote." She eyed me again. "Why am I seeing that same look?"

I told her about my meeting with Larry and Titus.

A few more terms escaped her lips—the kind of terms that get omitted in congressional records. "Tess Lawrence, deputy mayor." She shook her head. "That means if you miss a council meeting only three people will be there, and two are connected at the hip."

"I suppose I'll just have to make every meeting. I haven't missed one yet." I knew it was a stupid thing to say.

"You've never run for congress before. Your schedule is full now, it will soon be overflowing. When you win the primary, then the real work begins."

"We meet one night a week. I'll have to keep that night free."

"I have a feeling there is more going on here, but I can't put my finger on it."

I felt the same way and said so. I also had a question. "What do you think that photo was about?"

"I don't know yet but it unsettles me. A rumor campaign, perhaps. Maybe he's arrogant enough to think he's already won and that was his trophy shot."

That burned me. I don't like being manipulated. In fact, it makes me crazy. "When you came up to us in the conversation, you seemed to know Wentworth."

"I've seen his picture a few times. I was doing research for a couple of business magazines. It was just basic background stuff, but I touched on Rutger Howard's business. Howard is a bit of a recluse. He's extremely wealthy and oversees several businesses. The Bennie's restaurant chain is just one. If I remember correctly, he has fingers in pharmaceuticals, real estate, and several other areas."

"You have information tucked away on these guys, don't you?"

"Not much, but you can bet your panty hose I will by this time tomorrow."

Paul insisted on walking us to our cars. I stayed with Nat until she was situated in her uniquely equipped van. It was a new acquisition that allowed her to drive despite her paralysis and limited use of one arm and hand. Paul escorted me to my car, and I made my way home. My mind was buzzing like bees in a jar, and if I didn't quiet them I knew I wouldn't see more than an hour's sleep. To distract myself, I turned on the radio and found the sonorous voice of Robby Hood. Tonight's topic: a security guard with a ghost story.

chapter 22

The night passed slowly. I slept, but not well. I fought with the bed, the pillow, the sheets, and the comforter. I lost every round. When I'm upset or stressed I dream—bizarre, nonsensical dreams. H. Dean Wentworth kept popping up. In one dream we were back on the pier arguing. In a rage, he picked up Nat, wheelchair and all, and tossed her over the edge into the water where she sank like a stone. That sat me up in bed. Later I dreamed H. Dean and I traveled back in time. I was driving a covered wagon and chasing him across the prairie. When I woke up, I promised myself not to listen to Robby Hood again.

At five I rose, donned my jogging shorts and shoes, and hit the treadmill. I felt sluggish, and it took fifteen minutes to feel like I was awake and moving. I forced myself to stay on the instrument of torture until six. A hot shower, some Bible study, a cup of coffee, and a Danish later, I was ready to . . . go back to bed. I didn't. I left the house at seven thirty and drove to the office. I took the long way. I needed to see that the sun still rose according to schedule and that the ocean was where I left it last night.

I used the time to think and then to pray. I'm not good at praying, I admit it. And that brings me a great deal of guilt. I know I'm new to all this stuff about faith. I've come to believe what I read in the Bible, I enjoy church, and most of all, I feel changed. But when the truth is told, I often feel out of place. I watch people at church, and prayer seems to come so easily to them. I feel like a toddler trying to connect with adults. I have never been an unbeliever. My parents took me to church on the big holidays, Easter and Christmas, but one doesn't learn much when only three or four hours of the year are spent in the church. So while I never disbelieved, I've never been prone to believe.

Perhaps that was why prayer was so difficult. I'm used to one-on-one conversations where opinions are shared clearly and sometimes pointedly, or speaking before a group of ten to five hundred. I'm comfortable with all of that. But talking to God? That seemed out of my reach. I prayed anyway. All I could think of to ask for was wisdom. I knew I needed that.

I arrived at two minutes before eight. That's late for me, but I didn't begrudge myself the decompression time I spent in driving and prayer. I was feeling close to being alive although I doubted I looked it. Celeste was at the reception desk. She greeted me, looked at me, and then offered to bring me a large cup of coffee. *Great, Mayor-Just-Raised-from-the-Dead-and-Looks-It is in*. I told her I'd love a coffee and gave her my best smile. She gave me the it-must-be-horrible-to-be-your-age grin. It was a good thing we were close.

I plunged into my outer office, barked hello to Floyd, and then barreled into my home away from home.

"Mayor," Floyd said as I marched through the office, "there's—"

"Not now, Floyd—" I pulled up short. Someone was seated in one of the chairs facing my desk. He rose.

"Good morning, Madam Mayor." Judson West gave me a smile that slipped a little when he saw me.

"Yeah, rough couple of nights." I wanted to spare him the struggle of trying to be nice. "Sit down." I rounded my chair, dropped my purse in the drawer, and took a seat.

"Too much party last night?" He sat again. He was wearing a blue button-down shirt, tan sport coat, and black trousers. It was the first time I had seen him without a tie.

"Too much of several things, including coffee at midnight."

"Your date should have warned you about caffeine at such a late hour." His eyes sparkled.

"Nat did, and she hates it when people say we're dating."

He laughed. "I imagine so. I apologize for showing up without calling, but I thought I'd catch you before you started your day. I imagine you're pretty busy now."

"That's an understatement, and it's going to get worse."

He nodded, fidgeted a little, then said, "I'm sorry I didn't make it to the fund-raiser. I intended to come but I got caught up in other things."

"Don't let Chief Webb hear you say that. He might demote you if you start showing up at my campaign stops."

"He's not that kind of guy. True, he'll probably vote for someone else." He dusted off invisible specks from his shirt. He seemed nervous.

"I thought he might vote for me for congress just so I won't be mayor any longer. You know, a tactical vote."

"Tactical vote. I like that." He paused. "I have three things to run by you. The chief recognizes that finding a murder victim on city property might have ramifications for you and the council."

"For him as well," I added. "The police station is just around the corner from the murder scene."

"That's been eating at him some. He's been a little grumpy lately."

Lately? He was always grumpy around me. "What can I do for you this morning? Do you have some news about Fritzy's husband?"

"Yes." He straightened himself in the seat as if changing posture made the conversation official. "I was able to persuade the medical examiner to push the autopsies up. They're pretty busy, but once we had a second victim things moved more quickly. I must confess that I threw your name around a lot, reminding them that Mrs. Fritz works for you."

"Technically, she works for the city."

"It sounds better my way and carries more currency with the folks at the coroner's office. By the way, Dr. Egan wonders why you don't come by and visit anymore."

"Yeah, yeah, I bet you guys are still having a chuckle about that. Did Egan find anything useful?"

"Not much more than we already surmised. Both died as a result of a broken neck. The assailant is most likely a male, right-handed, and known to the victims. Mr. Lopez had been drinking but not in excess. No signs of drugs or alcohol in Mr. Fritz. The breaks were clean and apparently done in a single motion, indicating some training."

"Wait a second. How do you know the man is right-handed?"

He raised an eyebrow. "The marks on the jaw are bruises left by the right hand of the murderer. Based on the size and placement of the bruises we think that it was a man standing between five ten and six foot tall, but we can't hang our hats on that. That assumption is based on the size of the fingers and the height of the victims, but such things vary greatly."

"You said that the attacker was familiar to the victims?" That puzzled me.

"No defensive wounds on the body. No sign of struggle at the scene. If someone just went after the victims we would expect to see bruising on the arms or other injuries. Mr. Fritz wasn't a young man, but he was in good shape for his age. I bet he could still throw a punch but his hands showed just what you'd expect from a mechanic and nothing more. The same is true for Mr. Lopez, and he was younger and in better shape."

"They were killed by someone they *knew*? That's unsettling."

Celeste appeared at the door with a cup of coffee. She recognized West.

"I'm sorry. I didn't know you had someone with you. Would you like some coffee, Detective West?"

West, ever the gentleman, stood when Celeste walked in. His momma raised him right. "Hi, Celeste. No, thanks. I've already had three cups. I think I'm becoming an addict."

They exchanged pleasantries for a few moments, then Celeste went back to her desk.

"She's looking well," West said. "It's good to see."

"Life made her grow up faster than she should, but she has shown real resolve. I have her filling in for Fritzy."

"I didn't see her when I came in. I must have just missed her. They may not have known the assailant, but they were not initially frightened of him, or they would have fought back. We think that the killer is on the beefy side. In both cases it would have been difficult to break the necks of our victims where we found them. Especially Mr. Fritz. For that to happen, the killer would need to have been on the plane and directly behind his victim. For that and other reasons we think that he did his killing, then placed the bodies where we found them."

"Other reasons?"

He took a breath. "I don't want to be too graphic here, Mayor, but when a person dies suddenly, they often . . . lose control of some body functions—such as the bladder. When we found Mr. Fritz it was clear that had happened to him. We checked the area around the aircraft and found trace elements of urine. Tests aren't back yet, but we suspect that it is from Mr. Fritz, and if it is, it will identify the actual place of his killing. There was also trace evidence of dirt and oil on his face. At this point, we're assuming he acquired that when his body was lowered or fell to the floor."

If we weren't talking about the husband of a friend of mine, this would be interesting. At the moment it was striking me as grotesque.

"What about Lopez?"

"He didn't . . . have the same response. However, there was what looks like motor oil on an otherwise clean shirt and some dirt and grime in his hair, as if he had been lying on the asphalt."

"This doesn't make sense. Murder never does, but why move the bodies?"

He shrugged again. "Best guess is the killer moved his victims to delay their discovery. You know, to give him some extra time to escape."

"But he's not trying to escape," I said. "He didn't leave town. Instead, he crossed town and killed someone else."

"I can't argue that."

"Jerry thinks we ought to look at what they have in common."

"Dr. Jerry Thomas?" He studied me. I saw him stiffen.

"We were talking, and I was explaining what I knew. I kept talking about what made the scenes different, and he said he kept noticing what was the same."

"Such as both victims are men; both have wives, albeit one was estranged; both were in vehicles of transportation?"

"Exactly." I was surprised. "Almost word for word."

"I've done this work before." His words had chilled a couple of degrees. I thought it best to move on.

"You said you had three things. That was one."

He relaxed. "The other is we've released the body of Mr. Fritz. We're hanging on to Lopez for another day or two."

"Already? That seems fast."

"Like I said, we had a late night. Fritzy said she was eager to get on with the funeral."

"I'll let her know—"

"I already have. I called while I was waiting on you."

I said that was good and waited for the third item on West's mental list. He stared at me. I stared at him. Finally, I said, "And the third thing is?"

He didn't answer right away and when he started to speak, his cell phone sounded. He frowned, said, "Excuse me," and then answered it. His face darkened, his brow furrowed, and his lips drew into a tight line. "I'm on my way." He stood.

"That didn't look good."

He gazed down at me, looking both sad and angry. "There's been another murder. I'm afraid I'm going to have cut short our meeting." He started for the door.

"Wait a minute. Who? Where?"

He stopped and redirected his attention to me. I stood behind the desk. "I don't have the details yet. A security guard at the marina. He was found dead in his guard shack. That's all I know."

I slowly lowered myself back into my chair. "Same cause of death?"

"Unofficially? Yes. I'll know more when I get there."

"You know what this means."

He closed the door to my office and took a step closer. "It means we have a serial killer. It means we've had a year's worth of murders in less than a week."

That was what I was thinking, and it made me sick.

He glanced back to the door, then to me. "This is lousy timing, but the third thing on my list was personal business, not professional."

I looked up. My heart did a somersault. "Personal?"

"I think it's time we started dating. I was going to be a whole lot smoother than that but . . . Anyway, we'll talk later."

For some reason I had goose bumps. Maybe it was the news of the third murder, maybe it was my weariness, or maybe it was the man standing in front of me. I started to speak when my phone buzzed. I hit the speaker button. "Yes, Floyd."

"Doug Turner is on line one. He says it's important. Councilwoman Lawrence is on line two."

West smiled. "Life is never dull for you, is it?"

"Only in my dreams."

chapter 23

Doug Turner was insistent that I see him. He could be pushy—after all, he was a reporter—but I detected something in his voice that made me yield. When I asked what the urgency was, he demurred. I don't like someone keeping me in the dark, but I knew Doug well enough to know he didn't play games. I agreed to meet.

"I have an editorial meeting in a few minutes, but I can be at your office within the hour. How's that?"

"I've got a few things to do, too." I looked at the light on my phone that seemed to flash Morse code: "I'm waiting. I'm waiting." Tess would have to wait a few more moments. The light blinked out. She had hung up. She was an impatient woman. "I'll be here."

"Okay. I'll be there when I can." He paused. "This is going to be off the record, and I prefer that it happen behind closed doors."

Off the record?

"Doug, you're starting to freak me out—"

"I just got paged for the meeting. Gotta go." He hung up. Everyone was hanging up on me. I set the receiver back in the cradle and leaned back in my chair. A slight headache was making threats from the area around my temples. I hadn't slept well in several nights; I had a reporter acting like Woodward and Bernstein; and the night before, a man simultaneously offered me a bribe and threatened my campaign as easily as he might order an ice cream cone at a Baskin-Robbins. Add to that, I needed to confront a council member about behind-the-scenes deal making, the same woman who could turn a birthday greeting into an argument. Then there was Titus facing surgery, Fritzy planning the funeral of her dead husband, a murderer who—if West's call was accurate—had taken his third life.

Then there was West's bombshell. "I think it's time we started dating." That brought on a whole new set of feelings. My innards tingled when he said the words. The logical part of my mind shouted, "Not possible. I'm mayor, and you work on the police force." To which my heart—at least, I think it was my heart—replied, "So what?" Before West had finished crossing my threshold, the image of Jerry Thomas popped into my mind. That image was trailed by a larger picture of my deceased husband.

I was growing old just sitting in my chair thinking about these things. So I did what I always do. I got busy.

Someplace in his life my father picked up a saying, "Custer would have been a better general if he could have gotten the Indians to come over the hill one at a time." It was folksy, quaint, and historically inaccurate but it made a point: Take one problem at a time.

It was time for Indian number one: Tess Lawrence. I punched the intercom button on my phone. "Floyd, please call Councilwoman Lawrence and tell her that I'm coming over for a visit."

I rose, straightened my clothing—a peach cardigan-style coat, matching skirt, white shell top, and spectator pumps with a low heel (my feet still hurt from trotting the boards of the pier last night)—and marched out. Floyd was just hanging up the phone.

"She said she could come down here." Normally, I preferred to meet in my office. Sitting behind my large desk gave me a psychological advantage, but I'd had too much disrupting, even disturbing, news in there. I wanted a change of scenery, even if that scenery was just a few yards down the hall. Besides, I hated putting off confrontation. I waved him off.

I moved through the common area—several desks for secretaries, part-time help, and aides to the other members of the council. My office was the only one with two compartments and my aide the only one with an office to himself. It was one of the perks of being mayor. I walked into the corridor that led to the offices of council members. The offices bracket the hallway, two on either side. Titus and Larry were to my left, Tess and Jon to my right. The corridor had become our equivalent of the Mason-Dixon Line. I glanced to my left and was surprised to see Titus at his desk. I leaned in.

"Shouldn't you be home or something?"

He smiled at me but the grin lacked some of the brilliance I associated with Titus. No doubt the burden of tomorrow was weighing on him today. "Just cleaning up a few things. I don't want to come back to a messy desk. Besides . . ." He trailed off.

"Things are a little depressing at home?"

He nodded. "Yeah, my wife is a little worried. I keep telling her that everything is going to be fine, that they caught the cancer early, but she insists on worrying."

"Wives are that way. It's part of the contract. Wives who don't worry get kicked out of the union."

He laughed. "You speak to Tess yet?"

"I'm going there now, but I have different fish to fry."

He studied me. "Have you changed your mind about what Larry and I suggested?"

What they had suggested made sense, but having Tess as deputy mayor grated on my nerves, especially now. "I'll fill you in later." I turned away but not before seeing Titus's black face darken. This was important to him, and I felt the cold tide of guilt rising up to remind me that Titus didn't need more to worry about.

Tess's door was closed. She knew I was coming. The least she could do was have the door open for me. I knocked.

"Come in." It sounded more like an order than an invitation. I took a deep breath, suppressed my anger, reminded myself that I was a political professional, and charged.

Tess stood when I entered. I closed the door behind me. "Mayor," she said with a dip of her head. As usual, she looked impeccable. Prone to dark colors that contrasted with her very short, mousse-laden, bleached-white hair, she wore a charcoal gray pinstripe, very business-looking pantsuit. "Please have a—" I was already seated.

She sat in her chair. Her office, like all council member offices, was two-thirds the size of mine. In the years we had served together I had only been in her cave a handful of times. The desk was a custom-made affair with an Asian feel, made of some dark wood I couldn't identify. It was neat, orderly, and completely free of personal memorabilia. A few pictures of her with other officeholders adorned the walls, but they were small and not prominently placed. One large piece of art hung on the wall. It was a landscape of Santa Rita as seen from a boat at sea. It caught my eye.

"Is that new?" I asked.

"Three months."

Perhaps I was avoiding the inevitable but I rose and approached the painting. It was exquisitely done in oils. The colors were vibrant, the detail crisp enough to recognize but not so crisp as to distract from the art. "This is . . . lovely. Who's the artist?"

"Me."

I snapped my head around. "Really? I didn't know you painted."

She looked wounded. "I imagine there are many things about me you don't know."

That stung—twice. Once because she was right and again because I had it coming. I tried a diversionary tactic. "How did you get this perspective? I've seen many photos and paintings of the city but never one from sea. Did you work from a photo?"

"I went out on a half-day boat. My husband fished, I painted." Tess's husband was an architect, which occasionally required that she recuse herself when any of his projects came before council. "How can I help you, Mayor?" The words were chilly.

I took my seat again. "Two things. Let's get the nasty business out of the way first. After my fund-raiser last night I was approached by a man who first offered to bend the campaign contribution laws, then suggested that I help him declare eminent domain to obtain a piece of property so his firm can build a restaurant. He said he already had support on the council. I assume that's you and maybe Jon."

"Dean Wentworth?"

"So you do know him." My jaw tightened.

"I met him two days ago—"

I've been working on my temper, exercising my patience. All exercise is hard and uphill. This was no different. My tight jaw came loose. "Do you really think I would allow some hotshot executive to come into my city and start snagging people's property with my help? I will not do that, and I will fight you tooth and nail. How dare you work behind my back?"

"Mayor—"

"You know the council has leaned in the direction of the small business owner—"

"Mayor, please."

"No. You are out of line. Your actions are unethical. If he offered you money for your next campaign, and you took it—"

That must have struck a cord. She slammed her hand on the desk, filling the room with a pop that sounded like gunfire.

"That is enough! You're the one out of line." She stood and leaned over the desk and stabbed the air with a manicured finger. "I tried to tell you about it. I phoned your office to set up a meeting but you blew me off. If you made a little time for every member of the council and not just your favorites you could have saved yourself this meeting and been prepared for Wentworth. But no. Not you. It's your way or no way."

"My door is always open," I started, but she had more steam to vent.

"No, it's not. My access to you is limited, and it's limited by you. You've been pushing me away for years, acting as if I'm going to sneak up and stab you in the back."

"That's exactly what I think."

"Well, you're wrong." She sat down again. "We don't agree on many things. Truth is, I think you're a poor mayor, but you are the mayor. And I'm not pretending to be the good gal here. I'm acerbic, quick tempered, and driven. Yes, I know that. I do live with myself, you know. You're no peach either. I'll grant you that you're the darling of city hall, at least for most people, and I'm not, nor will I ever be. I've never been popular. I've always been on the fringe. Frankly, I don't care. I am who I am. But one thing I am not is crooked. How dare you suggest that I'd take inappropriate money."

I felt wounded and like an injured she-bear I felt compelled to fight back. "Oh, please. Lie to me if you wish, but don't lie to yourself. You're opportunistic and you know it. You're always looking for the next step up."

"I'm not the one running for congress."

That stabbed like an ice dagger. "No, but you were thinking about it."

"Yes, I was, and pulled out once you made known your decision to run."

"What?"

"I had been working a plan to run for the seat for two years." She took several deep breaths. "I put it on hold."

"Why?" It was the best response I could come up with. My blood was pumping so hard I was finding it difficult to think.

"Because I can't beat you. Is that what you want to hear? I can't beat you, Maddy. I never could. Your image is better, your people skills are better, your speaking is better, everything you do is better. You're even prettier. My running against you would be a waste of time and money."

I didn't know what to say. I knew she had wanted to run for the seat, but she never announced. I had assumed I had just beaten her to the punch.

She lowered her voice. She seemed to melt into the chair. "And for your information, I sent Wentworth packing. If he has someone on the council, it isn't me."

I sat there in silence trying to figure out if she was lying to me or telling the truth. "You didn't promise to help him?"

"Of course not. Have you ever known me to do something like that?"

Of course I did. There was that time ... well, surely the time she ... A light of understanding dawned in my brain. I was an idiot. Titus and Larry had said that Tess had never done anything to hurt the city. "I thought that maybe you and Jon ..."

"I can't speak for Jon," Tess grumbled. "You'll have to talk to him yourself, although you might try getting some facts before you do."

Another slap, but I was beginning to feel like I deserved it. I fumbled for something to say. I wanted to strike out, wanted to give Tess a verbal beating that would leave her bruised for the next decade, but I couldn't come up with the words, or the reason. I had drawn conclusions based on no facts whatsoever. I was mute, but Tess wasn't.

"Do you know what property Wentworth wants declared blighted?" I didn't, and I confessed it. She frowned at my ignorance. "It's the corner of Ventura Boulevard and Barker Road."

That was on the fringes of old town Santa Rita. I tried to imagine that area. It was close enough to one of the larger residential areas but still near to the freeway. Location, location, location was the realtor's motto. That corner had it. If memory served, one could see the ocean from that lot. "Johnny Jake's Tires?"

Tess nodded. "After I showed Wentworth the outside of my door, I did some research and took a drive. The tire store has been there since 1946. John Jake founded it after he returned home from fighting in World War II. He passed it on to his son in 1980. His grandson took over five years ago. It's been a family business all along. Did Wentworth tell you that he had made an offer on the property?"

"Yes."

"He didn't. At least according to Tony Jake, the grandson. He told me he's never heard of Wentworth or Rutger Howard. Wentworth never made an offer. The property is too expensive, and the Jake family knows it. What Wentworth wants is for us to declare it blighted, seize it through eminent domain, and then sell it on the cheap to Howard's company on the promise of improved business and a greater tax base. I'm smelling serious stink here."

I had come to Tess's office to set her straight, but she had turned the tables on me. Not only had she not agreed to help Wentworth and cronies but had given him the figurative back of her hand. Then she did what I should have done: she got the information and details.

A hot silence settled between us. I had been declawed. Like a child trying to catch bubbles in the wind, I was snatching at words. I needed to apologize. I really did. "You think he's trying to work us with smoke and mirrors?"

She nodded. Her jaw was clamped like a vise. "He lied to me the first five minutes we were together. I will assume he's lying about everything else."

"Let me ask you something, Tess." I cleared my throat. It didn't need clearing but my mind did. "Do you think his telling me he had help on the council was just to get us at each other's throats?"

"Since I can't read his mind, I can't say, but I know how guys like him work. He's the front guard, the guy who scouts out the terrain, and sows seeds of doubt. Rutger Howard is going to be the real problem. If the messenger is evil there's little doubt the message sender is worse." Then she shrugged. "Of course, I don't know that he doesn't have someone in his pocket. I can tell you, I'm not there. Maybe he got to Jon, but I doubt it. Jon's a criminal defense lawyer; he knows what such deals can lead to. Jon can be selfish, we all can, but I don't think he'd do anything that will ultimately end with the words 'five to ten years.'"

Tess always struck me as a cold woman, frosty in mind and heart. She was brutally blunt, impossible to intimidate, annoyingly persistent, and had several personal agendas. She was not a nice person. Not around me anyway. At the moment, I felt like I had become her clone.

"You said there were two things," she prompted. "Was there some other crime you wanted to accuse me of?"

"Larry and Titus came to me and convinced me that I was wrong in my resisting your desire to be deputy mayor."

"Well, at least you're consistent, Mayor."

"I want to say that I won't stand in the way. Even without my vote you'll be a shoo-in."

"Four to one, eh." She frowned. "No thanks. I don't know what brought about this change of heart, but I'm no longer interested.

You and I are too far apart on some of the issues and personally. Especially personally, now. Work out some other deal."

Titus was depending on her saying yes. I had just torpedoed my biggest supporter. "Don't say no yet. We vote next Tuesday. Perhaps you'll change your mind."

"I won't." Her phone rang, and she answered. "It's your detective friend. He says your aide told him you were here."

I leaned forward and took the phone. I listened for a moment then said a thank-you and handed the receiver back to Tess. Standing, I looked at the painting. I never imagined she had that kind of talent. The painting was . . . sensitive. Returning my attention to Tess I asked, "Will you be in this afternoon?" She nodded. "I'm calling us into a closed-door session at two. Can you make that?"

"Yes."

"Do you know if Jon will be available?"

Her jaw muscles began to swell in strain again. "You'll have to ask him. I don't keep his calendar." A moment later, she relented. "He said something about being in court today but that he would swing by around one."

"Thanks. I'll leave a message with his service." I headed for the door and opened it.

"By the way, Mayor," Tess said. "I take offense at you calling this *your* city. The city belongs to all of us, and I don't mean just the council."

A dark part of me wanted to take another verbal swing at my antagonist but I squelched it. We had knocked heads many times, and I believed that I had won every battle. But I had just gone ten rounds with her, and it had left me winded and bleeding in the corner. I looked at the painting again. "It really is a lovely piece of art, Tess."

I left and walked back to my office, head down like a dog too well-acquainted with a rolled-up newspaper. I would have spent the rest of the morning licking my wounds if I hadn't had other things on my mind.

I had one foot in the office when I said, "Floyd, I'm calling an emergency closed-door session with the members of the council. Make calls. It will be at two in the conference room. I want the city attorney there as well. Councilman Adler may be in court so leave a message at his office."

He stood. "Is there something wrong?"

"Just make the calls, Floyd, and be prepared to take notes at two. Oh, and Fred Markham. We were to meet at ten thirty. Tell him hold it until two."

"Yes, ma'am. Don't forget you have a meeting with Doug Turner."

My stomach took an elevator ride. I had forgotten. My confrontation with Tess had wiped my mental slate clean. "Is he here?" I looked in my office. Empty.

"No, but he called and said he was on his way."

"The day just gets better and better."

chapter 24

I had had enough of the office, and it wasn't even noon. Claustrophobia settled on me like a fog, which was unusual. I'm an office person. I like the security of four walls and the ability to control temperature and mood. While waiting for Doug Turner to show up, my office began to shrink and the air became stale. I knew nothing in the building had changed but things in me had. My emotional stew had come to a boil, and I didn't like it. What I wanted to do was ponder West's words about dating, but the heated exchange between Tess and me, and West's latest call forced all that to the back of the train.

I pulled Floyd off the Rutger Howard research I had asked him to do the day before and put him to work on the two o'clock meeting. Since Nat made her living researching events and people and she had committed herself to learning what she could, it was redundant to have Floyd do the same work, work he wouldn't be able to do as well.

I left the office, walked to the cafeteria at the north end of the building, and grabbed an orange juice. The cafeteria served not only city hall but the police station and courthouse, half a block down.

It's about the size of what you'd find in a medium-size hospital and could seat about 125 indoors and an additional thirty or so in the outdoor courtyard. For privacy and to lessen noise from the street, a wood fence enclosed the courtyard. Several patio tables and benches sat like mushrooms on the stamped concrete patio. I was alone. Lunch wouldn't begin for another half hour or so. From about eleven thirty to one thirty it would be buzzing. For now it was empty inside and out.

I took a seat and let the late morning sun bathe my back. I could feel my dark hair absorbing the sunlight and clinging miserly to the heat. January could be cool in Santa Rita, but it was seldom cold this close to the ocean. A gentle breeze massaged my face. I had brought no notepaper, no tape recorder, not even my handheld computer. I was carrying enough luggage in my mind.

Tess had dressed me up one side and down another, and I found myself agreeing with her. That galled me. For years we had battled, for years I had tolerated her nonsense, but today she had been right. I had rushed to judgment rather than gather facts. In the process, I offended her, nipped Titus's plan in the bud, and made myself a guilt cocktail, all in one meeting. Man, I was good. I frowned at my orange juice, glad that I couldn't make it feel bad.

Tess had even been helpful, in her own awkward, prickly way. When she said she was smelling "some serious stink" I knew what she meant. Something was happening, and we didn't know what it was. The question before me—one of a dozen—was, had someone on the council crawled into bed with H. Dean Wentworth? If so, then who? How much trouble could he cause?

I stuck my straw in the orange juice. It was partially frozen. I began to work the straw up and down, mixing the ice with the rest of the drink.

"Churn that all you want, you're not going to get butter out of orange juice." Doug Turner crossed the patio and took a seat opposite me. He had a folder in his hand. I looked down at what I had been mindlessly doing and thought of Nat and her cracker abuse at the Fish Kettle.

"Hey, Doug." I forced a polite smile and extended my hand. He shook it and set the folder on the table. "Sorry, I was daydreaming. Can I get you anything?"

"Nah." He looked me over. "Cat eat your canary?"

"Never had a canary. Never had a cat." I took a sip of sweet fruit juice. "Just have a few things on my mind."

"I imagine." He folded his hands over the file. "I may be the blemish on your day."

I had to laugh at that. I didn't bother explaining. "You made this sound urgent." I was prompting.

"Important, if not urgent. First, let me say that everything is off the record. I'm not here; we're not having this discussion." I agreed but did nothing to conceal my puzzlement. "You remember that Harper character? The guy who was supposed to be filling in for me?"

"Barry Harper. I remember. I doubt I'll forget anytime soon."

"He was annoying, all right. I went back to the paper and dropped the boom on my editor for sending someone like him out. I vented, then he told me that he hadn't sent Harper out. That Harper had come to him wanting work as a stringer. My editor said, 'Well, bring me something, and we'll talk.'"

"You didn't get fired?"

"No way. I've been there long enough that I can bruise a few egos and still show up the next day. Anyway, Harper strolls in this morning, with this." He pushed the file my direction. I set my orange juice aside and opened the folder. It was what I feared: A picture of me with Wentworth's arm around me. I had been surprised by the photo and my eyes were partly closed, giving me that lovely, I'm-too-drunk-to-stand-up-by-myself look. Nat was in the picture too, looking aghast at me, not the camera.

"It's from last night," I admitted. "This guy came up and started a conversation. Next thing I know I'm getting my picture taken. I didn't approve. What does Harper want done with this?"

"He said he wanted it printed, and he wanted us to pay for it."

There were a few sheets of paper held together with a paper clip on the upper left corner. I read the double-space type. "This is awful."

"On more than one count."

"You're not going to publish this, are you?" I pushed the photo and article back to Doug like it smelled of rotten fruit. "He didn't even spell my name right."

"Of course not. This is some of the worst writing I've ever seen. I volunteer as a consultant for the journalism class at the high school, and those kids write a dozen times better." He closed the folder and held it up. "This isn't anything more than what my neighbor's dog leaves on my front lawn."

"There's an unpleasant image."

"Trust me, I'm being polite. You should have heard what my editor called it."

"No thanks. So is Harper just a nitwit who has delusion of journalistic fame?"

"I thought so at first, but that conclusion doesn't feel right. There's something going on backstage, and I want to know what it is."

He leaned forward. I did the same. "Mayor, my instincts tell me someone is up to something. We reporters live for such things, but when someone tries to make me a player in a game I didn't know was going on, it gets my hackles up."

"I still don't—"

"Hang on. There's more. You know that when I first met him in your office I was less than kind."

"He had it coming."

"That and more, but here's my point. He brought a copy of the picture and the article to give to my editor, but he also made sure I got a copy by giving it to our receptionist. I found it on my desk. Why would Harper, whom I gave a tongue-lashing to, want me to see his work?"

"Because he's arrogant or stupid or both."

"He's not stupid. He knows how the journalistic mind works. The picture and the story aren't what's up. In the article he says you were seen in deep discussions with H. Dean Wentworth, associate of Rutger Howard. I looked at the photo, I read the article, and dismissed both out of hand, but I can't dismiss Wentworth. Why is he at your fund-raiser? So I do a little research—and so did my editor—and we learn that he lives in Atlanta. It's a long way from Atlanta to Santa Rita. He might be vacationing, but why would he be giving you a here's-my-best-buddy hug?"

"So you think there's a story behind the story, is that it?"

"That's it. Harper—probably Wentworth through Harper—wants us to raise our radar. The question is why."

"This doesn't make sense," I said. "Wentworth approached me and . . . You said this was off the record, right?"

"I did but if you reveal anything too juicy, I might go mad and throw myself into the sea."

He was doing me a favor, and I knew it. "Wentworth wants to build a restaurant in Santa Rita. It's a Bennie's. They're everywhere. Family dining and all that. He wants help in getting some property, I told him no." I left the juicy details out. There's nothing worse than a wet reporter. "There are many people in the city opposed to franchise or corporate-owned restaurants in the city limits. They feel it takes away the small-town charm."

"We haven't been a small town for quite a while."

"But the charm remains. What confuses me is why someone who wants my help would try to degrade me in the papers. Do you think he took it to other newspapers and media?"

"No. I've made a few calls, and no major paper from Santa Barbara south has seen anything yet." He paused. "I think Wentworth is firing a shot across your bow. You said you told him no."

"Yes. Pretty clearly, too." I thought about revealing Wentworth's offer of big money to the campaign but decided against it. I would be pushing the off-the-record agreement too far.

"You're holding back some things, aren't you?"

"It's my job." I picked up my orange juice and took another sip. "Do you think Harper gave you a copy because he assumed you'd bring it to me?"

"And because he wants us to investigate deeper. Which, by the way, is happening. That editorial meeting I told you about was about this article and the story behind it. Terri Slater is on it. Do you know Terri?"

"Can't say that I do. Who is he?"

"She. As you know, we're not a big-city paper so we double up on our duties. I handle crime and politics—redundant as that is."

"Cute."

"Terri does features and business. Since Wentworth is associated with the wealthy Rutger Howard, she got the assignment. I'm supposed to follow the political element. Be careful, Terri is young and out to prove something. She may come knocking."

"Swell. I still can't figure Wentworth's angle. It looks like he's biting the hand he wants to feed him. That doesn't make sense."

"Do you like magic?"

That caught me off guard. "What? You going to do a card trick?"

"I was never very good at those. When I was a kid I wanted to do stage magic. I didn't have what it takes, but I did learn a few tricks and, more importantly, a few lessons. When a stage magician is doing his bit he will do his best to misdirect your attention. If he holds something up in his right hand, you can bet he's doing something with his left. This article and picture is what Wentworth wants you to see. I wonder what he's doing with the other hand. Make sense?"

I said it did and thanked him. He rose, excused himself, and started for the door that led back into the cafeteria. Through the windows I could see the first shift of lunch-hungry workers. "Doug?" He stopped and turned. "Are we still off the record?"

"Sure."

"There's been a third murder . . . a security guard at the marina. I'm not revealing any secrets here, but I just as soon you didn't tell people you heard it from me."

"Thanks," he said. "Your secret is safe with me, but I already knew. I have a police scanner. I appreciate the gesture."

He left me with my orange juice and the puzzle of H. Dean Wentworth.

chapter 25

I fielded calls. I wrote memos. I had "hallway" meetings and did my best to put my universe in order. It wasn't working. I felt as if someone had taken half a dozen jigsaw puzzles and emptied them on my desk, then said, "There ya go. Have fun." I wasn't having fun.

The city manager had sent me a memo notifying me that the contract for trash service on all the city's property was going to double. We had just finished our budget and allowed for a 10 percent hike, but not doubling of fees. That contract would have to be renegotiated. The problem was, we couldn't just switch contractors. There was only one such service in the city, and bringing in a firm from Santa Barbara or other nearby city would be just as expensive.

County Disposal, a privately owned firm despite the name, had been servicing the city and its citizens for twenty years. Why the sudden change? The memo cited increased cost of doing business, cost of gasoline, and hikes in minimum wage. All valid but not valid enough to justify doubling their fees. They were taking advantage of my run for congress. My guess was they thought I'd roll over on this because I didn't want negative publicity.

I was becoming paranoid.

Fred Markham had sent a note informing me of a lawsuit being leveled against the city for a fall taken by an elderly woman in one of our parks. That was no surprise. Suits are filed against cities like clockwork. We're easy targets and have the appearance of deep pockets. I put that aside. It would be a subject for our next closed-door session. Not the two o'clock one I had called for today. That one was full enough. Lawsuits moved slowly.

I pushed more paper, fiddled with a speech I was to give next week to a local veterans' organization, and jotted down a few remarks for a dinner I was giving for my campaign volunteers. Work that needed to be done washed over me like a rogue wave. Normally, I thrive on pressure and a long to-do list, but today it threatened to overwhelm me. My mind was elsewhere.

Added to all this was the overwhelming task of education—my education. I had been in local politics for over a decade. I knew that field inside and out. The working of state government was familiar terrain also, but congress, well, congress is national policy. Some of the issues were like a foreign language. I understood the basic principles, the parts of government, the difference between a bill and a resolution. But I was now dealing with questions about the Homeland Security Act, terrorism, government-funded health care, military spending, Iraq, Iran, North Korea, Saudi Arabia, Supreme Court decisions, taxes, and a thousand other issues. A candidate could botch a question and sink a campaign with a single misspoken comment. Campaigns were hard enough to manage when things went right, but damage control was costly in time and effort and campaign contributions.

The real problem was my focus—I didn't have any. I tried to arrange my thoughts, whipping them into an orderly, manageable line, but my mind had different ideas. My thoughts were as obedient as cats in a sack.

What I really wanted to do was go to the marina. A third death. Going was out of the question. I had no business there, it would be of no help, it might look like grandstanding to my opponents, and I had work to do here.

Three murders. Three in four days. Three people died in the same fashion, and all related to the city. The gears of my brain seized. That thought had come from my subconscious. The first death was in one of the parking lots of city hall. The second, Fritzy's husband, had occurred at a small private airport—but the airport wasn't truly private. Its operation was, but the owners leased the property from the city. The same was true of the marina. Privately operated on property leased from the city. Coincidence?

The gears loosened up again. The connection to the city was there, but it was a bit of a stretch. How many people knew that the marina and airport leased our property? It was a stupid question. It was public information, and it didn't matter if thousands knew. What mattered was that one knew.

I had an itchy thought, one that stayed just out of scratching range. The city connection was interesting, but was there more? My intuition said yes, but what? I spun my chair around to face the credenza behind my desk. It was one of those that had an area for a computer and keyboard. The computer was on. It was part of Floyd's job to make sure my office was ready for me when I arrived: neat, files stacked, messages listed in order of importance, and the computer turned on. The screen was dark. I find screensavers distracting. I tapped a key and the monitor came to life. A second later I had the word processing program up and a blank page in front of me.

All my life, I've been a maker of lists. I find comfort in order, and I'm one of those weird people who feels momentary joy in crossing something off my to-do list as completed. Even if I didn't have a list on paper, I always had one in my mind. I followed my instincts.

WHEN	WHERE	WHO	HOW	?
Monday, early a.m.	City hall, front parking lot—old car	Jose Lopez	Broken neck	
Tuesday, early a.m.	SR airport, mechanic's bay— airplane	Jim Fritz, mechanic	Broken neck	
Thursday, early a.m.?	The marina, guard shack	??, security guard	Broken neck	

There were things I didn't know, and I filled those in with question marks. The chart could be more detailed, but I find it best to start small. It's the way my brain works. Start basic, then move to the complex.

I studied the list, looking for the Aha! but didn't see one. One thing I hadn't considered was the time of the killings. I knew that the first two had occurred in the wee hours of the morning but was guessing about the third. I felt safe in my speculation. After all, West was in my office early this morning when he got the call. It was fair to assume that the guard was found around shift change, meaning he was working graveyard, probably something like midnight to eight in the morning. West could confirm that for me. I added another column.

WHEN	WHERE	WHO	HOW	AGE	?
Monday, early a.m.	City hall, front parking lot—old car	Jose Lopez	Broken neck	Late 20s	
Tuesday, early a.m.	SR airport, mechanic's bay—airplane	Jim Fritz, mechanic	Broken neck	Early 60s	
Thursday, early a.m.?	The marina, guard shack	??, security guard	Broken neck	?	

Wednesday was an enigma. No murder. At least I had that to be thankful for. Still it begged the question, Why? Why no murder following the Tuesday/Wednesday show? Was the killer out of town? Busy? Maybe a murder attempt failed. Perhaps it was an effort to throw the police off. I couldn't imagine that it paid to be too predictable if you were in the killing business. Of course . . . there may have been another murder and the body is yet to be found. That thought made me sick.

I thought about what Jerry had said. He was making connections in ways I hadn't considered. There had only been two murders at that point. I chastised myself—*only two murders*. One was too many. I conjured up the discussion. He said that when I described what I knew about the crimes, he heard that both had been in vehicles, one in a car, the other in a plane; both had been "parked"; and both had wives, albeit Mr. Lopez was estranged. I couldn't speak to the security guard's marital status, but I was pretty sure the guard shack was not a mode of transportation. I didn't know the most recent victim's age, but guards were usually very young or retirement age. I'd have to leave that blank for now.

Another thing percolated to the top. I had been pushing it to the back of my mind because it made so little sense. Killing people on city property might make sense to a crazy person with a vendetta against the city, but . . . a radio station? The great thing about computers is that you can delete anything you don't like. I threw logic to the wind and filled in the chart a little more.

WHEN	WHERE	WHO	HOW	AGE	?
Monday, early a.m.	City hall, front parking lot—old car	Jose Lopez	Broken neck	Late 20s	Radio on—Robby Hood
Tuesday, early a.m.	SR airport, mechanic's bay—airplane	Jim Fritz, mechanic	Broken neck	Early 60s	Radio on—Robby Hood
Thursday, early a.m.?	The marina, guard shack	??, security guard	Broken neck	?	?

I felt ridiculous. What could a disembodied voice coming over the airwaves have to do with violent murders? Nonsense. A waste of time. I moved the cursor arrow to the red box with a white X in the upper right corner of the program ready to shut it down. It would ask if I wanted to save the document, and I would choose no. It had been a useless exercise. I hadn't stood a ghost of a chance . . .

If my mind had bells they would be ringing. Softly at first, but enough to get my attention. "Ghost of a chance," I mumbled. "Ghost of a . . ." Got it! Last night, I had been angry and offended by H. Dean Wentworth—Horace. His offer, which was nothing more than a bribe to me, and his subtle threat had gotten under my skin. I spent decompression time with Nat until midnight, then drove home feeling not the least bit decompressed. I remember turning the radio on and finding the Robby Hood show. Why not? Listening to the news wasn't going to make me feel better. I needed something less than serious. Instinctively, I had chosen him.

The program began to seep to the forefront of my thinking. Ghosts. He was interviewing someone who had seen a ghost—a security guard who had seen a ghost. I spun the chair around and skipped the intercom.

"Floyd! Get in here!"

chapter 20

"Show me." I popped out of my office chair and motioned for Floyd to plant his fanny. He hesitated. "It's a chair, not a throne, Floyd. Sit down."

He did and seemed to enjoy sitting in the mayor's seat. He had been with me for half a year. I thought the mystique would have worn off, but not for Floyd. Floyd was unique, and that's what I like about him.

"It's simple," he said, and pulled himself to my computer. "It's just like going to any other Web site. Start your browser." He did. "Type in *www.robbyhood.com* in the white address box." He typed. "Hit Enter and wait." We waited.

City hall was equipped with broadband three years ago so the connection came up in a second. Before me was a dark blue, nearly black background with a composite image at the center. The image moved, words appeared, and tinny electronic music trickled from my computer's speakers.

"Pretty cool Flash, huh?" Floyd said. "All the really neat sites have it. We should get one for the city's Web page."

"I'll think about it. What am I seeing?"

"It's just an introductory page meant to get your attention. That's what Flash is, an animated image that you can play over and over. It gets its name from the program used to make it, Macromedia Flash. They make Dreamweaver, Fireworks—"

"I know that, Floyd. I've been on the Internet before. I mean the background image."

He studied it for a second. "Oh, that's just composite artwork from some of the most popular topics. See, here's a UFO, here's a photo of Bigfoot, here's one of Mothman—"

"Mothman?"

"Yeah. It's a great story. See, back in the sixties—"

I put my hand on his shoulder. "What I want to know is if Robby Hood lists the topics of his programs."

"Oh, sure. In fact—" He moved the mouse and clicked on the word Enter just below the animated image. "In fact, you can listen to his past shows right online. I think . . . Yeah, here it is." He pointed at the image of an antique radio in the upper left corner. The word "Archive" was printed below it.

"Okay. Thanks. I'll take it from here." He rose and I took his spot in my chair.

"Aren't you going to lunch?"

I thought of my trip to the cafeteria an hour before. I wasn't hungry then, but I was beginning to feel a little empty. I took my purse from the drawer, removed my wallet, and gave him a twenty-dollar bill. "If you'll run down to the cafeteria and pick up a tuna salad for me, you can keep the change and take Celeste out. You won't be able to do anything fancy, but you should be able to find enough tacos to feed the two of you."

At the mention of Celeste's name a broad grin crept across his face. "Thanks!"

"I'm talking lunch, you understand? I'm not giving you two the afternoon off. I want you back in plenty of time for my two o'clock meeting. Got it?"

"Yes, ma'am." He was gone.

By the time my salad arrived, I had made myself familiar with Robby Hood's Web site. The guy was more than a talk show host; he was an industry. There were books for sale and tapes and CDs to buy. I found a link to "Just Who Is Robby Hood?" and followed it. A new page appeared on my screen dominated by the picture of a man in his thirties with brown hair as long as mine, wraparound sunglasses, and a black goatee. "You're kidding," I said to myself. As if in response, the picture changed, dissolving from the middle-age hippie to the image of a man who could be the anchor of a prime-time news show: black-and-gold silk necktie, sharply pressed white shirt, dark suit coat. His hair was bleached blond. It changed again. This time the photo was of a chimpanzee with a sun visor on his head, a cigar in his mouth, and playing cards in his hand. He was holding a full house.

"Cute." I spoke to the monitor and the air in the room.

The picture changed again, and this time a sentence appeared: "Wouldn't you like to know?" I wasn't going to find help here. I surveyed the rest of the site and found articles written by those claiming expertise in UFOs, cryptozoology, government conspiracies, alien abduction, mind control, privacy rights, crop circles, angel sightings, devil sightings, Mars archaeology—how could that be?—ancient civilizations, and more. It was a collection of every fringe idea I had heard of and a dozen more I hadn't.

I went back to the archive page. A long list appeared divided by date and hour. Since Hood's show was four hours in length, each day was marked off in four sections. The archive went back thirty days. I was only concerned with the last four. What I found was:

Wednesday p.m./Thursday a.m., January 11/12

- First hour: Open lines.
- Second hour: A security guard's remarkable ghost story.
- Third hour: Daniel Pat, mind-control expert.
- Fourth hour: Is the sun making us sick?

Tuesday p.m./Wednesday a.m., January 10/11

- First hour: Open lines.
- Second hour: Author Nicholas Templar, *UFO's and Cold War Soviet Union.*
- Third hour: Author Nicholas Templar, continued.
- Fourth hour: Open lines.

Monday p.m./Tuesday a.m., January 9/10

- First hour: Open lines.
- Second hour: Chemtrails. Poison from the sky?
- Third hour: Is the Hubble Space Telescope looking at you?
- Fourth hour: Open lines.

Sunday p.m./Monday a.m., January 8/9

- First hour: Open lines.
- Second hour: Chupacabra, trolls, gremlins, and other beasties.
- Third hour: The Mayan Calendar and the Prophecy of Doom.
- Fourth hour: Mayan Calendar continued.

Not the usual fare for talk show hosts, but I had already learned that from the few times I had listened to a portion of Hood's show. I was after a connection. Was it just coincidence that a security guard dies on the same night Hood's program featured such a guard with a ghost story? Jim Fritz died in the mechanic's bay of the airport while working on a rush repair job for a client. That was early Tuesday the tenth. Hood had an hour devoted to something called chemtrails. I caught a portion of the first hour where a caller mentioned chemtrails. Chemtrails, if there were such things, were laid down by airplanes. There was a connection.

Sunday's show was odd. I didn't know what a chupacabra was so I did an Internet search. I was surprised at the number of sites the search found. I clicked on the first one and learned more than I wanted to know. Stories out of Puerto Rico told of a sharp-fanged, aggressive creature that moved on two legs; stood no more than three feet tall; and attacked, killed, and sucked the blood from farm animals. *Chupacabra* means "goat sucker." And I thought politicians had bad press. Apparently sightings were now being made in the U.S. I frowned and returned to the Hood site. Goat-sucking critters hadn't killed three people in my city; someone who knew how to break a neck did.

What was I missing? When I saw it, I wondered why I didn't see it sooner. "Second hour: Chupacabra, trolls, gremlins, and other beasties." Gremlins! Jose Lopez was found dead in a green AMC Gremlin. I was stretching. I had to be. What kind of connection was that? Still, it was adding up. First night, Hood talks about mythical creatures, including gremlins, and a man is found dead in a car called a Gremlin. Hood has a guest on to talk about airplanes spraying chemicals in the air and Jim Fritz is found dead in an airplane. Last night—or probably very early this morning—a security guard is found dead after Hood has a guest talk about a ghost he saw while working as a security guard. Three hits. Too much for coincidence.

But wait. Jose Lopez died on the ninth, not the eighth. The dates weren't adding up for me. They seemed one day off. Hood's program aired Sunday the eighth. Lopez was murdered Monday the ninth. Was the killer just slow or . . .

The lack of sleep was making me slow. Floyd said that Hood's program began at eleven and went to two or three. I couldn't remember but that detail didn't matter. It explained the mix-up in the dates. Hood's Web site listed the day the program started. Technically, since it crossed over midnight, it was aired on two days.

I had a connection. I didn't know how to explain it, but at least it was a connection.

I leaned back and noticed that I hadn't started the salad I sent Floyd to get. It wasn't the first time I had lost myself and skipped a meal. I picked up the salad, removed the plastic cover, and then set it back down. Something had occurred to me. Clicking the home link, I was taken back to the start page of Hood's Web site. Not only did the site list past shows, but it had a section on upcoming guests.

I clicked the link and saw a page that showed the shows and topics for the week. I had seen the first three days in the archives section. It was Thursday—tonight's schedule—that I wanted to see. I found it.

I wished I hadn't.

chapter 27

I considered calling the police station and asking someone there to contact West. I could exercise my title and probably get what I wanted, but word would reach Chief Webb and I didn't want to give him another reason to attach swear words to my name. I looked at my desk clock: 12:40. I had an hour and twenty minutes before the start of the meeting I had called. It was less than ten minutes to the marina and another ten back. That left an hour, maybe a little less, for me to find and talk to West. I weighed the pros and cons, then grabbed my purse. Pro and con weighing took time. It was time to let my impetuous spirit free for a while.

I printed out my little charts and a few other notes I made and hotfooted it to my car. Thirteen minutes later I pulled onto the lot of the Santa Rita Crown Marina, the publicly owned parking place for boats and small yachts. One mile down the road was the Yacht Club that the really expensive boats called home. The parking lot was situated in front of a wide strip of lawn that framed the grounds of a long, Nantucket-style building. Its white walls reflected the sun and contrasted with the green of the grass and box-hedge planting that ran parallel with the exterior wall. The building held the rental office, a boat supply store, a small convenience store, and an all-purpose room for those hearty souls who preferred the narrow confines of a sailboat to a house.

West was easy to find. It was hard to miss the two black-and-white patrol cars, the white unmarked detective's vehicle, and the bright, broad yellow tape. This time there was no ambulance and no coroner's van. Too much time had passed. I guessed they had transported the body hours ago.

Clutching my purse, I dropped down from the driver's seat of my SUV and walked across the asphalt lot to the gate where the police activity was. The gate was ten feet or so north of the main building. A chain-link fence filled in the gap and continued around the property, turning at ninety degrees and extending past the water's edge a good ten or fifteen feet. Anyone wanting to sneak around the fence needed a boat or they would get their feet wet.

West was watching as one man and one woman in blue jumpsuits milled around. The jumpsuits had white lettering on the back; some small letters and two large ones. As I approached I could see that the smaller lettering read, "Santa Rita County," and the large letters, "SI." It was Scientific Investigations, the arm of the county sheriff's department that did the forensics work for the unincorporated areas and the chartered cities within its borders. The Santa Rita police department was too small to have its own forensics lab.

I continued forward as if I owned the place. It was a gift I had. I could look like I belonged in almost any situation. As I neared, I saw one of the uniformed officers look my way, then say something to West. He turned but didn't approach. He pulled out his wallet and removed a bill of some denomination. He handed it to the officer and returned the wallet to his rear pocket.

He smiled as I stopped at the yellow ribbon barricade. A small group of onlookers hovered around the scene, held at bay by the

Crime Scene—Do Not Cross ribbon. I put some distance between myself and the crowd. West followed. Only a few feet separated us, and I closed that gap with a couple of steps.

"You're late," he said.

"I'm what? I'm never late. We didn't have an appointment." I opened my purse and reached for the printout.

"No, but you're late nonetheless. I bet the officer you'd be here by ten thirty. You cost me five bucks."

"You cost yourself five bucks," I retorted. "You shouldn't be betting."

"I didn't want you to think I was perfect."

I grasped for the nearest witty remark but came up empty-handed. My heart was doing a jig. I was excited about my news. "I'm not that predictable."

"No, Mayor. Of course not."

I raised my eyebrows. "Did I just detect a whiff of sarcasm?"

"Nothing but clean, pure air out here. What can I do for you, Mayor?"

A few hours ago he had said it was time we started dating. He said it like he was making an observation about the weather. Here he was calling me by title. Of course, I would have been surprised if he had done anything different. We were both working in our official capacity—and there were other people around.

I had spent the short drive over practicing my speech. It was clear, short, and certain to avoid the appearance that I was meddling in a police investigation. I had acquired that reputation last year, and I didn't want to give any reason for the rumor to be resurrected. As an experienced speechwriter I knew that no matter how long or short the text, it should include an attention step, followed by a need step, satisfaction and visualization steps, and then end with a call to action.

"I prefer to leave police business to the police," I would begin and then lay out what I had discovered. Instead, I tossed the speech and got to the point. "Here." I thrust the papers at him. Not a stellar beginning, but it got his attention.

He took the folded papers, opened them, and ran his eyes over the material. He said nothing at first. "Where did you get this?"

"The Internet. I did a little research."

"A little research, eh?" He read it again, then, "I'll be back." He walked away. I hadn't expected that. I thought there would be a gentle reprimand for interfering and an admonishment to go back to the office and push my papers around. West was never cruel and never as acerbically blunt as his boss, but when he was in charge he stayed in charge.

I watched from my position behind the barricade as West walked to the guard shack that stood to one side of the open gate. He spoke to one of the SI people, then stepped into the shack. The SI detectives were packing their gear. A few seconds later, West reappeared, looked my direction, and wiggled his index finger in a come-here fashion. I ducked under the tape and ignored the curious glances of the spectators. I walked straight to West who stood just outside the door of the shack. He held my papers in his hand.

"You never cease to amaze, Mayor." He stepped inside. "Watch your clothing, there's fingerprint powder all over the place." I followed him in.

The shack was the size of a hall bath and was designed, constructed, and painted to match the main building. The white paint on the exterior was marred with black dust left behind by the SI folk. Inside was less glamorous. Bare studs and rafters made the place feel like a tiny garage on a 1940s home. A desk made of plywood and two-by-fours was screwed into the wall that faced the parking lot. A fixed pane of glass was on that wall, and a small sliding window was next to the door. A battered, gunmetal stool was set close to the crude desk.

"That's where we found him. His replacement showed up a little after seven thirty, saw the victim hunched over the desk, and assumed he had fallen asleep. Apparently he was prone to do that, but who can blame him? The guy was almost seventy."

"What was his name?" I was feeling a little ill.

"Carl DiMaio, a retired schoolteacher trying to make ends meet with a part-time job."

I could imagine poor Carl lifeless, his chest and head resting on the plywood table. "Who would kill a seventy-year-old man?" Indignity was added to my discomfort.

"Same killer that took the life of Jim Fritz who was in his sixties and Jose Lopez who was not yet thirty."

"You're telling me that his . . . that the killer used the same technique?"

"Yup. Everything is the same and you were right. Look here." He pointed to a small radio in the corner of the desk. "Same station as Lopez and Fritz. Initial estimates on time of death places the murder in the time frame of Robby Hood's show. I had made that connection on my own. What I didn't do was connect the deaths with the subject matter on Hood's show. I want to say it's all coincidence, but three murders in three days by the same means with radios tuned to the same station is pushing the coincidence idea a little too far, even for me."

"Do you think Robby Hood is connected somehow?"

West handed the papers back to me. He wouldn't need them. Sorting evidence was what he was trained to do. I had no doubts that he had memorized everything on the papers. "I won't rule out anything, but I doubt he's personally involved. He has the perfect alibi; he's on the air when the murders take place."

"Couldn't his program be recorded?"

He nodded. "Very possible. That will be easy to check. Your chart shows that he had open calls each night. A little research and phone records will tell us what we need to know."

"Then what?"

"Then I pay a little visit to Mr. Hood."

The thought that had pushed me out of my chair and into my car kept orbiting in my mind like an airplane waiting permission to land. "I did one other thing."

"You looked ahead to tonight's program." He was good.

"Yes."

"And?"

I took a breath and pulled another sheet of paper from my purse and unfolded it. "This is a printout of the Web page. It has the information that I used to create the charts. It also has tonight's program listed." I handed it to him. "The first hour is open calls. That seems to be the pattern of the program, on most nights anyway. The second hour has a guest who has his own Web site. I went to it. He's one of the conspiracy people. He's just self-published a book called *America's Secret Police, Past and Present.*"

"America doesn't have secret police," West said. "Who would there be to murder?"

I shook my head. "You're being too literal. Remember Lopez was found in his car on the night they discussed mythical creatures like chupacabra, trolls, and *gremlins*. Lopez wasn't a mythical creature but he drove a car named after one. Jim Fritz died on the night the topic was chemtrails sprayed in the sky by airplanes. At best, Jim was a weekend pilot, he certainly wasn't flying military aircraft at his age, but he did work around airplanes. Carl DiMonti—"

"DiMaio," he corrected me.

"Carl DiMaio wasn't the guest who saw the ghost, just a security guard like him."

"So since the word 'police' appears in the topic line you think the next target will be a cop?"

"I hope I'm wrong. I hope DiMaio is the last of it, but my gut tells me otherwise."

West studied the paper. "Did you read the topic for hour three?"

I thought. Nothing came to mind. "No, I was a little fixated with the word 'police.'" He handed the paper back. My eyes tracked to the spot. There it was. *Hour three: Mayor Judy Morrison discusses strange aircraft seen over her city.*

chapter 20

I was edgy as I steered my Aviator through the early-afternoon traffic. I had been so preoccupied with the idea that the next murder victim was going to be a cop that I hadn't noticed the next line. I comforted myself with the idea that all the murders had been related to the topic of the second hour, not the third. One of my problems is that my logical mind doesn't pay attention to my emotional side. When I lie to myself I expect the rest of my brain to play along. It never does.

It was the logical side of my personality that wanted attention. There had been three violent murders, each somehow associated with a topic that appeared in the second hour of Robby Hood's program. In terms of serial killings that was a lot, especially in three days' time, but three was an awful, small statistical number. I doubted there was a coincidence explaining the connection between the radio program and the murders, but I lacked the same conviction that the murder was somehow locked into the second hour. And who was to say the killer wouldn't find the idea of murdering a police officer too difficult and move on to something easier—like me.

As I pulled from the freeway and onto surface streets, it occurred to me that anyone on the council might be a target. I pushed the accelerator a little more. I had a meeting that had just become even more important.

I parked and headed for the office. I caught myself looking around more than I normally do, wondering if killers were behind cars or bushes. I walk fast but at that moment I was close to breaking into a jog. Very un-mayor-like. Just because my brain was buzzing didn't mean my body had to be.

"I was getting worried," Floyd said as I walked into the office. "You told me to be back well before the meeting, and you weren't here. It starts in five minutes."

"I only need three," I said and plowed into my inner sanctum, dropped my purse in the drawer after I removed my research. Opening my center desk drawer, I pulled a leather-bound notebook that I use to jot down thoughts during a meeting. I slipped the charts I made and the printout of the Web page into the folder.

"Also, while you were gone, someone from Mr. Elliot's office called. He won't be at the meeting. He went home with the flu."

Russell Elliot was the city manager. He was a quiet but efficient man; things just got done without even knowing he was around. "Okay. Take good notes. After the meeting type up an FYI memo and deliver it to his office. Put it in a sealed envelope."

"Ready?" Floyd said from my doorway.

"Go ahead to the conference room. I'll be right behind you."

"I can wait."

"That's very gentlemanly of you, Floyd, but I'm going to the little mayor's room. You probably don't want to be standing by the door."

"The little mayor's room? Oh. Oh, I get it. I'll wait in the conference room."

"Thanks, Floyd. I won't be long." He left and I exited close on his heels. I have a private bathroom but not off my office. In our remodel a few years ago, we considered adding an adjoining restroom but the cost persuaded us otherwise. As it was, my private restroom was out the office door and several steps to the left. I went in and locked the door behind me. Facing the mirror I tamed a few rebellious strands of dark hair and made certain that the emotions I felt didn't reflect in my face. A touch-up of lipstick and a straightening of the clothes and I was ready to go. I took several deep breaths to fill my lungs and aerate my brain. Right now, my brain needed all the oxygen it could get.

Notebook in hand, I stood before the mirror until my mayor mask was just the way I wanted it. Then I left.

I wasn't sure how I'd handle the meeting, and I reminded myself that there were several issues that needed attention. With long strides, I marched down the corridor and turned into the conference room at 1:59. I was the last one in.

The room had nothing about it to make it noteworthy. Situated immediately behind the council chambers, the conference room was where we held our closed-door sessions. The walls were a simple white and the carpet was the color of sand. A few pastoral pictures hung on the wall, the kind one finds in a doctor's office. Just twenty by twenty, it was too small to comfortably seat five council members, the city clerk, city attorney, and staff members for each council person.

The room was already full. I took my place at the head of the table and looked the group over. Only council members and the city attorney sat at the table. Aides sat in chairs that lined the wall. Jon Adler sat at the other end of the table, a Diet Coke in front of him. He looked bored. Tess sat to his right, my far left, wearing the same unhappy expression I left her with that morning. To my immediate left was Larry Wu who looked content and filled with ancient Eastern wisdom and ready to serve it up with his Texas barbecue accent. Titus was to my right and looked distracted. Between Titus and Jon was our city attorney Fred Markham.

"Thank you for being here on such short notice," I began. I sat. "I've received word that Russ is home ill and won't be with us today."

"It's a good thing I'm not due in court," Jon snipped. I wanted to ask if he meant it was a good thing for his client but stuffed the comment.

"There are four things we need to address, two of which we may be able to dispense with quickly. The first has to do with Councilman Overstreet." I looked at Titus for an indication that he wanted to make the announcement. I meant to ask before the meeting but I spent too much time at the marina. He returned my look and nodded. I took that to mean he preferred me to reveal the news. "Titus is having surgery and will be out of the office for a number of weeks. Perhaps two months or more."

Every eye shifted to him. Titus didn't like to be the center of attention, at least not after such an announcement. "It's a serious surgery, but the doctors feel everything will be fine." More silence.

"Colon cancer," he blurted. "Don't worry, I'll be back to make all your lives miserable. You'll just have to do without my keen insights for a while."

"Is there anything we or the city can do?" Fred Markham gazed directly at Titus. I noticed Jon and Tess were studying the table.

"Not a thing. I'd rather see us do something for Fritzy. I've arranged for a large arrangement of flowers to be sent to the funeral, but someone else will have to inform the florist when and where that will be. I'm going to be a little tied up."

"I'll take care of that," Larry offered.

I told them that Jim Fritz's body had been released from the coroner's office and that we should have details about the funeral soon.

"My offer to help with the funeral expenses still stands," Titus said.

"Count me in on that, too," Larry added.

I glanced around the room. Fred said he wanted to help, Tess gave me an approving nod, and several of the aides added their pledges. "I'll pass that information on to Fritzy. I imagine she and Jim had already made pre-need arrangements, but I'll double-check. I know she'll appreciate your concern."

"The next item?" Jon pressed.

"I was coming to that, Jon. In our last council meeting we left upon the matter of deputy mayor. Titus will not be with us this coming Tuesday—"

"Could you rephrase that?" Titus interjected.

It took me a second to get his reference. A few people tittered. "Right. Titus will be recuperating in the hospital and dancing with the nurses after an extremely successful surgery and so will not be in attendance at our Tuesday night meeting."

Titus gave a gracious nod. "I like the dancing part. Good addition. Of course, if my wife hears about it, I'll be spending an additional week in the hospital."

I gave a smile that I hoped didn't give the image of pity. "The matter of deputy mayor was left up in the air at our last meeting—"

"Whose fault was that?" Jon asked. "We were ready to deal with it right then and there."

"Shut up, Jon," Tess said. Her words were soft but hard as steel. Jon looked like she had slapped him.

"I hung things up. I admit that. Not only that, earlier today I jumped to a conclusion that was ... erroneous. I confronted Tess with something I should have checked out before I opened my mouth." I faced her. "My words were spoken in private, but I want my apology to be public."

I waited for Tess's response. It was slow in coming. She had glued her eyes to the conference table, her arms crossing her chest as if she felt the cold she normally inflicted on others. Eternity lasted five or ten silent seconds, then she lifted her head. Her eyes had softened. She made eye contact and gave the slightest of nods. Apology accepted. It was as gracious an act as I had ever seen from her.

"Sweet as this is—" Jon began.

"Tess was nominated for deputy mayor. Larry and Titus have informed me that they support the nomination. Even if I voted against the suggestion it would pass by four votes. I plan to make it unanimous." I looked back at Tess. Earlier she had all but told me what I could do with the nomination. The ball was now in her court.

This time she didn't shift her gaze. She stared at me, and I could tell the gears were grinding in her brain. I was certain she was calculating the ramifications of her decision. No doubt she knew that there was more to the issue than we had discussed. She looked at Larry, then Titus, as if she could read their minds. Tess was nothing if not politically astute. It didn't take a prodigy to know that she would be unable to hold the position two years from now and would lose the advantage of having the title deputy Mayor on the ballot— assuming she wanted to run for my office or some state office.

My nerves threatened to get the best of me. It took all my willpower to sit silently, allowing Tess as much as time as she needed. Frankly, it didn't seem all that important to me at the moment. I had thoughts of a serial murderer on my mind.

"Yes," Tess finally said. "Thank you."

There. It was done. My life had just become more complicated. Being mayor and running for congress was enough work for three people. Now Tess would stand in my place should I be absent from council meetings or unable to attend certain public functions. If I knew Tess, and I did know Tess, she would be in my face every week with some unsolicited advice or trumped-up emergency business. If I hadn't had more pressing issues I would have dismissed the meeting and drowned my sorrows in a double-chocolate sundae.

"Thank you, Tess."

"Is that all there is?" Jon asked. He made no attempt to hide his smugness. In his eyes, he had just won.

Fred Markham cut him a look but said nothing. Jon was an elected official, Fred as city attorney was an employee.

"The mayor said she had four items," Titus said. "I've only counted two. Larry's the accountant, but I'm pretty sure that leaves two more."

"That's how I figure it," Larry said.

Jon sneered. "Very funny. Our own Laurel and Hardy."

"Let's focus, folks," I said, standing. I wanted everyone's attention. "We have a problem that affects all of us and our city. As you know, the body of a man was found in a car parked in our front lot. You also know that Fritzy's husband was murdered. Both men were killed in the same fashion. Detective West tells me that . . ." Here I paused, not for effect but to steady my voice. "That each had his neck broken. This morning a third victim was found at the marina. He had been killed in like manner."

A word erupted from Larry that I hadn't heard him use before.

Tess leaned forward, her head tilted to one side as if she were trying to determine the punch line to a joke. Her eyes darted back and forth for a moment. "Each murder occurred on city property."

"That's right." I filled them in on the rest. I passed around the charts and let them study them for a few moments.

"Wait, wait, wait," Jon said, holding up his hands. "You're saying these killings are related to this Robby Hood character?"

"It appears that the killings are somehow related to the topics of his program." I explained those connections. Then I got to the fourth point, the point I didn't know existed until less than two hours ago.

"I did a little research on Mr. Hood's topics for tonight. In his second hour he's interviewing the author of a book titled *America's Secret Police, Past and Present.*"

"That's stupid," Jon said.

"That doesn't matter if it's stupid, Jon. It doesn't matter if we don't take the subjects seriously, the killer is, and that's where our concerns should be. My fear is that the murderer will target a police officer."

"Does Chief Webb know this?" Larry wondered.

"I don't know. Since Detective West is the lead detective I shared this information with him. I'm sure he's passed it along to the chief."

Titus cleared his throat. "There's more, isn't there?"

"Yes. So far, each murder has been tied to the topic in the second hour of Hood's four-hour show. Still, the third-hour topic is . . . troublesome." I recited the topic from memory. I hadn't needed to memorize it; it was branded on my brain. "'Mayor Judy Morrison discusses strange aircraft seen over her city.'"

"There haven't been any strange . . ." Jon began, then trailed off. The point had found its mark.

"*Mayor* Judy Morrison." Fred said. "Or should we be more concerned about the word *city.* I mean, the elements that tie the murders to the show's topics are tenuous at best: planes and chemtrails, mythical creatures and a model of car called a Gremlin, a security guard who thinks he sees a ghost and a security guard at the marina."

"It could be either, Fred. I think it's best that we all be on our guard. Please, folks, take no chances. Lock your doors; be careful whom you meet with."

"I hope you're taking your own advice," Titus said.

I dismissed the meeting, and aides and council members filed out like mourners passing a casket. I gathered my papers and put them in my notebook. Floyd excused himself. I fixed my eyes on the notebook, and then I slumped back into the chair. My clothing felt lined with lead, and my knees threatened to quit their job. I was a washrag wrung out and tossed to the side. Lack of meaningful sleep, stress from campaigning, tension caused by Dean Wentworth, the murder of Fritzy's husband, and everything else that had happened since I pulled in the parking lot last Monday began to press me down like a gigantic hand.

I lowered my face into my hands and wished for a few moments of blissful oblivion. I should have mentioned Wentworth's assertion about having support on the council for an eminent-domain action, but I didn't. I was done accusing people. If he had someone in his pocket, it would be known soon enough. I should have allowed time for Fred to share his findings about Rutger Howard and lawsuits brought against cities, but that too seemed inappropriate for the moment.

The chair next to me moved and someone sat down.

"I'll be there in a few moments, Floyd."

"No need to be insulting." The words were soft.

I lowered my hands and opened my eyes. Tess sat next to me. Her eyes were moist. She laid one of her hands on mine. To my surprise it was warm and soft. "You take care." She paused and gave my hand a gentle squeeze. "There are things more important than politics. Don't tell anyone I said that. If you do, I'll deny it." She smiled, and I wondered when I last saw a genuine smile on her face and not the one that came whenever a camera was present.

I smiled back, returning the favor. "Thanks, Tess. Look, about earlier in your office—"

"Don't." She stood. "I want to be mayor, but I don't want it because it suddenly becomes vacant. If you know what I mean."

I knew.

chapter 29

I dragged myself back to my office feeling I had done a week's work in the last few hours. The meeting had started promptly at two o'clock and let out just ten minutes later. It doesn't take long to deliver disturbing news. I formulated a short agenda on my walk from the conference room to my office. It included just two things for the next hour: one, have Floyd cancel any appointments I had on the calendar; and two, close my door and spend a solid hour in silence.

Floyd wasn't at his desk. Not too surprising. He was probably in the little aide's room. I slipped into my office, pushed aside the lined paper in the middle of my desk, and set my notebook down. Melting into my chair, I leaned my head back and ran a hand through my hair. First thing I would do when Floyd got back was send him to the cafeteria for an iced tea, extra sugar. Today was not a day to count calories.

Thoughts of what I should be doing floated like balloons. Not bright birthday balloons but black and gray and misshapen. I should call Fritzy to see if she needed any more help with the funeral and to be sure she had heard that Jim's body had been released. Surely she had, but the phrase "your husband's body" is overwhelming. I could still hear the words from nearly a decade before. I should alert the private security company that provided guards to city hall. I had never received a satisfactory answer about where they were the night Jose Lopez was killed in our front lot. That was a bone that needed more picking, but it would have to wait.

I should contact Nat and see what she'd learned about Wentworth and Rutger Howard. I should . . . I should . . . There had been no paper on my desk when I left for the meeting. I remembered seeing it clean and clear. I moved the notebook and pulled the lined paper close. It was the same paper Floyd liked to use when taking notes. It was printed. Floyd seldom wrote in cursive:

> *Things out of control.*
> *Need answers.*
> *Have gone to see Robby Hood.*

I punched a button on the phone, the one that connected me to Fritzy's desk in the lobby. Celeste answered.

"Celeste, it's Maddy. Did you see Floyd go out?"

"Yes, he left about five minutes ago. He seemed to be in a hurry."

I couldn't believe he would do this. Then again, I could. His brain was easily derailed, but his heart was never off course. He was trying, in his own way, to save me. "Celeste, have you ever been in Floyd's car?"

"Um, why?"

"I'll take that as a yes. What kind of car does he drive?"

"He has a Volkswagen bug. He told me his father owned it and then gave it to him when he started college. I guess it's an antique or something."

"What color, Celeste?"

"Brown, brownish. Something like that. Why? Is something wrong?"

"I doubt it but I want to find him. What else can you tell me about the car?"

There was a pause. "It has a sunroof-moonroof thing—except it's not like cars today, it's made of canvas or something."

"A ragtop," I said. I was pretty sure that was what they called it.

"Yeah, that's what he called it."

"Do you know the license number?"

"No. You're scaring me." I was. I could hear it her voice.

"Nothing to be frightened about, kiddo. Thanks." I switched off the phone and hoped I hadn't just lied. My next move was to call West. I punched in the number for the police station, identified myself, and asked to speak to Detective West. I learned that he was out of the office but that he had called and said he was returning to the station. "I need to see him. Could you call his cell phone or ask dispatch to radio him to stop by my office first?"

I struggled with what to do next. I didn't know where Robby Hood lived, and judging by his Web site, he wasn't inclined to give out that kind of information. I went to Floyd's desk. Maybe he left an address or something else to help me find him. I doubted he was in danger. At least I told myself that. While there was no solid reason to believe that Robby Hood was involved in the murders, his show certainly was, and whoever was intent on breaking necks might take exception to Floyd asking questions. Another thought, one I had tried to ignore, elbowed its way to the front. Floyd was a city employee. If the killer was intent on adding me or a council member to his list of murders, he might find Floyd a more convenient target. Granted it was still daylight; granted it had yet to be proven that there was a direct correlation between Robby Hood's program and the murders; granted . . . granted nothing. I'm not comfortable rolling dice for anything.

Files covered Floyd's desk and were kept company by papers and notes. I pushed a few around and found the file he had begun on Rutger Howard before I shifted that responsibility to Nat. I set it aside and noticed that the file drawer in his desk was partially opened. A file folder had been stuffed in at an awkward angle, preventing the drawer from closing. I removed it and found "Robby Hood" on the tab. I sat at the desk, laid the file on top of the other scattered papers, and opened it. Inside were printouts of pages from Hood's Web site but little more. Words were scribbled on the inside surface of the file. I read through them. It was a checklist.

Floyd's thinking could drift and scatter but when he was on his game, he was as methodical as they came. Apparently, this assignment had triggered the best of his administrative abilities. The list read:

✓ *Start file.*
✓ *Visit Web site.*
✓ *Google "Robby Hood" for more Internet info.*
   Check for blogs.
✓ *Does Hood need bus. lic. to operate in S.R.? Ck with Thayer.*
✓ *What network handles Hood?*
   Make list of advertisers?
   Make timeline of Hood?

Several of the items had check marks by them. I was holding the file that Floyd had started, and it held information from his Internet research. I scanned those pages but found nothing that would help me locate Floyd. He must have found something, must have come up with an address somewhere.

I looked at the list again.

✓ *Does Hood need bus. lic. to operate in S.R.? Ck with Thayer.*

It was easy work to decipher Floyd's abbreviations. *S.R.* was Santa Rita. *Ck with Thayer* had to mean check with Dana Thayer, our city clerk. *Bus. lic.* was business license. And that was it! Monday Floyd had said that Hood was in Santa Rita. I didn't push for more information. I wished I had. If Hood operated a business within the city limits, then he'd need a license and that license would be on record with the city clerk.

I snatched up the phone and dialed the necessary extension. "Dana Thayer."

The image of Dana flashed on the screen of my mind. She was a woman enamored with detail and organization. She was a great clerk because, best I could tell, nothing mattered more than everything having a place and everything being in its place. She was a severe-looking woman, black hair pulled back over her ears. Reading glasses were always present, either hanging from her neck or stuck to the end of her nose as if someone had welded them there.

"It's Maddy, Dana. I need to ask a question."

"Good afternoon, Mayor. How can I help you?"

"Did my aide ask you to check for a business license?"

"He did. He's an insistent young man, almost to the point of being rude." I heard papers shuffling. "He did, and I gave him an answer."

I waited. "Dana, he's not here right now. Could I trouble you for that address?"

"There is no address because there is no business under the name of Robby Hood. You know, someone from the police called and asked the same question this morning. They were unhappy with my answer. It's not my fault. If someone files for a business license, then we have it here. If they don't, then we don't."

"No one's blaming you, Dana. I'm just trying to find out where Robby Hood lives."

"He's a radio personality, right?" I said he was. "I imagine Robby Hood is a pseudonym."

I started to say thank-you and hang up, but then had an idea. "Dana, if *you* wanted to find where this man worked and lived, how would you do it?"

"I'm not a private detective, Mayor."

"No, but you are an administrative genius who has helped keep this city on track for over twenty years. I bet you could find Robby Hood if you wanted to."

"Now you're just trying to flatter me into helping you."

"Is it working?"

"Yes." She paused, and I gave her a few moments to think. "The key is to find the man's legal name. Learn that, then we could check with the county tax assessor. Of course, I'm assuming that he owns property in or near Santa Rita. If he's a voter, there would also be a record of his registration. Of course, you could ask the police to pull strings with the Department of Motor Vehicles and get an address that way."

"Great ideas, but I still need to find his legal name."

"That's what your aide said. I suggested he start with the radio station."

A figure appeared in the door to the office. I raised my eyes. West stood at the threshold looking puzzled. "You wanted to see me?"

I raised a finger. "Thanks, Dana. If you come up with any other ideas, let me know. You've been a big help."

"You're at the wrong desk," West said. "Did Floyd launch a successful coup?"

"He's gone looking for Robby Hood. He was in a meeting where I shared about the apparent connection between Hood's radio program and the killings."

"Why would he go to Hood?"

"To protect me, I guess. The mayor connection seems pretty strong. It certainly is in the mind of Floyd." West swore. "Ease up, Detective. He's young and a little imprudent."

"A little?" He frowned, then smiled. "I guess I should admire his chutzpah. Does he know where Hood lives?"

"I assume so, since he left a note saying that's where he's headed, but he didn't leave an address." I told him about my discussion with Dana Thayer. "Apparently the man likes his privacy."

West grimaced. "There's no such thing as privacy in our society. It's gotten to where you can't buy groceries without leaving some bit of personal information behind. May I use the phone?" I pushed the phone across the desk and he picked up the receiver, then dialed. "Do you remember my saying that I was going to interview Hood? Well, I've had someone trying to track down his location."

The next few moments were filled with West getting an update from whomever he had on the line. "Give me the number." He repeated it aloud and I jotted it down in the folder. A second later, West was placing a long-distance call. He looked at me. "Terminal Radio Network, Cincinnati. They have the rights to Hood's program."

"Cincinnati?"

He shrugged. "Distance means nothing anymore. You want to listen in?"

I did and moved to my office, picked up the phone, and punched the line with the light. I covered the mouthpiece so neither I nor anyone else could hear my breathing.

"Thank you for calling Terminal Radio Network, this is Mindy, how may I direct your call?"

"Good afternoon," I heard West say. "This is Detective Judson West, Santa Rita Police Department, homicide division. Who's in charge there?"

There was a pause. "Did you say homicide?"

"Yes, I also asked who was in charge there."

"Um, well, it depends what you mean by in charge. There's the president of the company, but he's out of country right now, and there's our chief operations officer."

"I'll take him."

"I don't normally put calls through to him. He has his own line and number—"

"Mindy, let me stop you right there." His tone hardened. "When I conduct a murder investigation I take a piece of paper and draw a line down the middle. On one side I right the word 'helpful' and on the other I write 'hindrance.' Now which column am I going to write your name in?"

"One moment please."

"A little rough on her, weren't you?" I said from the office.

"I have a thing about people who hide behind titles. It's a character flaw."

A new voice, male and irritable. "This is Charles Lubbock. Who am I speaking with?"

West identified himself again and then got straight to the point. "I'm investigating a series of murders and believe one of your on-air personalities may be of assistance. I need the address of—"

"Robby Hood?"

"Yes."

"Don't sound surprised, Detective. You said you were in Santa Rita and that can mean only one thing—Robby Hood. I can't give you any information about him."

"I don't think you understand, Mr. Lubbock—"

"Actually, I understand very well. Do you have a warrant? I doubt it since you can't deliver a warrant over the phone. No warrant, no information. Hood likes his privacy."

"I can get a warrant in short order and have someone from the Cincinnati Police there to pull apart your files until he finds what I'm looking for."

"Go ahead, pal," Lubbock said. "Hood is under contract with us, but contracts go both ways. We place him on as many radio stations in the country as we can. He's hugely popular and has developed a persona of secrecy which he wishes to keep intact. We're contractually bound not to release any personal information without either his permission or a duly executed warrant. A phone call out of nowhere doesn't qualify. For all I know, you're a slightly batty ice-cream salesman pretending to be a cop."

"I assure you I'm not, and I wouldn't have called if this weren't important."

"Exactly what a batty ice-cream salesman would say. Bottom line, bring a warrant."

For a moment I thought I could feel heat from West pouring through the phone line. "This is no joke, Lubbock," West said.

"You don't hear me laughing, do you? And one other thing, if you ever call here and intimidate my receptionist again, I'll unleash every lawyer we have and we will fill your office with every flaming lawsuit, injunction, and whatever the law allows. You have her in tears."

The phone rang and the light on one of the other lines began to flash. I started to ignore it but couldn't. After all, I had asked Dana to get back to me with any other ideas. I switched lines. "Mayor Glenn," I said.

"I think I have something that belongs to you." The voice was familiar.

"Who is this?"

"You don't recognize my voice? Now you've hurt my feelings."

"Robby Hood?"

"Live and direct. And like I said, I have something that belongs to you—or should I say, someone who belongs to you. Do you know a Floyd Grecian?"

I said I did. I must have sounded frightened, because he said, "He's fine, Mayor. In fact, he's sitting in my dining room eating a tuna fish sandwich. I offered him a beer, but he chose milk instead. I have trouble trusting someone who drinks milk."

It sounded like Floyd. "We've been trying to track him down."

"We?"

"Yes, Detective West and I."

He groaned. "Oh, not the police. They make me nervous." There was a pause. "Floyd told me about the murders. I imagine your detective wants a word with me."

"I know he would appreciate that."

"Okay, here's the deal. Your Sherlock Holmes can come up here, but you must come along with him. I've never met you, and I hear that you're something special—at least according to Floyd."

"I'm willing to do that."

"Okay, I'm going to give you my home address. I don't want it going beyond you or Detective What's-his-name. I value my privacy. In fact, I depend on it."

I made the promise, hung up, and walked out to see a red-faced West hanging up the phone. I held up the piece of paper with Hood's name and address.

chapter 30

The measure of a man—or a woman for that matter—is how they respond when things don't go their way. West had tried his best bluff on the phone with the COO of Terminal Radio Network and had the door resoundingly slammed in his face. When I showed him the note with Hood's name and address on it, he just rolled his eyes and said, "News I could have used before getting my ear chewed off." I told him that Hood called and that Floyd was noshing a sandwich in the man's house.

He shook his head. "Would you object if I shot your aide?"

"Yeah, I would. Help is hard to find."

"How about if I just wing him a little?"

"There will be no wounding of city employees today, Detective. Now are you going to take me to Mr. Hood's home, or do I drive myself?"

"I'll take you. If you went up there alone and something happened to you, the chief would have my hide hanging on his wall."

"He doesn't like me, remember? He might pin a badge on you."

"Great, so my hide would be sporting a badge. No thanks. I need to interview Hood anyway. You are to follow my lead. Got it?"

"I'm a good follower." I disappeared into my office to grab my purse. I heard him whisper a remark but couldn't make out what it was. I chose to remain in ignorance. When I returned five seconds later, West was already in the corridor looking impatient. "Let's go, James. I have an aide to beat up."

The drive to Hood's residence seemed longer than the odometer indicated. We were there in twenty minutes, and the whole drive was done on surface streets. We found Hood's place easily enough. It was near the top of one of our hills and tucked among the expensive houses with large lots. His home was a pseudo-Tudor style done in the way only a California builder can do it. It wasn't a true Tudor, just Tudorish with decorative timber and stucco exterior walls. Where there wasn't stucco, there was a stone facade. It looked considerably larger than my home and more elaborate.

At first we could only see a portion of the house through the wrought-iron gate. An intercom box firmly attached to a pole was stationed a few feet from the gate. West pulled his car close and depressed the Page button.

"Talk." It was Hood's voice.

"It's Detective West and Mayor Glenn," West said.

"Ah, you're here to pick up the lost puppy." The gate began to move, sliding sideways along its track. West pulled through. Once beyond the wall and gate, we could see a large lot with a finely trimmed lawn and professionally landscaped grounds. Apparently, Hood had a preference for purple.

We turned down the drive that curved until it reached the front of the home. West pulled behind a beige, ragtop Volkswagen. Celeste had done a good job describing Floyd's car. We exited and walked up the three steps that led to the porch. West reached forward to knock but the door opened before knuckle met wood.

Before us stood a woman of singular beauty. Her hair was short and curled in such a way that I flashed on pictures I had seen of

1920s' flappers. She was an inch taller than me and had skin so smooth that I wondered where she bought it—it couldn't be real. She was dressed in a red almost-bikini that must have shrunk in the wash. A gossamer robe hung open on her shoulders. I looked at West and felt a sudden sense of jealousy and an urge to violence. I reminded myself who I was. It did no good, but it gave me something to do.

"I'm Detective Judson West," my police escort said as he showed his identification. "This is Mayor Madison Glenn."

"I don't have a badge," I said and forced a smile.

"Please come in," she said. Her words were almost lyrical. *Great*. We crossed from Eden into Camelot. A suit of armor stood to one side of the lobby and an arrangement of swords mounted to a thick panel of wood hung on the opposite wall. The almost-dressed doorwoman led us from the lobby past a formal dining room, a set of heavily carpeted stairs, and into a great room that was—great. I judged it to be twenty-five feet by forty if it were an inch. Thick pile carpet, white as snow, cushioned our footfalls. To our left and right were walls that ran to a paneled, barrel ceiling trimmed out in ornate crown molding. We had crossed from Eden into Camelot and now into a forest. The walls were white but difficult to see. Trees in planters lined north and south walls, and a few were scattered around the floor.

"Sherwood Forest?" I asked West softly.

"What else? Look at that view."

The west-facing wall was all glass, from the floor to the ceiling fifteen feet overhead. Through the massive panes I could see the city below and the ocean beyond. I couldn't imagine a better view was available in Santa Rita.

"This way, please." Apparently we were gawking, and our greeter wanted us to move along. "They're on the deck." She led us through a tall arched opening into another dining area. Since this one was situated next to the open kitchen, I knew it to be the dinette. A pair of French-style doors was open, and I could feel the January ocean breeze inviting itself into the house.

The house was built on a slope of hill and the deck extended into the air above. The deck was made of a wood I didn't recognize. What I did recognize was Floyd Grecian sitting at a picnic table I was pretty sure wasn't bought at a Home Depot. He was playing chess with the thinnest man I had ever seen.

The bikini model approached the thin man, kissed him on the back of the head, and then said, "Watch your queen's knight."

"Hey, no fair," Floyd said. "Chess is a one-on-one game."

"Floyd?" I said, trying to strike a chord between parent and supervisor.

"Oh, hi, Mayor." He popped up. "I'm sorry, real sorry. I didn't think things through."

I looked at his chess opponent who had switched his gaze from the board to West and me. Floyd caught my intent. "Oh, Mayor Madison Glenn, this is Robby Hood. And that is Detective Judson West."

Hood stood slowly as if it took more work than he expected. Bikini-woman took a quick step forward, her eyes glued to him. Could this really be Robby Hood? He approached and offered a smile. He wore thick, round glasses, and his brown hair was thin and short. A T-shirt with the words TAKE MY LEADER, PLEASE hung on his shoulders like he was a coat hanger. Two white threads hung from his black shorts. The threads were his legs. He took my hand, bowed, and gave it a small kiss. I have never had my hand kissed. I could learn to like it.

"The Honorable Madam Mayor. You honor my humble home." It was Hood's voice.

Humble? My house was large, and I could fit it inside his. "Um, thank you." I was trying to remember how to curtsy, then let it pass.

I wasn't dressed for it. He stood erect and turned to West and offered a hand. West hesitated.

"I won't break, Detective. I'm thin but wiry." West shook his hand. "Come and sit down. I have a few minutes before I have to run you off.

"You've met my wife, Katie. Can we get you anything?" We both deferred. "Well, let's have a seat." He returned to the picnic table and took a place on one end. Katie sat next to him. West and I took seats opposite them and next to Floyd.

"I'm not what you expected, am I?"

"Well," I began.

"No need to fabricate excuses. I am what I am by the random activities of genetics and no fault of my own. My body doesn't process food like yours. I'm able to retain enough nutrients to live, but I won't be going out for the Olympics in this life. I assume you have questions for me." He looked at West.

"Yes, sir, I do, but I have one for Floyd here."

"Don't be hard on him, Detective. He thought I was a danger to his boss and reacted."

"I can admire that, but my real question is—" West turned to Floyd—"how did you find this place?"

Floyd smiled. "I kept striking out. I tried business licenses, tax records, the Internet, and everything else I could think of. Nothing. So I asked for help."

"What kind of help?" I asked.

"I have a friend who works for one of the parcel delivery services. I had learned that Mr. Hood's radio program was handled by Terminal Radio Network. I called them but couldn't get past the receptionist."

"You were lucky," West said.

Floyd looked puzzled, but went on. "So I figured that that TRN must have sent packages of mail or gifts or books and stuff to Mr.

Hood. I also figured that some of those would come through the parcel delivery services. So I called my friend who delivers packages and asked if he made any deliveries from Terminal Radio Network. He said he did, and gave me the street name and a description of the house, and that was that."

"Unbelievable," West said. "I think I'll turn in my badge."

Floyd looked confused again. "He's paying you a compliment," I said. "You outthought him and me together."

"That part of his thinking was good," West groused. "Coming out here was a different matter."

"I'm no murderer," Hood said. "Floyd filled me in on what he knows. You think that someone is killing people based on my shows?"

"It's an avenue of investigation," West said. "You can understand why we want to talk to you. I hope you'll forgive me for saying so, but you are a bit reclusive."

"I like my privacy," he said sternly. "I have a right to my privacy." I thought of West's earlier comment about there being no more privacy. "Besides, it helps my radio show."

"How so?" I asked.

"I'm in a tough field, Mayor—or should I say, Congresswoman?"

"That hasn't been decided yet. I'm still mayor."

"We have something in common, Mayor; your running for congress, I mean. How many congressmen or congresswomen can there be from the district you live in?"

"Just one, naturally."

"How many talk shows are there? Don't answer, there are scores of them. It's a tough business to get into and rougher still to make it for very long. Now I deal in the odd, the bizarre, the out-of-the-ordinary. I don't want to be like other talk show hosts who rant and rave and who seem to find fulfillment in alienating most of their listeners. They're a dime a dozen. Only a couple are worth their salt. I want to deal with what few will touch."

"UFOs and little green men," I said.

"And conspiracies and alternate universes and ancient civilizations and anything else you won't find on the front page. Oh, I know, you probably want to dismiss it as the imaginings of overactive minds. I say, so what? Who cares? If every topic we touch on is artificial and contrived, so what? At the very least, we've had a good time, we've stretched our brains, we're bold enough to ask questions, and if we have no answers, then at least we've enjoyed the journey."

He wrung his hands a few times, folded them, interlaced his bony fingers, then continued. "Of all the talk show formats only a handful do what I do successfully, and the few of us who do battle for the same time slots. My competition is minimal but tough. Every listener that tunes in to Art Bell, George Noory, or Jeff Rense is a listener I don't have. I'm up against giants, so I have to use every trick in the book. Keeping my identity a secret is part of that."

"Would murder increase your ratings?" West asked.

"Of course it would, but I wouldn't participate in anything like that."

"Not even if it meant being number one?" West pressed.

Hood's expression soured. "Look at me, Detective. How long do you think I'd survive in a federal prison? I want to be number one, but I'm not willing to lose my wife, my home, and my life over it. Truthfully, I think you're more gullible than me and far more gullible than my callers. They might believe in flying saucers, but you believe that I can orchestrate a series of murders from my home—a home I never leave."

"Never?" West said.

"I'm an agoraphobic, Detective. I haven't left these grounds in months and that was for a trip to the hospital. But wait, that doesn't preclude me from hiring someone to do the deeds, does it?"

"No, it doesn't." West was in professional mode. I looked at Floyd. He seemed nervous.

Hood smiled. "I like that. You're a chronic doubter, Detective. I can see it in your eyes; more importantly, I can hear it in your voice. That gives us something in common. My job is to doubt. I make a living by questioning reality and the status quo while being brave enough to consider what others have dismissed as foolishness. Have you listened to my show?"

"No," West said.

Hood looked at me.

"Just recently. I've heard a little."

He nodded. "I know I'm not everybody's cup of tea, but people find me interesting enough to tune in every night. Even my reruns garner great ratings."

"Just how does your operation work?" West wondered. "If you never leave the grounds, then how do you get to the studio?"

"He has a studio here," Floyd said. "He showed it to me. You should see it."

"I thought you came here to do battle," West said to Floyd.

"No, I came here to find out what was going on and to ask Mr. Hood to change his program."

Hood rose and motioned for us to follow. "Come, I'll show you what few have seen."

He led us back into the house, through the dinette, to the stairs, and began a slow ascent. He spoke as he went. "I've had the house designed to meet my unusual needs. The upper floor is my office. What were three bedrooms now serve as studio, storage space, and Katie's office." Katie was a few steps behind me.

At the top of the stairs Hood pointed to a door on his left. "Since this room faces the street instead of the ocean we use it to store supplies, tapes of previous shows, and everything else we don't want in our offices." We took two more steps to a pair of doors that opened to another room. I looked in. "This is Kate's office. She handles all my correspondence and e-mail. She also handles the business side of things." He motioned for us to follow. The hall was crowded with the five of us. We fell into single file. West followed Hood closely. Floyd stepped on my heel. He apologized profusely.

At the end of the hall was another onetime bedroom. Hood strolled inside, and we followed like ants. "This is the studio," Hood said. I was surprised. I expected a mixer board with a hundred knobs and slides, electronic meters, and strange and fascinating things. Instead there was a wide maple table pressed against the windowed wall, overlooking the city and ocean. On the table was a computer, a digital clock with large red numerals, a phone, and a headset with a microphone.

"Like me, it's probably not what you expected. True?"

I confessed to being surprised.

"I work from here, Detective. It used to be that someone like me would have to go to a studio and have a producer operating most of the electronic details. Technology has changed all of that. I do my research throughout the day, and my producer does his from his office. He works in a studio in LA. Everything is done by computer and phone."

"Wait a minute," West said. "Someone calls a number, and it doesn't ring here?"

"Of course not. It can be done that way, but why would I want all the calls to ring in my house? During the show, I have two people operating things for me. One makes sure my voice is going out as it should, the other is screening callers and sending me info over the Internet. You ever use a message program to chat with someone over the Internet?"

"I have," Floyd offered.

West remained silent.

I admitted that I had.

"Then you know that you can type messages back and forth with anyone almost anywhere in the world. When I'm on air, one of my producers tells me who is next in the cue and what they want to talk about. They also remind me when we're coming up on a break. Bumper music is arranged in advance."

"Bumper music?" West said.

"The music you hear in the span between a break and the show. It serves as a transition and covers time discrepancies."

"I don't understand," I said.

Hood looked at me, then explained. "The show is national. That means I'm being heard in four time zones and over scores of radio stations. The show has prescheduled breaks. For example, most stations want some local news time. Places like San Francisco, Los Angeles, Houston, and many more give traffic information even at two in the morning. When we break at the top of the hour for station identification and local news, the local affiliates kill our feed and do their own, then they come back on. Unfortunately, not everyone can come back on at the same second. The music gives a little padding."

"How much did Floyd tell you?" West asked.

"He told me about the murders, but I had already read about them in the papers. Tragic."

"He mentioned that there may be evidence linking the murders to your show?"

"Of course. I assume that's why he came all the way up here and rang my intercom."

Katie spoke up. "Are you suggesting a publicity stunt, Detective? Because if you are, then you're way off base. Ratings are one thing. Serial murder is another. You would do well to remember you are a guest in this house."

"I'm not suggesting anything. I'm gathering information. And you would do well to remember that I'm trying to prevent a fourth murder."

"Everyone, take a deep breath," Hood said. He turned to West. "I don't envy your situation, Detective. Not one bit. I specialize in the strange, and whoever is breaking the necks of your citizens is definitely strange." He looked around the room. "Let's go back out on the deck. I'm getting claustrophobic in here with all of you."

"You still have to finish preparing for tonight's show," Katie said.

"There's time. There's time." Hood showed no sign of anxiety.

The interview lasted another thirty minutes and took place on the deck where we first saw Hood. Katie brought tea and cookies, which Floyd downed with enthusiasm. I caught West eyeing her as she moved in and out of the house. Nothing dissolves a man's brain faster than a pretty woman in a bikini. I started to kick him but refrained.

West ignored his tea and asked questions, taking notes in a small notebook, just like on television. I had a feeling the notes were spare, just enough to jog his memory come report-writing time. He asked questions in short sentences, and Hood answered in the same manner. It was like watching a verbal gunfight. I kept my mouth shut but took in every word.

"What's your real name?" West asked.

"That's private and part of my on-air persona," Hood retorted.

"We have your address. I can get it from the tax records."

"My home is owned by my corporation."

"Corporations are matters of public record. I can find the information there, as well."

Hood frowned. "You see, Katie? This is what I've been talking about on air. There is no more privacy." It was an echo of West's words earlier. I had a feeling that these two men shared some of the same sentiments on that topic. Then I heard him say, "Robin Hoddle, born and reared in San Francisco and now a resident of Santa Rita. Robby Hood is the name I go by now and would prefer to be called by it."

On it went until my mind numbed. Each question seemed sharper than the previous and each answer came in terse tones. These men were building a nice hatred for each other. Floyd seemed uncomfortable, like a child watching his parents argue.

"Who plans your show schedule?" West asked.

"In large part, Katie does. She serves as my primary researcher and sets the schedule. Other producers have input, but Katie and I make the final decisions."

"So you can choose what makes it on the show and what doesn't?"

"Yes. Are you wondering if I'm directing the killings by the topics I choose?"

"Perhaps. I look at all avenues."

Hood smiled. "Have you ever heard of the Cydonia area of Mars?"

"No," West admitted. "My jurisdiction is limited to this planet."

Hood ignored the remark. "It was in the summer of 1976 ... July, I think ... that the Viking Orbiter One was taking pictures of Mars. Its mission was to find possible landing sites for the Viking Lander Two. Late in July it photographed an area called Cydonia. The area has fewer craters and some interesting hills and escarpments. One such hill looks very much like a face when seen from altitude. Ever since the photo was released there have been those who argue that the facelike hill is artificially made. Are you following me?"

"Artificially made means someone had to have been on Mars to make it," Floyd interjected.

"That's right, Floyd. Others have argued that it's nothing more than a hill. Over twenty-five years later, people are debating the issue. Believers say that NASA and the government are covering up the truth; nonbelievers say the believers are caught up in wishful thinking."

"What's your point?" West pressed.

"People see what they want to see. They hear what they want to hear. You see three horrible deaths and compare them to my schedule and see the face of a murderer. I look at it and see coincidence."

"I didn't think guys like you believed in coincidence."

"Guys like me? You mean people who discuss off-the-wall topics. It's true, my mind is more open than most, but I don't believe everything that comes my way. I'm not stupid, Detective West. You look at me and think I'm gullible because of the topics I choose to discuss on my program. I look at you and the mayor and see people far more gullible than I."

That stung but I pretended not to notice.

Hood looked at West. "You'll find no murderer in this house."

chapter 31

We left the house. West and I remained long enough to see Floyd crank up his car, pull a U-turn, and drive off. Overhead the blue of the sky had deepened as the sun began its slide toward the ocean. There were a few hours of sunlight left but not many. Days are short in the winter. West was working through the afternoon traffic. We spent the first five minutes in silence. I couldn't tell if he was tossing water on an emotional fire or if he was simply digesting what he had learned.

I was trying to make heads or tails out of it all. Hood was nothing of what I anticipated, although I didn't know what I expected. Whatever it was, he wasn't it. I was also a little uncomfortable. West has always struck me as genteel and polite. With Hood, he was as cuddly as sandpaper. His tone had been dark and threatening, his approach cutting. Why the change? What was he seeing that I wasn't?

He broke the silence. "Did you see the body on Hood's wife?"

That I wasn't expecting. My face grew hot. "I'll admit that I noticed, but I didn't dwell on it like some people I know."

He shot me a confused glance, then returned his gaze to the road ahead. "What are you . . . Oh, I get it." He smiled. "Careful now, or we'll need another seat belt for your jealousy."

"I'm not jealous."

"Of course not, but just in case you were, let me put that to rest. I'm not talking about sexual attraction—although she was easy on the eyes."

"If I pop you one, would you arrest me for assaulting a police officer?"

He laughed. "Probably. My point isn't that she had a beautiful body, but that she had a fit body. In fact, I wouldn't doubt she throws the weights around on a regular basis."

The image of the little red bikini came to mind. When Katie first came to the door all I could see was how much I could see. I was set back by the little amount of cloth, and I felt embarrassed for her. "She likes to work out. So what?"

"I'm betting that she isn't just his wife, if she's his wife at all."

"What else would she be?"

He looked at me, and I expected to hear something about her being his live-in lover. "Bodyguard." He made a turn, then asked, "What was your first thought when you saw Hood?"

That was easy. "This guy couldn't break another man's neck, even an elderly security guard."

"Exactly, but I bet Katie could."

"Really? She didn't look that strong."

"That's because you didn't look as closely as I did."

"No doubt about that."

"I'm wondering what Katie Lysgaard does while hubby is entertaining the late-night masses." He had verified names before leaving.

"I assume she handles the loose ends of the program, brings him coffee—I have no idea. You think she might go out and prowl the streets looking for people to kill."

"It's not as impossible as you make it sound. It looks like she has the physical ability to do the deeds, especially if she's had some martial arts training. I suppose she could even have been in the military. That's pretty common now. We have women on the force who could get pretty physical in an altercation. I've seen it. There's a couple I wouldn't want to go rounds with."

"But how would she go about killing the men?"

"Your problem is that you don't have a man's brain."

"Odd, I've always thought of that as an advantage."

"Funny. Katie is a babe, and your jealousy just goes to prove it."

"I'm not jeal—"

"With her looks she could approach most men, and it wouldn't be fear that they'd be feeling. If a man steps close to another man there is instant suspicion. When a beautiful women moves closer a different emotion surfaces."

"And you think she's strong enough to not only wring a man's neck but lift his body and place it back in a car, an airplane, and on a stool in a guard shack."

"We think the guard was killed right where we found him, but your point is well taken. I know one thing. I'm going to do a little more investigating on Ms. Lysgaard."

"Try not to enjoy it too much."

"At this point, it's nothing but background checks and fingerprints."

Something occurred to me. "You were pretty pushy back at Hood's home. In fact, I could be forgiven for using the word *rude*. Did he bother you that much or was that an act?"

"Both. He was a little too smug for my tastes, but I pressed him to see what his response would be. More to the point, I pressed him to see what his wife would do."

"She didn't do anything."

"Another reason to be suspicious. If your husband was still alive and someone like me was making implications like I made with Hood, what would you do?"

"Show you the door."

"She didn't do that. She let every innuendo pass. She was cool—too cool. Sometimes it isn't what people do that reveals their nature, it's what they don't do."

I hadn't thought of that. "What now?"

"I take you back to your office, and you do whatever you do. I go watch my third autopsy. Then around seven tonight, I pick you up, and we go out for steaks."

I eyed him. "How do you know I don't have plans?"

"Do you?"

"Yes. I'm meeting with Nat and my issues team."

"Oh." He nodded as if my statement didn't matter, but there was enough change in his expression to let me know that it did.

"There'll be food but not steaks. Pizza."

"The world runs on pizza," West said.

"It wouldn't be a date, but I could make sure there was enough food for one more."

"Is that an invitation?" He smiled. There were those white teeth again. I felt soft in the middle. It must have been the talk of pizza.

"You haven't lived until you sit in a room with political junkies talking over the details of unemployment rates, taxation laws, military spending—"

"Please, no more. I can scarcely contain my enthusiasm." He chuckled.

"Laugh if you will, some of us think it's better than television."

"I think I'll pass. How about something afterwards? Maybe drinks."

"I don't drink."

"Fair enough. Do you pie-and-coffee?"

"I've been known to send a piece of chocolate cream to its final resting place."

"Pie it is. Will eight be too early?"

"I'm not sure we should be dating," I said. The words sounded strange coming from my mouth. "There might be repercussions."

"I was wondering when that would come up. That's why I've put off asking you out. I knew you'd feel that way and turn me down." If he was hurt, he didn't show it. "What repercussions?"

"I'm the mayor, and you're a detective on the police force. It might seem inappropriate."

He shook his head. "To whom?" I hadn't expected that and in truth, I hadn't been honest enough with myself to ask. He pressed. "The other members of the council? Voters? The media?"

"I suppose. I'm more worried about the ethics."

"Having pie with a cop is unethical?"

"Of course not, at least not in this county."

"Mayor . . . Maddy, listen. I'm just a regular guy who happens to be a police detective. I'm not the police chief who responds to you directly. I don't argue budget, ask for money, or make policy. I investigate crimes."

"Still, it may be misconstrued by others. This is a difficult time for me."

"Why? Because you're running for congress?" He shook his head and turned on the street that led to city hall. "Do you think I'll cost you votes? Let me tell you what I've learned, Mayor. Decisions made out of fear usually cost more than those made in courage."

"I don't consider you a liability." I was feeling defensive. "I resent you suggesting that I would be that petty. My life is more complex than you imagine. There are issues I have to deal with."

He didn't reply but his grip on the steering wheel was noticeably tighter. "Issues? Do you know anyone who doesn't have issues? We all do. Yours are no different." He pulled around the block and into the back lot and stopped by the rear entrance.

"I think my issues are different and quite honestly, I don't think you can understand." My jaw was tightening and the muscles in my neck stiffened.

"Why? Because you lost a husband? Lopez may have been estranged from his family, but his kids still lost a father; Fritzy lost a husband, and . . . others have lost special people." He frowned, reached across me, and shoved my door open. "I have to check in at the office. Forgive me for not walking you to your office."

There aren't many times when I'm wordless. I wasn't sure what had just happened, but I knew something had gone sour and gone quickly. I released the catch on my seat belt and exited. I searched for the right words, the last phrase to utter at that tense moment. I came up empty. I pushed the car door closed.

West drove across the lot toward the police station.

He didn't look back.

chapter 32

The last volunteer had left Santa Barbara's Jimmy's Mafia Pizzeria. It was renowned in the area for having the best Sicilian pizza on the west coast. This despite the fact that Jimmy was not part of the Mafia and wasn't even Italian. Thankfully, there was no law prohibiting a short Irishman from making the world's favorite food. The pizzeria was tucked away on the east side of the freeway and just inside Santa Barbara's southernmost border. It had a large dining area with the required battered wood tables and red-and-white checkered tablecloths which were more plastic than cloth. At the back of the restaurant was a meeting area for private parties. Nat had rented it for our meeting.

Ten others had joined us, all volunteers, but each with a set of credentials that made them especially useful on the issues team. We had a banker, a tax accountant, a middle school teacher, the head of a large construction company, an attorney, a computer scientist, and a handful of others with special experience. Their job was to educate me, alert me to possible areas of dissent, and help form policy. It was heady stuff. We had met many times and I ended every meeting feeling as dumb as a post. The amount of information I needed to have at my fingertips when I spoke to women's groups, chamber of commerce gatherings, senior advocacies, homeschooling organizations, and a hundred other mix of voters was enormous. I used to become frustrated with politicians who gave vague answers or answered questions not asked. Like many I assumed they were being evasive, not wanting to say what they really believed. I now know that they often did this so as not to reveal that they didn't yet have a position.

The large room had now grown empty. Employees gathered up dirtied plates and empty pizza trays. Half-empty water bottles stood like lone sentries, marking the place where their owners had used them, then left them for the Dumpster. Crumbs and soiled napkins remained evidence that a short while ago, the room had bustled with smart, opinionated people. Now, just Nat and I remained, a basket of cold breadsticks between us.

"So what is it?" She and her wheelchair were positioned at the head of the long table. I sat to her left.

"What is what?"

"I had only 60 percent of Maddy tonight. Where was the other 40 percent—the fun part?"

"I'm here. I heard everything that was said."

Nat nodded her head, her blond hair swaying with each motion. "Your mind was here, but not your heart. Maddy ain't Maddy without both." The last sentence she uttered with her best I-done-lived-all-my-life-in-these-here-hills accent.

"Too little and too much, I guess. Too little sleep, too many murders, too much to think about. I'm starting to run out of gas."

"Uh-huh." She looked smug.

"Uh-huh what?"

"Spill it, girl, Dr. Nat is listening."

"There's nothing to spill," I protested.

"Oh, please. Dump before you explode and I have to go home and wash all the Maddy off my clothes."

I sighed. It felt good but brought only a little relief. I was spent, the mere remains of an empty toothpaste tube—hollow and mis-shapen. She reached out and took my hand. She said nothing else. Moments became full-fledged seconds that expanded into a minute. I told her about what I had learned about the murders and the sus-picion I had that they were related to Robby Hood. I described my meeting with the council, my earlier confrontation with Tess, Floyd's big adventure, Titus's pending surgery, and whatever else came to mind.

"You have a right to your privacy, Maddy, and I'm the last one to interfere, but I think something else is bothering you."

"Murder and running for congress isn't enough?"

"It's more than enough and it would crush ninety-nine out of a hundred people you meet, but none of the folks are Madison Glenn."

"I'm not that special."

"You are, and that's the crime of all of this. You're special, and you don't know it. Your mind is as sharp as any I've ever seen, and remember, I've interviewed the best and the brightest. Your heart is pure gold, your ethics beyond reproach, your motivation is selfless and sacrificial. Maddy, you should have a halo."

"Nonsense."

"Object all you want. The only difference between your opinion on this and mine is that I'm right and you're wrong."

"If only you could muster a little confidence, Nat."

"So which one was it? Dr. Thomas or Detective West?"

"You're fishing."

"That's because I see fins and scales. Which was it? And don't forget, I was a journalist." She gave my hand a squeeze, then shifted in her chair like she was preparing to watch a movie.

"Detective West said he thought we should start dating and—"

"He made a move! I didn't think he would."

"You want to hear this or not?"

"Sorry. I'm ready. Dish me the details."

I watched her for a moment. She was making light of the topic, but I knew she was doing so for my benefit. "He offered to take me for pie after this meeting. I balked. We talked, and it went downhill from there. I just don't think that a mayor should be dating someone on the police force."

"I see."

"Jerry was over last night. He brought Chinese food and brownies. We sat on my deck and watched the tide come in. We had a good time. He made hot chocolate to go with the brownies."

"He brought Chinese food to your home *and* brownies. I assume you proposed marriage."

"I'm trying to be serious here, Nat."

"That's the problem. You're too serious."

"It's the way I'm wired." I reached for a breadstick and broke it in half, setting both pieces on the napkin in front of me. I had no desire to eat it. Breaking it was enough.

"So you spend some time with Jerry and feel good and then spend a little time with West and feel uncomfortable."

"It goes beyond that. As I said, I'm uncomfortable seeing a man who's on city payroll. Besides, he said some unkind things."

"West said unkind things? Judson West? Are we talking about the same person? What did he say that was unkind?"

I recounted the drive in the car and conversation. It was distasteful. When I was done Nat was shaking her head and giving me that you're-the-most-loveable-moron look. "What was unkind?"

"I told you. He as much as said that I'm preoccupied with my work and my dead husband. I don't need to hear that from anyone."

Nat stared at me but said nothing. Her eyes were somehow sad and steely at the same time. I don't know what she was thinking, but it was making me uncomfortable. Finally she asked, "How's our friendship?"

That surprised me. I had known Nat for less than a year, but we had become the best of friends. I trusted her in everything. If I hadn't, she wouldn't be running my campaign. "To my knowledge it's fine."

"That's how I see it. I also see you as God's gift to me. I haven't embraced your newfound faith, but I believe that whatever God there is, he put you in my life. That's a lot for me to say, seeing as I lost the use of two legs, one arm, and a stellar career."

Hearing the phrase "whatever God there is" unsettled me. A year ago, it wouldn't have.

Nat leaned forward. "At the risk of losing the only real friend I have, let me say, West is right. We all have issues. You're unique in many ways. Your beauty, your brains, your drive, your wit, your commitment, your selfless acts—but in other ways you're like the rest of us mere mortals."

"I never claimed to be special—"

"It's time to shut up and listen, Maddy. You can walk out if you want, I won't chase you. My battery is almost dead so I wouldn't make it very far if I did. You lost a husband, I lost most of a body, Jerry lost a wife to someone she thought was better. The list goes on. Celeste almost lost a mother last year and even though she lived, both Celeste and her mom lost the sense of security we all need. I suppose some losses are more painful than others, but you'd be hard pressed to convince some people your pain is greater."

"I've never tried to do that." I was getting angry.

"Of course not. I'm not saying you have, and I doubt that was West's intention. You do, however, keep some people at a distance, even those who love you."

"I do not."

Nat said nothing. The air between us soured, and my heart began to beat like I was on my treadmill. I was already worn to my last thread. I didn't need pop psychology. The comebacks came to me, sharp phrases that would put an end to the conversation. I used none of them. I didn't want to hurt her feelings—Who was I kidding? It wasn't her feelings I feared hurting, it was mine. Maybe if I wasn't so tired. Maybe if I wasn't so wearied by work and concern over the crimes I had seen. Maybe ... maybe ... maybe.

"Maddy," Nat said, her voice just a decibel or two above a whisper, "you have a great career and a better-than-average chance of walking the halls of congress. You have friends and family who love you. And you have two men interested in you. One brings you brownies and the other offers pie. Frankly, if Quasimodo showed up at my doorstep with an invitation for pie, I'd go." She gave me a look warm with love. "Have some pie, woman. Have some pie."

I watched as Nat drove off in her van, thankful to God that someone could speak to me in a way that I could hear. I hated every moment of that conversation, and it still tightened my stomach, but I loved and admired the woman who forced it down my throat. My final words to her that evening were, "I don't know if God—and by the way there's only one God—put me in your life or not, but I am certain he put you into mine."

I took a chance and pulled into the police station. It was almost nine and I assumed that West had gone home. I was wrong. He was at his desk, his head down, an open file before him.

"Excuse me, Officer. I believe I was promised coffee and a slice of chocolate-cream pie."

He looked up, smiled, and the light in his eyes danced. "You sure?"

"I am as long as we don't spend the time apologizing to each other."

He stood and reached for his coat. "That's more than fine with me. I found a little place south of the pier. It isn't much to look at, but it has great coffee and better-than-average pie."

"Butch's?"

"Yeah, that's the place. How'd you ... Oh, that's right, you're mayor of this place."

"He made a nice contribution to my last campaign. We'll have to tip heavy."

"What do you mean, 'we'?"

chapter

"Ask me about the murders and your security," West said. He sipped decaf coffee from a white mug that looked like it had been on duty for many years.

"Why?" I had just finished the last bite of chocolate-cream pie and there was nothing else for my fork to do. I set it down. I took my own cup of decaf. It was close to ten, and Butch's was still buzzing. A good dessert menu will do that. It was also one reason I avoid the place. I didn't need more temptation to eat. Lately it seemed that my life revolved around my office and the next restaurant.

"Because if asked, I want to say we discussed the case and your security."

"Okay, but I have a different question. You were making a case that Hood's wife Katie could be the killer, but earlier you said the bruising on the victims' jaw indicated a man had done the deed."

"That occurred to me also. She had rather large hands but not what I would have expected. Still, a set of bruises are not the same as a handprint. Different people bruise at different rates and in different ways. It's a puzzle, but not enough for me to write her off yet."

"Even if she has the ability, what would her motive be? Boost ratings? That seems extreme."

"Motive is for the prosecutors to determine. My job is to link evidence to a suspect and make an arrest."

"And what evidence do you have? Anything new from today's autopsy?"

"I'm still waiting on the SI team but we don't have much. You're not going to believe this, but the marina has a video-security system. It wasn't working and hasn't been for weeks."

"You're kidding?"

"Not at all. People watch television detective shows and think that everything falls into place. My experience has been that it's the other way around. It's Murphy's Law: if it can go wrong it does. Take security at city hall. A man is killed in the front lot and the guards who are supposed to patrol the buildings and grounds don't find the body, you do."

"I'm still waiting on an answer about that." I made a mental note that three days was more than enough time for the security company to come up with an excuse.

"No need to bother. I called today. I'm impatient about these things."

A moment of regret upset my content stomach. I was supposed to follow up on that and had promised to do so on Monday. It was now late Wednesday night. "And?"

"And, the guard who was working that night started vacation the next day. Jim Lynch, head of Atlas Security, was furious. Apparently the guard wanted to get on the road a little early and left his post sometime after one that morning. He had worked it out with the guard who was due to relieve him to help cover his early departure. There are two guards out of work now."

"Is the world filled with that many incompetents?"

"Based on my experience, yes. Now let's talk about your security. This connection you dug up between Hood's topics and the murders has me a little on edge. For your safety, I think you should stay somewhere else tonight."

"The only connection to me is in the third hour of the program." I called the description up from memory. "'Mayor Judy Morrison discusses strange aircraft seen over her city.' I'll grant you that the word 'mayor' appears and it refers to a woman mayor, but it also refers to aircraft. More to the point, all the murders have been based on the topic found in the second hour, not the third. I doubt I'm a target."

"I'm not willing to bet your life on the difference between hour two and hour three. Stay someplace else—a friend's, your parents', a hotel."

I gave it some thought but then said, "No. I'll be safe at home. I have a good security system. I should be fine."

"You are the most stubborn woman I have ever met."

"I hear that a lot." I sipped my coffee. "It's not that I'm stubborn; it's that I don't think evil should push us around. If we don't rule it, it will rule us."

"That's very noble and foolish, but I figured you'd say something like that. You have before, so I've made arrangements. I spoke to Chief Webb about your detective work—"

"I bet that went over well."

"He mumbled something about an interfering woman intent on getting herself killed. Nonetheless, he's ordered increased patrols of your neighborhood and those of every council member. I also asked Jim Lynch to arrange for a guard at your house. He was embarrassed enough to volunteer himself, but I convinced him that that wasn't necessary."

"Don't you think you should have spoken to me first?"

"I considered it, but I knew you'd object, so I did it anyway. You can have the chief fire me in the morning."

I wanted to be angry. West was meddling in my life again, but as a charter member of the International Meddling Society I had little room to talk. "Lynch understood that I will be paying for that guard out of my own pocket and not the city coffers. I am to get no special treatment."

"You are a hard woman to please, Maddy Glenn. Did you give your parents this kind of trouble when you were growing up?"

"I was the perfect child. At least that's how I remember it."

"I bet they tell a different story."

"I'm the apple of my father's eye and the joy in my mother's heart."

"And a royal pain in my—"

"Watch it. I outrank you." We exchanged a little laughter, and I looked at the handsome man across the table from me. He was gorgeous to behold, a pleasure to talk to, possessed an admirable intelligence and a noble dedication to his work.

So why was I suddenly uncomfortable? Why did I feel out of place? Each time I saw West I had experienced a sense of joy and a soft feeling just behind my sternum. But this moment wasn't right, and I didn't know why.

"You okay?"

"Yes—of course—why?" Three statements in four words. I was overcompensating.

"You seem . . . distant." He leaned forward. "If you're still bothered by things I said early today, don't be. I said things more firmly than I meant to. Serial killings do that to me."

"You didn't say anything wrong. I suppose I had it coming." My uneasiness grew. Emotions detached from facts bothered me. If I was to be angry, then I wanted a reason for my anger. If I'm disquieted, then I wanted a reason for that. I had no reason for what I was feeling. I should experience joy and relief. I had finally let loose enough to go out with Judson West. So where was the schoolgirl euphoria? Had I been mourning the loss of my husband for so long that I could no longer have strong emotions for a man?

I had just finished a piece of pie, but for some reason I wanted a brownie and hot chocolate. I wasn't hungry. I didn't need the sugar fix. I wanted the simple, relaxed emotion I felt with Jerry last night as we watched the surf roll in and the moon paint the ocean.

This was a surprise, and I was too weary for surprises. That had to be it. I was just too worn out to process my emotions properly.

"I'm beat," I said. "Sleep hasn't been my friend lately. I think I'd better call it a night."

West studied me for a moment, then reached for his wallet. Instinctively, I reached for my purse. "Oh no, you don't. My male ego won't allow it. Put that away."

"How do you know that I wasn't just reaching for my keys?" We had chosen to meet at Butch's. It didn't make sense to drive there in one car, then drive back to city hall to retrieve my car so I could drive home. I'm nothing if not fixated upon efficiency.

"I'm a detective, remember? That makes me a keen observer of all things human." I put my purse aside and waited for the waiter to make change. A few minutes later I was in my car driving home and wondering at what point I had fully and completely lost my mind.

chapter 34

It was nearing ten thirty when I pulled onto my street and made my way toward home. My weariness was taking no excuses. I had put it off long enough. My blinks were getting longer, and I was glad that I only had a short distance to go. Sleep was what I needed and sleep was what I intended to get, if I could get my mind to cooperate. It was still mush, little more than Jell-O in the sun. My time with West had been disappointing, and I still didn't know why. He had been the perfect gentleman, witty, humorous, and concerned. It should have been the perfect date, but it never felt right, ill-fitting. I began to think that I needed psychiatric help.

I slowed as my house came into view. The front porch light shed yellow light across my tiny front lawn and spilled out on to the street. I decreased speed more than normal. West had said that an Atlas Security guard would be waiting for me. I didn't want to startle him. The house was dark as I expected it to be at this hour and the front yard was empty. No guard. I pulled into the drive and waited, assuming that he must be around the back of the house. A guard isn't much of a guard if he doesn't check the parameter. Nothing. Finally, I pushed the button that sent a signal to my garage door opener and waited for it to finish its slow rise, then I pulled in.

I switched off the engine, reached for my purse with one hand while pushing the same button that opened the door. It began its noisy descent, clanging and popping. There had to be a quieter contraption than what I had, and if there was, I would buy it in a heartbeat.

Stepping from the SUV, I moved toward the door that opened into the house. The garage light was on a timer. It came on whenever the big door opened and then extinguished itself sixty seconds later. Since I didn't want to be fumbling around in the garage looking for the light switch, I wasted no time entering the house. The Uniform Building Code requires that all doors leading from a garage into a house be fire rated and have a self-closing device. My house was no different.

I stepped across the threshold and reached for the light switch that would turn on the foyer light. Instantly the gloom was replaced by warm illumination. There was a beeping. There was always an electronic beeping when I entered. It was my security system reminding me that if I didn't enter a code in the next few seconds, calls would be made, police would arrive, and I might be facing a stiff fine for a false report. I obeyed my electronic master, approaching the living room control box and pushing buttons on the keypad to let the system know I belonged there. Red and green lights gave me information. Once the code was entered the beeping stopped and a green light shone next to the word Disarmed.

While driving home I had considered a short walk on the beach. I frequently took leisurely strolls along the sand bathed in the ivory moonlight. But West's concern had turned up my own, and I thought it unwise. Instead, I'd have a glass of milk and call it a night. Before I did, I had one more bedtime routine to perform. I punched in my code and a button with the word Stay printed on it. Once done the perimeter with its doors and windows would be armed but the internal motion detectors would be deactivated. A good thing, too. Having the alarm go off every time I get up to use the bathroom would wear thin real quick.

I waited for the green light by the word Stay to come on. It didn't. I reentered the code and pressed the right button. A red light stared back at me.

"Now what?" I said to myself. I looked closer at the control panel. A red light was shining next to a label reading Doors. It meant a door was open. But how could that be? The alarm was fine when I entered the house and the only door I had touched was the one from the garage. It must not have closed completely. That was the problem with self-closers. Sometimes they didn't do what they had been designed to do. I had a more detailed control panel in my bedroom. From there I could determine which doors and windows were open, but that was upstairs. I decided to check the door I had just used first. It couldn't be anything else.

My cell phone rang and I jumped. I opened my purse and found the annoying device. I looked at the caller ID. It was Jerry.

"Hello," I said.

"It's me. I just wanted to make sure you were doing all right."

"I'm fine. I just got in and was locking up."

I turned and stepped toward the door. Sure enough, it hadn't closed all the way and there would be no setting the alarm until it was completely shut. I raised my free hand and pressed it against the unclosed door. What was the children's joke? When is a door not a door? When it is ajar—

The door swung open with a bang, hitting me on the wrist, and crashing into the wall. I cried out in pain and instinctively backpedaled. My cell phone fell on the carpeted floor. I screamed in pain.

"Maddy? Maddy!" Jerry's voice sounded tiny and miles away as it percolated out of the cell phone's speaker.

Someone charged through the door, erupting from the black sepulcher of the garage and into the thin light from the lobby chandelier. I was doubled over, holding my throbbing wrist, which sent lightning bolts of pain up my arm and through my body. I felt sick to my stomach but that lasted less than a moment. The frigid water of fear filled my belly the next second. Before me stood a figure dressed all in black. A black ski mask covered his head and face. Equally black leather gloves were clinched into knotted fists.

"Who—"

The right hand opened and struck me on the right cheek. My head snapped to the left, then sensations ran amok. Pain filled the side of my head, my neck popped at the sudden movement, I tasted blood, and my brain seemed to rattle in my skull. All this before I hit the floor.

For a moment, I forgot my wrist.

"Maddy! Maddy! Talk to me." Lying on the floor I could hear Jerry's voice better but it didn't matter. The phone was four or five feet from me and if my rational mind hadn't just been slapped out of me, I might have reached for it. My uninvited guest had other ideas. A giant step later he had the phone in hand. Coolly, he pressed a button, closed the flip lid, and then threw it at the opposite wall, where it gouged the drywall and clattered to the floor, now more paperweight than phone.

He watched it fall. I let him. I rolled on my stomach and pushed myself up, sprinting for the stairs, hoping to put some distance between us. I felt something move in my wrist; something I've never felt move before. It conjured up a fiery gorge of nausea. I pushed it down. There would be time to vomit later, if I lived. And if I didn't . . . well, then it really didn't matter.

Driven by fear as deep as any I had ever felt, I made for the stairs. I took the first two in one stride, the third in one, then watched as the steps rose to meet me. My left leg wasn't working. I commanded it to move but it was weighted. I turned. My attacker had seized my foot. I pulled. I yanked. I kicked. I stayed put. Then came the tug and it was hard. I felt the stairs dig into my ribs despite the carpet and padding. I clutched for the handrail and missed, but managed to seize one of the turned balustrades.

He yanked my leg but I held on. The force was enough to make me certain that my knee would separate or my hip would slip out of joint. He stopped, and I turned in time to see he had chosen a different approach. He was starting up the stairs. I had only made a few risers so the trip was short.

The black figure stood above me. From my supine position he seemed to tower. The light from the foyer silhouetted his masked face. He reached down and grabbed a fistful of hair and began pulling me up. My heart had stopped beating; instead it quivered without rhythm. I couldn't breathe. I was being suffocated by fear.

He yanked my head around and my body followed. Something pressed against my jaw—a hand. The pain searing my scalp from where he held my hair lessened as he let go. He placed that hand on the back of my head. I felt my head turn slightly and my neck twist. His fingers wiggled on my jaw. I thought of Jose Lopez. I thought of Jim Fritz. I thought of a guard found dead in his guard shack. So this was what it was like for them.

My fear melted away. My heart steadied. My mind came back online. For years I had watched old movies and had always been critical of the way they portrayed women as helpless, good only for screaming and stepping to the side until rescued by the hero. If I was going to die, I wasn't going to die like one of those silver-screen goddesses.

He moved my head to the right as if measuring the distance it would travel, then eased it to the left. I had never seen someone break another person's neck, but I knew that the next second would bring a snapping motion that would end my days. I could yield to it and it would all be over in moments.

I thought of my mother. I thought of my father. I thought of Nat and Celeste and Fritzy and Titus and Larry and West. And I thought of Jerry. Poor Jerry. This act would surely kill him as it killed me.

I pulled at the arm with the hand that held the head God built. At best, I could hold him off a second, maybe two. But if I tried, his practiced move might not work, and I might lie on the stairs suffering a slow death.

If I were to be another victim, I decided, I'd be one he'd remember for the rest of his miserable life. I placed one foot on the nose of the next tread, then the other, and pushed backward as hard as I could. If he wanted to break my neck, maybe I could return the favor.

He rocked backward, and I fought for purchase and pushed again. Legs that pounded a treadmill five days a week and fueled by fear-laced adrenaline did their work.

We fell backward. He landed on the stairs. I landed on him. And I heard the glorious sound of his head bouncing on a stair tread. He let go on the way down, clawing for the rail to one side and the wall on the other. His body cushioned my fall. The stairs knocked the wind from him, which spewed out in a guttural grunt.

I kept pushing backward hoping that he wouldn't have time to regain his composure. I raised myself up, scrabbled up the stairs, but felt the fleshy vise of his hand clutch my other ankle and pull. I went down again, my face by his feet.

If my face was by his feet, then maybe my feet were by his face. I kicked for all I was worth. One heel hit something soft; next my other heel hit something hard. I knew it was the treads on the stairs. I had also gotten some part of his head.

Again I was free. I crawled up two more steps before he was on me. Arms wrapped around my waist, and suddenly I was in the air, then falling. He had lifted me and tossed me over the handrail.

I landed on the floor hard, and it was my turn to feel my breath leave my body. Had I been farther up the stairs, the fall would have broken something. Air or no air, I had to get to my feet. I was beyond pain. Survival was at the forefront of my mind. I must have caught him a good one with my foot, because it took a second for him to gather himself and start down the stairs.

A second was a blessing. I staggered to my feet. My vision was blurred, and my lungs demanded air. I heard a thud behind me but I had no time to wonder about it. I started for the front door, but it was too near the staircase. I'd never make it.

On the wall near the staircase was the alarm panel. It had a panic button, but the odds of me battling my way past my assassin long enough to hit the alarm was nil. Instead, I turned and charged for the dining room. If I could open the sliding glass doors, I could make it outside. If I could do that, I could scream loud enough and long enough to be my own alarm.

If only I could get outside.

I would try. I took a step and wobbled on legs that had been yanked, pulled, and forced to do work they were never designed for. The kitchen was right off the dining room. If I couldn't make it outside, then maybe I could reach the knife set next to the stove. Could I stab a man? I decided I could. I would work out the morality later. The dining room was dark and the kitchen darker. I ran for the dark.

Thump. Thud. There was noise from outside.

I preferred to hear sirens. I reached the door, my gaze welded to the handle and the lock. I'd have to flip a lever releasing the lock, then slide the door to one side. There was the screen door. Mustn't forget the screen door.

My hand touched the handle, its cool metal chilling my fingertips. Thud, thud, thud . . . "Mad . . ."

The handle receded from my grasp. No. I was receding from it. He had me by the back of my coat and blouse. This time his arm went around my throat, and I felt my feet leave the ground. I had seen police shows where this was done. They called it a sleeper hold. His arm tightened around my throat, not choking off my air but pinching off the arteries that took blood to my brain. I kicked. I clawed. Lights sparkled in my eyes like stars. Then there was a loud bang, and the stars poured into the room and showered me.

The image was right; the logic wasn't.

Not that it mattered.

I was free. He dropped me, and I fell to my hands and knees. Now what?

I raised my head and my neck protested painfully. Something was coming through the sliding glass door. But I hadn't had a chance to unlock it. The stars. The stars that showered me were bits of broken, tempered glass. The door had shattered into a thousand little cubes and coming through the opening was Jerry—a Jerry I didn't recognize. His face was pulled back in a sneer that would terrify the Grim Reaper. At least, I hoped so.

My strength was gone, my brain was demanding more blood, more oxygen, and my arms were overcooked noodles. I fell on my side and watched Jerry's feet tromp across the glass, crunching with each step.

Jerry wasn't a fighter. He had never been in the military, didn't play any sports in high school or college, hated confrontation. He was a passive, gentle, thinking man—a teddy bear in a doctor's smock. At the moment he was a stranger. He was the best, most welcome stranger I had ever seen.

"Get out!"

You tell 'em, Jerry. It took a moment for me to realize he was talking to me.

I forced myself to my knees. Not far from where I had fallen was the small, wood side table I kept between the lounge chairs on the deck. My brain had enough oxygen to do the math. The thumping I had heard was Jerry trying to get in through the back door. The garage was sealed up tight and the front door bolted. The glass door was his only possibility.

Grunts and sick-sounding thumps came from behind me. I pulled myself up using one of the dining room chairs as a crutch. Jerry was faring badly. He was up against an experienced fighter. Jerry blocked as many punches as he could, but soon every other one was getting through. It must have taken the greatest and most desperate courage for him to do what I saw next.

Jerry lunged, wrapping his arms around the assailant. "Run, Maddy. Run!"

The man in black pulled his head back and head-butted Jerry straight between the eyes. Jerry's arms dropped. His knees wobbled. A fierce blow caught Jerry just under the ribs and he went down. The brave man was on his knees before the demon in black.

He stepped behind Jerry. A gloved hand reached for his jaw. Another found its place at the back of Jerry's head. I found enough strength to charge, to jump, and to land on the back of the man who was about to kill my friend.

My weight and momentum took all three of us to the ground. I held on. I didn't try to break my fall. There could be no more pain. I held on, my arms wrapped around the man's head. I held on, my legs around his torso. I squeezed with all my might, which wasn't much and was becoming less each second that ticked. I squeezed anyway.

The attacker had amazing strength. He was able to lift himself to his feet with me attached to him like a leech. I didn't care. I was beyond caring. I had one goal: not to let go. If he was going to kill me, he was going to have to do it while I was still attached. He staggered and clutched for me. His gloved hands reached for my head, my hair, but missed its mark. He bumped into a wall, then the dining room table. That's when it occurred to me that I had his eyes covered. I found more strength to squeeze.

I knew I wasn't hurting him, although I wouldn't have cared if I had, but I had taken away his vision. The problem was, I didn't know what to do next. I prayed I would live long enough to see a next.

He moved toward the shattered door, still clutching at me. Twice he bent forward so quickly I was certain I was on my way down, but my muscles hung on a little longer. He stumbled forward, then caught his foot on the upturned table Jerry had used to break in the door. We fell through the opening and onto the deck. We went down hard and that was it for me. I could hang on no longer. My arms and legs gave way, and I lay in a heap on the wood deck, the ocean beyond, the sky above.

It was a good place to die.

Sounds of sirens sliced the night like razors. The assailant rose, swayed, then took an abrupt two steps back. He fell over something, landing hard on his back. The something was looking at me. The something wore a white shirt and dark pants and a badge that read Atlas Security. The something stared back with unmoving, vacant eyes. His head was tilted at an odd angle.

The sirens grew louder. Jerry appeared, blood trickling from his forehead, nose, and mouth. His face was swelling like a boxer in the twelfth round. The man in black sprung to his feet, started toward Jerry, then froze. Jerry jumped between the man and me.

The sirens screamed. The man ran down the side yard. Jerry started after him.

"Jerry! No!"

He spun; anger had frozen his face into a sneer. He looked back down the side yard.

"Jerry, no. I need you. Stay."

The mask of fury melted like ice in an oven. He blinked twice, then rushed to my side. "Let me look at you. Where are you hurt?"

"No. No, Dr. Jerry. Just hold me." I began to weep. "Just hold me."

He sat on the deck and cradled me in his arms.

I sobbed. I didn't care about appearances. I didn't care about the media, about congress, or about city government. I let it all out as I shivered in Jerry's arms, no longer able to control my emotions or my body.

Jerry held me. It had all happened over the eternity of minutes, but it would live on in night terrors and every unexpected sound in the dark. We sat on the deck under a canopy of cold, staring stars, and heard the sounds of an apathetic ocean. In houses up and down the street, children slept safely in their beds, and parents watched televisions. Some would wonder about the sirens that sounded so near. A few might turn up their TVs.

Jerry said nothing but his arms didn't budge as he held me and we rocked gently.

The sirens stopped. Through the shattered opening I heard a knocking. I also heard footsteps in the side yard. I tensed and Jerry held me tighter. Pulling my face away from Jerry's chest, I looked at the man who rounded the corner. He wore the familiar uniform of the Santa Rita Police.

"Ambulance," Jerry demanded. "I want an ambulance right now!"

The black of the night invaded my mind, and I could no longer hear the ocean or see the stars.

chapter 36

They gave me a private room. The time between the arrival of the police and when I was wheeled from the ambulance into the emergency room of Pacific Horizon Hospital was fuzzy. I remember being moved from the gurney to the ER bed well enough—it hurt. Jerry was there each moment. He refused to be seen by any doctors until my initial exam was complete. There had been poking, some prodding, a blood draw, a cold stethoscope to the chest and back, eyes peering into my eyes, ears, and mouth. All of that was followed by a short stay in radiology. By two the next morning I was in a room with pale green walls, a bulletin board with leftover get-well cards from the previous occupant, and the dark eye of a switched-off television staring back at me.

I lay with the back of the bed tilted up, which eased the pain in my head. My arm throbbed and itched. A temporary fiberglass cast ran from my elbow to the palm of my hand.

Pacific Horizon Hospital is a four-story building. It sits on the east side of the freeway, nestled in the side of a gentle hill. Almost all major buildings in the city were designed after the California mission style. PHH was a glass and concrete edifice whose very difference drew attention to itself. It lacked architectural style but it was a solid hospital with an intelligent, cut-above-the-average staff. I was thankful for its presence.

Two people stood near my bed. "Dad, you need to take Mom home," I said. "She's tired."

"No, I'm not." Mom pretended to act offended, but she was too worried to pull it off.

"Okay then, Mom, you need to take Dad home. He's tired."

"Nonsense, young lady, we're old, we don't sleep anymore."

I loved it when he called me "young lady." With forty just around the corner I'd learned to appreciate anytime someone called me young, even if it was out of parental habit.

Greg and Agnes Anderson were the best parents any human could hope for. Both were intelligent, funny, talented, and loving. Mom had retired from teaching music at the local high school, and my father continued to teach history at the University of Santa Barbara. He was close to retirement age, but they were going to have to extract him from the school like a dentist removes a molar. He wasn't going to go quietly.

I wasn't sure how long they had been at the hospital, but they were waiting for me when I was delivered by wheelchair to the place I would call home for the night. I wanted to be discharged, but since I had been knocked about the head and shoulders, choked, and tossed over the handrail of my staircase, the doctors decided I needed some observation. They were a cautious bunch.

"I appreciate you coming, but I'm all right. I'll be going home in the morning."

"No, you'll be coming home with us," Mom said. It wasn't an invitation.

"I appreciate that, Mom, but no."

"All right then, we're coming to stay with you." Again, it was a statement, not an invitation for discussion.

"I'd love to have you, but I charge rent. I'm thinking a large taco casserole should cover a couple of nights."

She smiled and tears filled her eyes. Her baby was going to be fine, but she couldn't push the imagined scene from her mind. Nothing will start a woman crying faster than seeing another woman cry. I had to act fast. "And pound cake. I need it to keep my strength up."

"It's a deal," Dad said. Mom had put him on a diet, and any reason to break it was welcome.

I looked at them. Each sporting hair more gray than not, more wrinkles than I recalled, and masks of deep concern. The corners of my father's mouth turned down, making his closely trimmed beard droop. The sparkle that was always in his eye was dimmer than I had seen it.

"I'm sending you two home. I'm mayor, I have the authority. The entire police force is at my disposal, so don't trifle with me." I grinned. That really hurt. I had seen my face in the mirror of the bathroom. I was confined to bed for the night, but some things demand attention. The bathroom was one of them. The image that came back from the mirror nauseated me. I had a monster bruise on my right cheek and dark bruises along my jaw, marks similar in size and shape to fingers. I knew how they got there and the realization that I was one quick, snapping motion from meeting my Maker fired up the nausea I had been fighting. While in the bathroom, I was tempted to remove my gown and see what other bruises awaited discovery. I decided they could wait until I was home.

"We're fine, honey," Mom said. "You don't have to worry about us."

"I won't be able to sleep if I know you two are standing vigil. Give me a kiss, then go home and rest. I'm putting you to work tomorrow."

Mom stepped forward and looked at me. She seemed puzzled.

"What is it, Mom?"

"I'm trying to find a place to kiss that won't hurt you."

"The forehead's in pretty good shape. Try there."

She did. I felt her warm lips on my skin and a tear that fell from her eye to my cheek. I was getting close to losing it again, and I had cried all I wanted to for the night. Dad followed suit.

"Will you get someone to come out to the house and fix the glass in the back door?" I asked, trying to hold myself together with the glue of distraction.

"Already done. I called and left a message at one of the glass shops in town. I'm sure they'll be out first thing in the morning. Detective West tells me he had a couple officers put up some plywood to secure the house."

"That's good. When did you see him?"

"In the ER waiting room. He sat with us for a good while, then said he had to check on a few things."

"Careful what you say about me." West walked into the room. "Look what I found nosing around your door."

Jerry walked in behind him. Mom gasped. So did I. I hadn't seen Jerry since they had wheeled me down to radiology. He had taken a beating and was examined by another ER doctor. I heard him objecting to the exam, but emergency room doctors are not to be messed with, even if there is an MD after your name.

In the dim light of the room, I saw the sweet, mildly rugged face of Jerry looking the worse for wear. One eye had closed to little more than a slit; his jaw, nose, forehead, cheeks—everything really—was puffy.

"Oh, Jerry," was all I could say.

He smiled and it looked excruciating. "Do you like my new look? I think it gives me the rugged he-man appeal so many men wish they had."

"Forgive me for saying so, Doc," West said, "but you look more like a man who tried to kiss a moving train."

"Yeah, that's the look I was going for."

West shook his head. "Well, if it's any comfort, you're bound to look worse in the morning."

"Are you all right?" Mom asked.

"I'm fine. Some bumps, some bruises, a sore side, and couple of other things I'll brag about later."

Mom stepped to Jerry and gently put her arms around him. "We owe you so much. If you hadn't arrived when you had—"

"Hug easy, Mrs. Anderson. I'm a little tender from slamming my ribs into that guy's fist." He gave her a gentle hug, then Dad shook his hand.

"You up for a few questions?" West asked me.

"Only if you'll boot my parents out. I was telling them you'd arrest them if they didn't go home and get some sleep." I didn't want them to hear the details that West might ask for.

"Okay, okay, we'll go," Dad said, giving me a wink. He didn't want Mom to hear the details either. "But we'll be back to nag you later. So get some rest."

I promised and waved good-bye.

"I get the first question," I said. "How did the intruder get past my security system?"

He motioned for Jerry to take a seat in the large padded chair near my bed. Jerry put up no argument.

"I have an idea, but I need to hear your story first. Start from the beginning."

I did a play-by-play from the moment I pulled onto my street until I lost consciousness in Jerry's arms. It was painful to recount, and at times I had to beat my emotions back into the cave of logic. The weeping time was over for now. I'm sure there would be other times soon.

"You were lucky Jerry called when he did," West said. "And even more fortunate that he was nearby."

"It was more than luck. I don't think I believe in luck anymore. I don't know if this will make sense, but I was terrified beyond words but I never felt alone."

West shifted his weight as if uncomfortable with the topic. "I'm glad that works for you." In an obvious effort to change the subject he turned to Jerry. "How did you get there so quickly?"

"I had just been to the house and nobody was home," Jerry said. "As I was driving away, I caught a pair of headlights in the rearview mirror. I thought it might be Maddy so I called. That's when I heard the struggle. A moment later, the line went dead. Of course, I called 911 and turned my car around. I wish I could have been there sooner."

"If you had, you both might be dead." West looked at his note sheet. "The attacker killed the guard who had been posted there. If he had seen you, he or she would have taken you out first. You were the greater danger."

"It was a he," Jerry remarked. "No way was it a she."

"How can you be so sure if the attacker was masked from head to foot?"

"It's the first thing they teach you in medical school—men and women are very different. This was definitely a man. A skilled man."

"Detective West thinks that a woman we met might be the killer," I inserted.

"I can't speak to that," Jerry said, "but I can tell you my fist hit a man, and he grunted like it. I wrapped the guy up in my arms. I was close enough to tell the difference."

West seemed disappointed.

"Now," I repeated, "how did he get past my security system without setting off the alarm?"

"Here's my take on that." West closed his notebook. "We examined your property and house, top to bottom. You have an automatic sprinkler system, right?"

"Yes, it comes on late at night. What of it?"

"We looked at the timer. They're set to come on at ten and run for ten minutes. It left a flower bed muddy. The flower bed I refer to is the one on the north side of your garage. We found his footprints there. They weren't simple prints like he was walking through your daisies. They were a mess. I think he was crouched down in the bed, hiding from you when you returned. The perp had mud on his shoe.

"You came home," he continued, "and he hid just around the corner of the garage. As you pulled in, he followed you, hiding behind that big SUV you drive. We found mud next to the right rear tire. You walked to the door between the garage and your home. The door began to close behind you. Moving quickly, he caught the door before it closed all the way."

A light went on in my head. "That's why the alarm indicator showed the open door."

"You walked in and turned off the alarm and its motion detectors. You only have a few moments to do that. That's how these systems work. I'll bet you tried to reset the alarm."

"Of course. When I have it set to Stay the motion detectors are off, but the parameter is set. So . . . he waited until he heard me disarm the system, and he also knew I couldn't reset it until that door was closed."

West nodded. "When you started to push the door closed he came charging in. The alarm is deactivated, and he could do what he came to do without setting it off."

"But he failed," Jerry said.

"Thanks to you and to the fact that we have a mayor with some attitude. Some people would have just given up."

"That's not in my nature."

"I take it the attacker is still at large," Jerry said.

"Unfortunately. We're still working." He looked at me. "I owe you the world's biggest apology. I should have seen you home after our ... meeting."

Jerry gave us the eye but didn't say anything.

I shook my head. "You arranged for extra police coverage in the area and the guard. You don't need to apologize for anything. On the other hand, I should eat a little crow. I had convinced myself that the attacks were not only related to Hood's program but also confined to the second hour of the show. You said that may just be coincidence and that we should take the third-hour program seriously."

"I guess you haven't heard," West said. "They changed the schedule at the last minute."

chapter

Morning came all too quickly. With the help of pain relievers and a mild, prescribed sedative, I went to sleep around three. West had left to oversee the evidence gathering at my home. Jerry stayed until I had fallen asleep, sitting in the chair, his watchful eyes on me. I woke up once just as the sun was beginning to peek in my window. Jerry was gone. At home, I hoped. The man earned a lifetime of leisure as far as I was concerned.

A nurse brought an electronic thermometer and an ice-cold stethoscope. An orderly brought breakfast, which I was sure was designed to empty hospital beds, and the admitting ER doc came by before calling his night a day. He was a stout, bald man who insisted I could go home at noon but not before. "A few more hours of rest will do you good. Otherwise you're looking great."

"I've seen my face, Doc. I'm not looking all that great."

"I meant healthwise, you're doing fine. The bruises will take some time to go away. You may need a touch more makeup for the next few weeks."

"Makeup. I don't need makeup, I need a stucco job."

"If you do, choose the hand-trowel look. It has more character." He studied me for a second. "Compared to what I see most weeks, you look pretty good. Be thankful."

"I am, Doctor. I'm thankful for many things. You wouldn't happen to know where Dr. Jerry Thomas is, would you? Did he go home?"

"Hah! That's a good one. At least your sense of humor is intact. We couldn't get him out of here with dynamite. He's in the doctor's lounge sleeping on the sofa."

I thought of Jerry curled up on a worn sofa, trying to be comfortable with his bruised ribs. Guilt, the gift that keeps on giving, crawled into bed with me. "I'll try to make him go home and rest."

"Good luck. I'll make sure all the discharge papers are in order. You should set up an appointment to see your personal physician in the next day or two. Don't want anything new to develop."

After the doctor left, I played with my food, pushing it around on the plate until I was convinced that I lacked the courage to eat any of it. Around eight o'clock, people began to show. First came West, who had nothing else to report other than Chief Webb was hopping mad about the whole thing and didn't know who to blame. He looked as tired as I felt and when I asked if he had slept at all last night, he changed the topic.

Floyd arrived, looking pale and upset. I reassured him that I'd live to torment him in the days ahead, then gave him instructions about the next few days. I would be working from home until my face would no longer frighten little children and small dogs. I also asked him to call Nat. I was going to be off the campaign trail until I could present a proper public figure. There would be media to think of, speaking engagements to cancel, and damage control to undertake. I had no idea what impact this would have on my candidacy, and since my pain relievers were wearing off, I didn't much care at the moment.

I dozed off for an hour or so, and when I awoke Jerry was sitting by my bed. His face was still puffy but he appeared more like the man who came charging to my rescue.

"You owe me a new sliding door," I said. My mouth was thick with some nasty film. I smacked my lips. He stood and poured water from a plastic pitcher on a nearby table and handed me a cup with a flex straw in it. I frowned as I tasted it. "This isn't a double latte. It's tap water."

"Well, you must be feeling better, just awake and already demanding home improvement and expensive coffee."

"It's all an act. I plan to milk this for a few years." I pushed up in bed. "I need to make a few calls. What time is it?"

"A little after nine." He sat down again. The act made him grimace. "I've already called your parents and told them I'd bring you home. They said they were heading to your place and that they had a key. Your dad wants to supervise the installation of the door I broke."

"I need to call Nat."

He shook his head. "No phone calls."

"I can't just hang around in bed until noon."

"You can. You will."

"You said it was nine?" I said. He nodded, and I added, "I'm going to take a little walk."

"You can walk to the bathroom and back. I'm a doctor. You have to listen to me."

"You're a pediatrician, and you took as bad a beating as I did, and you get to move around."

"I didn't break anything."

"If you don't help me, I'll remedy that."

"What are you thinking of doing?" He rose again.

"First, I'm headed to the restroom. Then you're going to take me for a walk. I'll need a robe; this gown is ventilated in an unfortunate area."

I shooed him out the door and made use of the facilities. I washed my battered face and tried to straighten my hair. When I was done I congratulated myself on moving from hideous to mere bone-melting scary. When I exited Jerry was standing behind a wheelchair holding a knee-length robe.

"This is a compromise," Jerry said, keeping the robe just out of my reach. "You're a politician, you know about compromise."

"All right, all right. I'm starting to think the wrong one of us is mayor." He handed me the robe, and I slipped it on. New pains from places I didn't know I had began to tour my body. I eased myself down into the chair. "Didn't they have anything sportier? This looks like a wheelchair my mother would drive."

"Ah, chronic complaining, the first sign of recovery. Where are we headed?"

"Surgical waiting room. Titus Overstreet is having his surgery today." I told him of Titus's sudden announcement. "Are you going to be all right pushing me around in this thing? It must hurt."

"I am Dr. Steel." He grunted. "Okay, it hurts a little but I'll manage."

The twilight pall of the hospital in the wee hours had evaporated and the corridors were buzzing with activity. Jerry moved at a measured pace, and I started to prod him on, letting him know that I could endure the speed. Then it occurred to me that the reduced rate wasn't for my benefit.

Surgeries often start early in the mornings. Patients arrive and get their final prep. Family get to wait in a room designed to be efficient when it should be designed for comfort. The room was crowded with people of various ages. Some looked unperturbed; others looked on the verge of nervous breakdowns. In the latter camp was a statuesque black woman with high and prominent cheekbones, a soft jawline, a narrow chin, and dark eyes tinged with red. She was the one I had come to see.

As we entered, those who waited looked at us, some with pity, others with confusion as if we had mistaken this place with the ER. The black woman had her gaze fixed on a well-worn carpet. I motioned for Jerry to push me closer.

"Hi, Cindy," I said. She looked up and her reddened eyes widened. "Mayor, what—"

I shushed her. "Let's go with Maddy for now." I looked around to see if anyone heard her or recognized me. I didn't mind being recognized. At this point, I'd consider it a miracle, but I didn't want to answer questions from the lobby. "I had a bit of an accident."

Cindy looked up at Jerry. "Same accident?"

"In a manner of speaking," I replied. I introduced her to Jerry and Jerry to Mrs. Cindy Overstreet.

"I came to see how you and Titus were doing. I assume they've taken him in already."

"He was to be the first surgery of the day. We came in at five this morning. They said surgery would begin around six thirty or seven."

"So no word yet?" I asked.

She shook her head and dabbed at her eyes.

I rose from the wheelchair and moved to the empty chair next to her. Jerry replaced me in the wheelchair. He seemed glad for it. "Titus tells me that it was found early and that things should go very well."

"That's what the doctors say, but I'm still worried."

"It's your privilege." I took her hand with my good one and gave it a squeeze.

She smiled and dabbed at her eyes again. "I don't know what I'd do if I were to lose him. He means everything to me."

I gave another squeeze. "Titus is strong and so are you. It's the waiting that is hard."

"I was hoping it would be over by now."

Jerry leaned forward. "Surgeries almost always start late and sometimes word doesn't get out here even after it's over. It's a different world back there."

"Minutes spent waiting are hours long," she said. "Things moved so fast. First the test, then the diagnosis, then the surgery. And he was working so hard these last few weeks. He wanted everything in place. He was so worried what you would think."

That jarred me. "What I would think? About his surgery?"

"No, about the restaurant thing. He knew you'd be opposed to it, and he admires you so much. I don't think you know how much my Titus thinks of you May . . . Maddy."

The restaurant thing? Bennie's? Wentworth had mentioned support on the council and I naturally thought it was Tess, and when she convinced me that it wasn't she who had partnered with Wentworth and his boss Rutger Howard, I made another assumption. Jon Adler would sell his mother for Lakers tickets. I never would have expected Titus.

"Why would . . . Never mind. It doesn't matter." There were more important things at hand. I could talk to Titus later. I'd have to wait.

She looked at me and her eyes widened. "Have I . . . I mean, I haven't said something I shouldn't, have I?"

"Nothing to worry about, Cindy. Just some city matters. You've done nothing wrong, and there's nothing to worry about." Those words came out smoothly, but my mind was a jumble. I had completely missed my guess.

Cindy shifted her eyes from me to someone over my shoulder. I snapped my head around, and my heart began skipping. Instead of seeing a man dressed in black I saw a man dressed in surgical greens. My heart continued to pump even though there was no danger to me. I had a feeling I'd be doing a lot of unnecessary jumping in the future.

Then I felt a new tension. The man was making his way toward us. He looked at Cindy, then Jerry and me. He raised an eyebrow.

"Dr. Thomas? Jerry? What happened to you?"

"Hey, Ben." He stood. "Ben, this is Maddy Glenn, and you've probably already met Cindy Overstreet. Maddy, this is Dr. Ben Clark."

"*The* Maddy Glenn? Mayor Glenn?" His voice carried and several people looked our way. "It's a pleasure." He extended his hand, then noticed the fiberglass cast. He substituted a smile. "I'm dying to hear the story behind all this, but first . . ."

He took the other empty seat next to Cindy, then gave her a pat on the knee. "First, let me say, he's fine. He came through the surgery without a hitch. We got a late start and the surgery took about half an hour longer than expected. We did find cancer. There was more than we anticipated, but we're pretty sure we got it all. It was localized in about a footlong section of colon. We removed that. We examined the area thoroughly and could not find evidence of spread outside the colon, so that's good. There will be some follow-up treatment, but he should be fine."

Tears began to run down her cheeks. One or two slipped from my eyes as well.

"When can I see him, Doctor?"

"It will be a little while. He's in recovery and will remain there for another hour or two, then he'll be moved to ICU for observation. You can see him after he gets settled in. If he doesn't develop complications, he should be in a regular room sometime tomorrow afternoon. You should plan on his being in the hospital for a week."

He patted her knee, then stood. He looked at Jerry again. "I wish I had time to hear the story now but I have another surgery waiting, but you will tell me soon."

Jerry agreed and Dr. Clark left. I watched as Cindy dabbed her eyes. "I'm so relieved. I don't think I could live without him." I was relieved too and said a silent prayer of thanks.

Jerry wheeled me back to my room. I was exhausted. The short excursion had tired me more than I thought possible. As he pushed me along the corridor, I said, "It's good to see that kind of love."

"It's better to feel it."

I climbed back into bed, biting my lip to avoid grunting in pain. I left the robe on. I was feeling cold. "Don't you have patients to see?"

"I have a man covering it. I'm taking a couple of days off."

"Good for you." I closed my eyes and hoped for sleep, but Jerry's words kept whispering in my ears. *It's better to feel it.* I had felt such love once, and it was taken away from me. One experiences love like that once in a lifetime. My own thought tripped me. Was that true? Who was to say that a person only had one chance at love?

"Can I ask you something?" I watched him push the wheelchair into the corridor, then return to the seat by my bed.

"Sure. Unless it's about cooking. I don't know anything about cooking."

"Oh, I don't know, you pick up a mean take-out meal."

"That's true. I spend more time sitting alone in restaurants than I care to think about." That image bothered me. "What's your question?"

"Why haven't you given up on me?"

He looked puzzled. "Given up?"

"It's been almost a decade since my husband was killed and almost that long since your wife left you. You've been attentive, supportive, but never pushy. And you've never hidden your feelings for me."

"True enough."

"Yet, I've not repaid you in kind. I've never let us be more than friends."

"Also true."

I looked into his still-swollen face. "So why haven't you given up?"

The answer came without deliberation or hesitation. "Because a man doesn't give up on his heart." He leaned forward, rested his elbows on his knees, and studied his hands. "Sometimes it seems to me that you refuse to fall in love with anyone else because it will somehow steal away your love for Peter. Your husband was a good man, and you should always love him. I have never tried to compete with him for your affections. Never if he were alive and not now that he is dead." His eyes moved from his hands to my face. "I'd rather be in second place with you than in first place with anyone else."

Jerry had been open about his desire for me, about his love, but he had never been this blunt, this plain. He looked different to me. His swollen nose, puffy face, and still-squinty eye had changed his face for a few days, but it hadn't changed him, and I was beginning to see him in a new way.

"You are a wonderful man, Dr. Jerry Thomas."

He smiled in an embarrassed way. "Yeah, I know. I keep telling people that."

I closed my eyes again and the unbattered face of Jerry appeared in my mind. It felt good. It felt comfortable.

Sleep took me in its arms.

chapter 07

As Jerry pulled his car into my driveway I felt conflicting emotions. Home looked good. It was my place of peace, my sanctuary, but last night's violence had breached its walls. Mixed with the joy of being home was the bile-tasting fear that had taken up residence in my gut.

"It's a good thing I followed the ambulance last night instead of riding along. Because of my forward thinking, I was able to play chauffeur." Parked at the curb was my parents' car and Nat's van. I was glad to see both.

"Were you really thinking ahead?" He switched off the car. I looked at the closed garage door in front of us, then to the side yard where my attacker had hidden. I had an urge to buy a big, foul-tempered, ugly dog.

"No. I was barely thinking."

I could imagine what he was thinking. I was in the worst shape so he wanted the paramedics to focus on me. That would be Jerry's way. He probably threw his I'm-a-physician weight around to get what he wanted.

Jerry exited and rounded the car to get the door for me. Normally, I just bounded out once parked, but this afternoon I was in the mood to be pampered. I had slept another two hours before waking an inch or two more refreshed but in serious need of ibuprofen. At six minutes past one I was sprung and thankful for it. Hospitals are lousy places to rest. Too much noise, too many people, and they smell too much like hospitals.

After helping me down, Jerry offered me his arm. I took it and leaned a little on him until I found my legs. No serious damage had been done beyond the broken wrist, bruised face and body, and sore muscles. I was already feeling better, but was certain it would be a couple of weeks before I felt good.

The afternoon sun was high overhead, doing the same work it had done yesterday, oblivious to our brush with death. The air was still and birds in a nearby fruitless mulberry tree sang a song whose meaning was known only to them. God's creation was looking pretty good to me.

The front door opened before we reached the concrete stoop. My mother stood at the threshold, putting on a brave face, wearing a big smile, and her arms outstretched toward me. I hoped she wasn't going to hug. We could hug next week. Over her shoulder I saw Dad, looking simultaneously pitiful and fiercely angry. Nothing angered him more than someone trying to hurt his family.

"Welcome home, sweetheart." Mom's smile broadened enough to fight back her tears. She leaned forward and placed her hands on my shoulders as gently as if I were as fragile as cotton candy. She gave me the tiniest kiss on the forehead, then gave way so that I could enter my home.

Despite my best intentions, my eyes immediately traveled to the stairway where I fought for my life less than fifteen hours before. It looked as it always looked. Once fully in the house I let my gaze wander to the dining room and the sliding glass doors that had rained in on me the night before. They had been repaired and no little cubes of glass could be seen. The rug bore track marks from the vacuum and I could make out a few spots on the rug that appeared lighter than the rest. Mom must have cleaned up the blood that had poured from Jerry's nose and mouth. The chairs were put back in place and the dining room table repositioned. On the table rested a dark briefcase.

Through the window I could see the deck, the lounges, and the small table Jerry had used to shatter the glass door. My memory reran the image of the dead guard. I forced it away.

I moved toward the sofa, Jerry constantly by my side. I was feeling like an invalid. This had to stop. Releasing Jerry's arm I found my favorite spot on the couch and dropped my aching body onto it.

"Hey, stranger." I turned in time to see Nat wheeling in from the kitchen. She pulled close and took in my appearance. "Purple's not your color."

"I wanted to try something new." We made eye contact that lasted a very long second. Without words, we exchanged what needed to be said. She was sorry it happened, and I was going to be fine. "I didn't expect you to be here."

"I invited myself. I'm rude that way."

"Feel free to be rude anytime."

"What can I get for everyone?" Mom asked. "We have soda, tea, coffee—"

"I don't have soda in the house," I said.

"I went shopping. You know your dad enjoys soda."

"I'm surprised you didn't rearrange my closets." For years I've teased my mother about her tendency to mother a middle-aged woman.

"I'm almost done with that." She was quick. I asked for a cup of tea, then decided that it would be too hot for my swollen lip. I opted for ice water. Everyone else went for coffee, except Dad. He was now obligated to have a soda.

When Mom got back with the drinks, I said, "The place looks great."

"Your dad took care of the door," she said. "The poor workmen could have been done an hour earlier if your father hadn't been hovering over their shoulders."

We chatted, just light conversation, everyone judiciously avoiding the terror of the previous night. Mom was constantly on the verge of tears. I held her hand for a while, then fought off her suggestion that I take a nap. "I haven't slept well for several days, but if I sleep any more today I'll be staring at the ceiling while you all are snoring in your comfy beds."

"Well then, I've got a taco casserole to prepare, and since I don't fix things out of a box I have some work to do. Your dad's going to help me."

"I am?"

"Yes, you am."

They disappeared into the kitchen. Seconds later I heard water running, pans being shuffled, and other cooking hubbub. I looked at Jerry. He had taken one of the corners of the matching loveseat, his head rested on his hand, his eyes closed, and his breathing revealed a man fast asleep.

"He's been a peach," I said. "I owe him my life."

"I doubt he'll ask for anything in return," Nat said. "He doesn't seem the kind."

"He's not." Something warmed inside me as I watched him snoozing.

"So what do you want?" Nat asked.

"What do you mean?"

"After my accident, everyone wanted to take care of me, to do things for me, fetching this and that. They meant well and I needed their help, but I used to wish someone would simply ask, 'What do you want? Do you want to talk or be left alone?' So I'm asking. We can talk or not talk. We can avoid the attack or address it. We can skip work or do some. You get to call the shots."

"I wish it hadn't happened."

"It did."

"I know. To tell you the truth, I'd like to work. That's my best therapy."

"I'll be back." Nat wheeled away. I watched her move to the dining room table, pick up the briefcase, and return with it. "You had assigned some work for me." She removed a folder and handed it over. I took it and set it on my lap.

"What am I looking at here?"

"I did the research you requested on Rutger Howard and H. Dean Wentworth."

"Ah, Horace. Find anything good?"

"I knew Rutger Howard was a big operator. He's CEO of the Bennie's restaurant chain, and he pilots its parent company, Howard Enterprises. I'll spare you my research technique but between the Internet and the people I know, I've learned that Howard likes the eminent domain ploy."

"As I said before, it's being abused in many cities."

"I know. I've been able to locate six occurrences in the last year where they've tried to obtain property through a municipality by orchestrating an eminent domain situation. In two cases allegations of under-the-table payments to elected officials were leveled. Both cases were dropped. In all six attempts at eminent domain it was granted and Howard Enterprises got a deal on the property—usually less than half what the fair market value would be."

"In all six cases?"

"All six. What are the odds of that?"

"Not good. Do they have that much influence, or are there too few honest city officials?"

"It gets worse," Nat said. "I found a report that alleges as many as 10,000 pieces of private property have been seized by cities for private developers in recent years. In Atlantic City a middle-class neighborhood was condemned to allow a tunnel to be built to a new casino. A man lost four commercial buildings he owned in New York because the city wanted to set up a parking structure. In Washington, a city took the home of a woman well into her eighties. It had been her home for over fifty years. Why did they take it? They said they wanted to expand a sewer plan, but when it was all over, her home went to an auto dealership. There's one horror story after another."

"What about legal challenges? Surely the property owners can sue."

"Sure they can and they win—40 percent of the time."

"That means they lose 60 percent."

Nat nodded. "That's right, and that only counts those that had the financial means to launch a lawsuit."

"You know this is not new," I said. "Eminent domain is derived from the Constitution. The Fifth and Fourteenth Amendments are supposed to limit how the government can use the power. The Fifth Amendment states—" I had to think, and my thinking was a little muddled. "That no person shall be deprived of life, liberty, or property without due process of law. That applies to the federal government. The Fourteenth Amendment says the state cannot deprive any person of life, liberty, or property without due process of law."

My mind was chugging but at least it was moving. I called for my father. He stepped from the kitchen and looked glad for it. "Okay, Professor, didn't you tell me that the railroads used eminent domain to gain the rights they needed to build the tracks?"

"You always were a good student. The railroads would come to town, have property condemned, and the owners given a dollar with the advice, 'If you want fair and just compensation, take us to court.' Of course, not many people could afford to sue the railroads. It happened with the highway system, too."

"Thanks, Dad."

"You going to tell me why you ask?"

"Not now. I don't want to get you into trouble with Mom." He looked disappointed and went back to the kitchen. I felt badly for him, but if he knew I was talking shop, then Mom would know, and if she knew . . .

"What's happening, Maddy, is this," Nat said. "Businesses are learning that they can acquire property without going through the bidding process and that they can obtain the property for less money. Assuming they can get the city council to go with them on it. If they do, then they can force themselves into neighborhoods that don't want them."

"So Rutger Howard sends his man to pave the way. He tries to buy me off with a big contribution, and when that doesn't work, he starts to play dirty. He has his photo taken with me to imply I'm already on board. He works behind my back to try and influence council members and has some luck—although I was wrong about whom he had won over." I explained about my debacle with Tess and what I had learned this morning about Titus.

"From everything you've told me about Titus, it seems so out of character. Why would he do that?"

I handed the folder back to Nat. I was too tired to read.

"Maybe he genuinely believes that having that new restaurant would be good for the city." It was Jerry.

"Have you been pretending to sleep?" I asked. "You were eavesdropping."

"I've dropped no eaves. I was just resting my eyes, at least for the last few minutes. I may have blacked out for a while. Don't be jumping to conclusions."

"You looked asleep," I said.

"Not about me, about Titus. His wife didn't say anything about eminent domain, only that he had been working on—how did she put it?—the restaurant thing. She didn't say anything about eminent domain. Maybe he just likes Bennie's. Some people do."

Now I was feeling rotten inside as well as out. First I drew a wrong and hasty conclusion about Tess's role in the matter, and now I may have repeated the error with Titus.

"So Howard Enterprises is doing all this to gain property at a reduced price," I said.

"We don't know everything they're up to," Nat added, "but that's how it appears on the surface, and there's sufficient history to back it up."

"No one ever said this job would be easy." I leaned my head back. Weariness was starting to win. "I need to make a call."

"You need to rest," Jerry said. "There's no one who needs to hear from you today."

"Yes, there is." I started to reach for the phone next to the sofa but Jerry beat me to it.

He handed it to me, and I dialed information. A few minutes later I was talking to Jim Lynch, president of Atlas Security. It was time for me to offer my condolences for the man who died on my deck.

The next five minutes were rough.

chapter 38

inner had been wonderful. Mom's taco casserole was as good as it had ever been, and I wished I felt well enough for seconds. It was the first food I had since turning my nose up at the hospital breakfast. I had slept through lunch. My parents reminded me that they were moving in for the next few days. I insisted that they didn't need to, but was glad that they overruled me. I was also glad that Nat and Jerry had stayed for dinner.

Mom served pound cake, replete with a scoop of vanilla-bean ice cream and chocolate syrup. I managed to force that down. We moved outside through the new sliding glass door for decaf coffee and to watch the sun set. The yellow ball had turned orange as it neared the horizon, and the band of light it painted on the undulating ocean glistened gold. The air smelled sweet, and the gulls and terns performed airborne gymnastics.

Still, it was hard to forget that a dead man had breathed his last on this same deck. I went back into the house. The thought was too much for me. Besides, something was nagging me. I lay down on the sofa and closed my eyes. Thoughts bounded and rebounded like ping-pong balls. I thought of the eminent domain problem. Money and expediency were the motives. Greed was a motive. At least I understood that. People always did things for a motive. The motive might not be logical or reasonable to anyone else, but it made sense to the possessor.

Then I thought of Robby Hood and Katie Lysgaard. What an odd pair. He was not an ugly man, but he was hardly a trophy. On the other hand, Katie was knock-dead gorgeous. What did she see in him, the man who spent his nights in an upstairs room in his house talking about ghosts, goblins, monsters, UFOs, conspiracies, and who knows what else? Maybe it was his intelligence. Maybe it was his wealth. Maybe West was right, and she was nothing more than a bodyguard.

Why would a killer go to such lengths to kill people somehow related to the Robby Hood show? I was no expert, but serial killers usually had some internal, dark motivation. They killed women because they hated their mothers; they killed young men because they were homophobic; some killed for pleasure. But these murders were tied to one man and his radio program. Each killing connected to a topic on Hood's show. What did that achieve?

The newspaper ran articles about each death, and although I hadn't had time to see it, I imagine the events had made the radio and television news. To my knowledge, no one was making the connection to the show. Four people had died and an attempt was made on my life, but the killer's fascination with Hood's show was still too dim for others to see.

If the killings weren't for public attention, then they must be for some private reason. What? The joy of killing? There have been those who loved the hunt and the act of extinguishing a life, but why bother with Hood at all? Why not pick a target at a bar, or in the park, or a store perhaps? That didn't seem right.

I sat up. Something was stirring in my mind. Maybe the killer didn't want public attention. He wanted Hood's attention. But what could Hood have done to make someone so angry as to kill on four consecutive nights? Had it been a business deal gone bad? Perhaps Hood ridiculed the man on air, and he was seeking revenge. How sensitive an ego would a man need to be pushed off the edge of rationality—to start breaking necks? And who would know the identity of the one being ridiculed? Hood didn't allow last names on the air. I had heard that myself. Only on-air guests used their full names.

At first, I thought Hood was paranoid, hiding as he did in that big house, behind the tall wall, but I wasn't much different. My phone number was unlisted; my address a secret. I began to wonder if Hood had been threatened at one time. That could make a person paranoid. I know my own paranoia had climbed a few notches since last night.

The doorbell rang and I rose to get it. By the time I rounded the sofa, Jerry and my father had shot through the dining area and into the living room.

"I've got it," Jerry snapped. His tone removed any possibility of debate. Apparently paranoia was contagious. My mother stopped at the threshold of the deck. She was holding a coffee cup like it was a shield. Behind her was Nat. It was just a doorbell, but the sound of it conjured up all manners of evil.

Jerry bent over and peered through the peephole. He stood straight again and frowned. Unlocking the door, he opened it. "Good evening, Detective West."

A chilly, "Dr. Thomas," wafted through the opening.

"Ask him in, Jerry," I prompted.

He did and West entered. He wore a tan coat and black slacks. The ever-present tie was still missing. In his hand were a dozen long-stem roses. They were beautiful. I was certain he didn't get them at the supermarket.

"You're looking better," he said and brought the flowers to me. Jerry closed the door.

I laughed. "I'm pretty sure that's a lie. Only a paper bag would make me look better today. Have a seat." I motioned to the love seat and took my place on the end of the sofa closest to where West sat. Conversation was easier that way. I could face him, and he could face me. If we both sat on the sofa, I would have to turn to speak to him and I was too stiff to want to do that for very long.

"Mom?" I held out the flowers. "Do you mind?"

"Oh, they're lovely," she said. "How sweet. I'll put them in a vase."

I thanked him for the roses. He waved it off. "I wanted to see how you were doing."

"I'm alive and kicking, not very high, but I'm kicking. I don't suppose you ever—"

"No. Nothing has changed since this morning. We've scoured the area, but he's long gone. I imagine he's ditched his black outfit."

"What about the murders? Any progress on that front?" I noticed Jerry hovering. "Sit down, Jerry. This concerns you, too." That invitation was interpreted as open to everyone in the house. Moments later, my living room furniture had people perched in every available spot. Nat was the last to arrive.

West seemed uncomfortable. Detectives seldom talked about ongoing cases openly. They played their cards close to their chest, but this was a different situation. "I've just returned from the medical examiner's. He's getting pretty tired of doing these. No unexpected news on that front. The guard was killed in the same fashion as the others, and the marks on the jaw match. I showed him the pictures I had taken of you and Dr. Thomas. He agreed that they matched also, at least as far as he could tell from the photos." West had taken photos of our injuries while we were in the ER. It was one of the most embarrassing things I've endured. There was no need for embarrassment, but it reared its head anyway.

"I've also done some background research on Robin Hoddle, aka Robby Hood, and Katie Lysgaard. There are a few interesting things, but nothing earth shattering. Hood's program has been on the air for several years. Last year he moved his side of the operation to his home. Before that, he worked out of an LA station. He started doing late-night news soon after college. Someplace along the line he gained an interest in the wacky stuff. I spoke to one of his former station managers who had nothing but nice things to say. It seems Hood is a natural. About seven years ago the station let him have his own show. It was only late-night weekends at first, and no one thought it would go anyplace. Two years later his show was on seven days a week."

"The guy works seven days a week?" Jerry asked. "He doesn't take any time off?"

"I questioned several of the station managers for affiliate stations that carry the show. They tell me Hood is live Sunday through Friday. Saturday night is usually a repeat of an earlier show, or the stations run some other programming. I got the same word from Terminal Radio Network. Those guys are real close-lipped, but since that info was public knowledge, they let me have it. They clammed up when I asked anything personal about Hood. He has them under some kind of contract."

"What about Lysgaard?" I wondered. "Is she really Hood's wife?"

"Yes, as of two weeks ago." West paused and waited for our reaction. He got one.

"Two weeks?" I said. "They're newlyweds? You'd think he would have mentioned that when we were there."

"He wasn't very forthcoming. The man wants his privacy. If you ask me, he's beyond paranoid."

"You'd expect that from someone like him," Jerry said. "It's certainly part of his on-air persona. Sometimes the actor evolves into the character he plays. The few times I've listened to him, I assumed he was playing his audience's desire for such things."

"I think it's real for him," I said. "What else about his wife?"

"Ah, well, you'll be happy to know that my cop instincts are as sharp as ever. There's more to her than meets the eye." West looked at me and smiled, enjoying the little dig about Katie's almost bathing suit. "Her full name is Katherine Lysgaard. The name is Scandinavian. She's Hood's junior by nearly ten years. She went to school in San Francisco and served in the military." He smiled.

"I assume the smug smile is rooted in your comment that you thought she might be his bodyguard?"

"Precisely," West said. "She served four years in the army. Military police. She left with an honorable discharge in hand and started a security company with a partner. They did some detective work, but their bread-and-butter was personal security to business execs and pop stars. Apparently she was good at it. That's how she met Hood."

"He hired her?" Nat asked. She had that look I've come to know, a look that said her mind was absorbing information like a sponge sucks up water.

"Indirectly. Hood's network hired the H & K Agency when a fan turned stalker. A woman who tracked Hood down at the station one night came ready for love if he returned the feelings. She also came with a knife in case he was less than interested. Some people at the station were able to run her off before she could do any damage, but it had a profound effect on Hood." I could understand that. "It wasn't long after that he moved out of the studio and into his home. A few months later, he moved out of LA to Santa Rita and set up shop. He bought the house we saw and had extra security added."

"And overseeing the security was Katie Lysgaard," I said.

"And love blossomed. I said she looked more like a bodyguard than wife. Turns out she's both. Two weeks ago, she left her company. Apparently she didn't need the money anymore.

"And there's something else I've discovered," West continued. He looked straight at me. "Do you remember when Hood told us that his calls are screened? Well, that wasn't always the case. He used to brag on air about his show being free of screeners. That changed quickly. I got interested in Hood's sudden change, so I tracked down the man who does the screening. He's an employee of the network and works out of the same LA radio station Hood did. I asked him why Hood switched to having his calls screened. At first he said that most shows are screened now because several big-name hosts let people on who say or do something obscene. The FCC cracked down on the radio hosts and the networks that air them. Lots of money in fines was paid out. So now all calls are screened, and a delay is used so if someone gets out of hand, the host can kill the line. Hood started getting calls—threats. It changed his mind."

"So the motivation for murder is what?" I asked.

"We don't know," West admitted. "Someone wants attention. Hood doesn't appear to be the target. Each death occurred miles away from his home. I still think Katie Lysgaard is somehow involved. She has the training, she's invested in Hood's success, she's the one who posts the upcoming schedule. No one knows more about what Hood is going to do than she does."

"We've already told you, Detective," Jerry said. "The attacker we faced was a man, and there's no doubt about it."

"And you said the finger marks on the jaw are too big for a woman of Katie's size," I added.

West raised his hands. "Easy, guys. I said I thought she was involved. I didn't say she was the killer. It's not unusual for serial killers to have a partner. Raymond Fernandez and Martha Beck killed women for money in the 1940s. They became known as the Lonely Hearts Murderers. Paul Bernardo and Karla Homolka, you don't want to know what they did. David and Catherine Birnie in Australia buried nine bodies in the backyard of their home. Myra Hindley and Ian Brady in Great Britain lured children to their death, Alton Coleman and Debra Brown, and Gerald and Charlene Gallego were thrill killers. There are couples who plan and implement murders and team murderers. It's a long list, folks. Murderers often travel in pairs."

"So you're saying that Katie may be feeding information to someone who actually commits the murder?" I said.

"How long was it from the time we were at the Hoods' home to the attack on you?"

"Not long," I admitted.

"Exactly. And remember the guest who was to be in the third hour was moved to the second hour of the show. All the killings have been related to that one hour. Katie was in a position to make that change."

"So was Hood."

"True."

It didn't feel right, but I couldn't say why.

West stood. "I have to go but I wanted to bring you up-to-date— and to bring the flowers. I wish I could have brought you better news."

I stood to walk him to the door. My muscles protested, but I ignored them. "The roses are lovely. Thank you." I led him to the door. "I appreciate the update. I wish I could be of more assistance."

"Mayor stuff is your job, catching criminals is mine." He reached for the doorknob. "Jim Lynch is sending a few more guards over. They should be here soon. They'll be in uniform."

"I don't think the attacker will be back."

"Chief Webb insisted. He said if you were killed on his watch, he'd never live it down."

"It's good to hear of his concern. I suppose you're calling it an evening."

He shook his head. "No. I'm off to visit the Hoods again. They don't like it since it's getting too close to showtime, but I didn't give them much choice."

"Be careful." I was worried for him.

He said he would and left. I locked the door behind him, then I checked it twice.

chapter 39

The conversation in the living room continued for another half hour, then three uniformed guards showed up at my door. They identified themselves and showed identification. I invited them in but they declined. Each was broad in the shoulders, tall, and wore a serious expression. They were standing near the place where one of their own had died on duty.

They were older than most of the guards I had seen from Atlas Security. Most of those who strolled the grounds and halls of city hall were young. These were in their early thirties. I didn't ask, but I guessed that they were the best Jim Lynch had. I expressed my sorrow at the loss of their friend. They thanked me, then took up positions around the house. If the attacker came back he was going to receive a greeting he would never forget—if he lived.

Before I could close the door, Nat excused herself. It was time, she said, to take herself home. Jerry and I walked her to the van. One of the guards escorted us and another watched from the front lawn. I longed for anonymity. We watched as Nat drove off, and I was once again amazed at what the lady in the wheelchair could do.

Back in the house, I told the others that my spring had run down and I was going upstairs to lie down. It was still early, not even eight, but I had expended enough physical and emotional energy in the last twenty-four hours to deserve an early bedtime. Jerry gave me a small kiss on the forehead, then gave me the look.

"Maddy, I think it would be good—"

"If you can find a place to sleep, you're welcome to stay." Finding a place to sleep would be no problem. Mom and Dad needed only one bedroom. There were two other rooms to choose from. Jerry needed to go home, needed to sleep in his own bed, surrounded by his own things, but I knew there was no way I could convince him of that. There might be three beefy guards out front but Jerry wouldn't feel I was safe unless he was here to witness it.

First, I would take a shower. For some, showering is a process to be endured in the name of cleanliness. For me it was the best place to let my mind run free and the place I could best shut out the world.

Standing in my master bath, I turned on the shower and disrobed. I let my clothing fall to the floor and left it there. A long mirror spreads across the wall over my sinks. The woman who looked back at me was pitiful. My face was swollen in spots, and bruises hung on the surface of my skin. My eyes traced my naked body, and I was reminded why I was so sore. There was a large, angry bruise on my left shoulder, and an equally angry bruise under my right arm, both from being knocked to the stairs. My right hip was red. Several bruises and scrapes decorated my legs. The only clothing I wore was a fiberglass cast. I shook my head at the image, and it returned the gesture. I was the poster girl for home invasions.

Enough, I told myself. I was battered and bruised, but praise God I was alive. There were four people in four days who couldn't make that claim. I climbed in the shower. The hot water stung my skin, and the force of the jet made my injuries complain. Being careful not to get my cast wet, I adjusted the shower, lessening both heat and force. I backed into the water and let it caress my neck and back. A few moments later, the drone of the showerhead and the warmth of the water put me into a meditative state.

At first I thought of nothing. Then I thought of the gratitude I felt to God for another day of life, for Jerry, and for family and friends. I had changed a lot from the time I embraced faith, but I had a long way to go. The way I handled Tess, the conclusions I jumped to with Titus, my quick temper, all of it reminded me that I was a long way from being what I should be, but that was to be expected.

I thought of poor Fritzy and of my parents who had been injured in the attack. Not directly, but no parent could see their daughter look the way I did and know what I experienced without being forever changed.

Pie with West came to mind and I puzzled over what had gone wrong there, what hadn't happened and why. To those thoughts came Jerry, his bravery, sacrifice, and kindness. And his poetic soul. "Because," he said in response to my question about his persevering attention to me, "you don't give up on your heart." It wasn't finely crafted iambic pentameter, but the beauty of it was undeniable. "You don't give up on your heart," I said aloud.

I turned and dipped my head beneath the flow. Hot water ran through my hair and fell in a torrent to the drain below. My thoughts returned to the information West had brought and the thoughts about Hood's connection to the murders. The mulling began anew.

Why? It kept coming back to why. West had rattled off some information about couples and partners who had worked in deadly tandem. I had no doubt that such things happened but something wasn't right. I don't believe in women's intuition. It's a myth. It's silly and it's not something a woman of the twenty-first century relies upon. That being said, I trusted it anyway and my intuition was saying that I was overlooking the obvious.

Katie Lysgaard. Military trained, personal security expert, bodyguard; walks away from her business to marry the man she . . . she . . . what? Loves? Maybe. Respects? Perhaps. Desires? Why not? Would she kill to increase ratings? Would she conspire to create deadly interest in Hood's show? No, I decided. Four murders in five days was too much, and the media had yet to make the connection, something necessary for such a plan to work.

So, if the killings weren't for personal benefit, then what were they for? Thrill? No, not just thrill, otherwise the killings could be done without a connection to Hood. The connection was the key. If not for the audience, then for the . . . players?

Mental bells began to chime. I raised my head and let my drenched hair cling to my face. The water pounded my chest. If there was a message in the murders, I couldn't see it, but what if someone else could? What if the message was for Hood? I pushed my hair back.

Steam filled the bathroom and covered the shower doors in condensation. I pushed the showerhead down and stepped from the cascade. I'm one of those people who thinks best with a pencil in my hand. I didn't have a pencil in the shower, nor did I have paper, but I did have a finger and a steam-covered shower door. With the pounding sound of water in my ears, I raised my hand and wrote:

4 in 5

Four murders in five days. Then I added—

4 in 5 — 1 wk

They had all died in one week. Okay, it was redundant, I told myself, but the emphasis was different. This all began on Monday.

There were no murders in the city prior to that nor did I recall any in other cities nearby; not by broken neck anyway. Another idea occurred to me, so I added another line.

$$RH + K = 2\ wks$$

Robby Hood and Katie had been married just two weeks although they had known each other longer. West had said Katie left her business, a business she had with a partner. H & K Agency. A business partner I assumed, but could it have been more? I wrote:

$$H\ \&\ K - K = Katie$$
$$H = ?$$

I looked at my slowly disappearing scribbles . . .

$$4\ in\ 5 - 1\ wk$$
$$RH + K = 2\ wks$$
$$H\ \&\ K - K = Katie$$
$$H = ?$$

Could it be . . . ? I turned off the shower, slid my makeshift blackboard open, and grabbed a towel. I didn't realize how difficult it was to dry oneself with just one hand. I did the best I could, then ran a brush through my hair. I moved into my bedroom and slipped back into my clothes. I toddled down the hall, into my home office, and turned on the computer. I sat in my leather desk chair and wished that computers were instant on. I rose from my seat and began to pace. Questions were colliding with ideas, but I felt that I was close to tripping over the truth.

My office had once been the game room, the place my husband spent hours playing billiards with my father or a few of his friends. I don't play billiards and the table reminded me of a time that would never return. I converted the space into a large office. It was roomy with large windows that faced the ocean on one side and small panes that faced the street on the other.

The computer came to life, and I retook my seat. I was intent on doing an Internet search. Within seconds I had my browser up. I did a search for H & K Agency. The search engine returned several addresses that looked promising. I chose the most likely and was taken to a Web site. It was dark with silver letters. "H & K Agency, the First Choice in Personal Security." Down the left side were a series of links in boxes. The rest of the page was a collage of limos and men and women in sunglasses with serious expressions on their faces. The links read: Introduction, Personal Security, Business Security, Background Checks, Identity Protection, References, and About Us. I clicked on the last one. A short paragraph in reverse type set against a black background read:

"H & K Agency is a client-oriented personal and business security firm bringing the best in personal guards, electronic protection, and business security services to the private and government sectors. Experienced, government-trained owners who take your needs seriously lead highly trained personnel. With us, everything is life and death. If you must place your life in the hands of someone, make sure they're the right hands. Make sure they're our hands."

"Cute tagline." I scrolled down and found a section that said "principal" and found two photos. One of a woman with long black hair and unforgettable features. She was wearing a black pantsuit instead of a bikini. Her hair was longer in the photo but I knew it was the same woman I had met at Hood's home. I read the brief bio. "Katherine Lysgaard received her police training in the United States Army, where she was assigned several top secret duties and decorated for bravery." It didn't say what kind of bravery she had exhibited.

It was the photo below that took my breath away. The caption read, "Harper Barrymore is a former Army Ranger who brings his skills and training to your special needs." What stunned me was Mr. Barrymore's photo. Although it had clearly been taken several years before, it showed a man in a neat black turtleneck sweater and black pants—a man I had met before. But he hadn't introduced himself as Harper Barrymore. He had used the name Barry Harper. The annoying stringer who tried to intimidate an interview out of me. It had been a ploy, but why pretend to be a reporter? Why interview me? Then I recalled that he had been the one to take my picture with H. Dean Wentworth.

There's an old saying that if you have enough monkeys and enough typewriters and an infinite amount of time, sooner or later the monkeys will type the complete Encyclopaedia Britannica. I don't know if that's true, but my monkeys had just put it together. It wasn't the world's most famous encyclopedia, but it was enough.

I placed a call to West's cell phone but got no answer. I tried again, this time leaving a message. Odd. Disappointment settled over me. I wanted to share my insights but I couldn't reach him. I called the police station and an officer named Rodriguez answered. After identifying myself I asked if West was in. He had told me he was headed to Hood's house, but maybe he had stopped by his office.

"No, ma'am. I haven't seen him since I came on shift at six."

"May I trouble you to leave a note for him? Have him call Mayor Glenn as soon as possible."

"I can try his cell phone," the officer said.

"I have that number. He's not answering."

He commiserated with me, then promised to leave the note. There was no chance of sleep now. My mind was running at race-car speed. I moved back to my bedroom, ran the brush through my hair again. It was still wet, but I was too impatient to dry it. I combed it straight back and found a scarf. It wasn't my best look, but I was so battered a scarf wasn't going to make a difference. I stuck my feet into a pair of white slip-on shoes, comfy and easy to don with just one working hand.

Moments later I passed my office and started down the stairs. "Jerry!"

He was at the foot of the stairs before I eased down the first third of risers. "Yes?"

"We're going out."

"I don't think that's wise. I thought you were going to bed." He looked puzzled.

"I changed my mind. Get your keys."

He took a firm tone. "You're not going anywhere except to bed."

I reached the bottom of the stairs. Mom and Dad looked at me as if their daughter had just sailed beyond the horizon of sanity. "Sweetheart—" Dad began.

"No debating. No buts. No questions." I looked at Jerry. "Get your keys because either you're driving or you're moving your car off my driveway so I can back out my—"

"Okay, okay. You'll find trouble if I'm not there to watch over you."

Three minutes later I was seated in the passenger seat of Jerry's SUV giving him directions to Robby Hood's home.

"Will you tell me what's going on?" Jerry sounded irritated. He had every right to be. He was just as battered as I was and needed rest. I doubt he had more than half the sleep I had since last night.

"Of course." I looked at him and smiled. The dark of night kept him from seeing it. "I know who the killer is." My Internet search and my ideas poured out. Then I said, "You deserve all the credit."

"Me? This is your idea."

"It was something you said." I looked at him and watched his face as splashes of light from street lamps fell on his skin. "Remember when I asked you why you haven't given up on me?" He said he did. "You said—"

"A man doesn't give up on his heart."

"Exactly. Unless I'm off my rocker, Harper Barrymore and Katie Lysgaard were more than business partners. West said she and Hood were married two weeks ago. A week later the killings began. He's seeking revenge against Hood and Katie."

"But why not just attack them directly?"

"Because Hood is paranoid. He uses a pseudonym; his house is in the name of a business. He was hiding behind his corporation, his persona, and the walls that surround his house. He was hard to find. If it wasn't for Floyd's parcel delivery friend and Floyd's off-the-wall thinking, we might still be hunting for him. Sooner or later the police would have gotten a court order to force Hood's network to reveal his location, but that might take another couple of days. Harper would have had the same trouble. Network headquarters is in Cincinnati, you know. In the meantime, people were being murdered each night."

"This Harper guy is angry at being tossed off for Hood, so he's trying to ruin Hood's show by attaching murders to the topics." He didn't sound convinced. "That seems extreme, even for a wacko."

"People have done worse, but I think there's a different motivation. I just can't figure that part out. Not one killing, but several. Certainly that would raise the interest of the police to a new level. It's almost as if he were taunting them."

"I'm no expert on criminal thinking, but don't serial killers sometimes do just that?" Jerry said as he took the next right. He was driving like my grandmother. "What about that guy in San Francisco, the ... the Zodiac Killer. He wrote letters to the police."

"But there hasn't been any taunting, bragging, or baiting. The killer would have to know that the police would find Hood and protect—" The mental monkeys stopped typing.

"What?" Jerry said.

"Where is your cell phone?"

"On my belt where it always is." I didn't wait for permission. I reached for it. "Hang on. I'll get it." He shifted in his seat and pulled the flip phone from its holster and handed it to me. "Who are you calling?"

"Whoever I can get to answer." I tried West again. Nothing. I dialed the number for the police station. Officer Rodriguez answered again. I identified myself and got right to the point. "Can you reach Detective West by radio?"

"If he's in his car. Otherwise we use his cell phone."

"He's still not answering. Can you get an unlisted phone number for me?"

"No, ma'am. I could get in big trouble doing that. I have no way of verifying who you are and—"

I knew the answer to the next question but I asked anyway. "Chief Webb has gone for the day?"

There was a chuckle. "Yes, ma'am. It *is* getting late."

I hung up and tried to remember Webb's home phone number. If I had my cell phone then retrieving the number would have been easy, but that phone met a violent end nearly twenty-four hours before. Instead I called home. Mom answered and I assured her I was fine and hadn't lost my mind. I then asked her to go to my office. I had an address and phone book for all key city personnel. A few minutes later I had Webb's phone ringing.

"Yeah."

"Chief, it's Maddy. I'm sorry to bother you at home, but I need a favor."

There was a long pause, and I could hear the television playing in the background. "What favor?"

"I need someone to call Robby Hood's home. Detective West is there, and I think there may be trouble on the way."

"What kind of trouble?"

"I promise to explain later, Chief. This is one of those cases where you have to trust me."

"You want me to get an unlisted phone number, is that it?"

"You can do that as part of police business, right? I have the address of the home."

Another long pause. "Give it to me."

I did. "The house belongs to Robby Hood. His legal name is Robin Hoddle and the phone may be in the name of a corporation."

"How do I reach you?" I gave him Jerry's cell phone number.

"Sit tight." He hung up.

We didn't sit tight. I pushed Jerry to press the accelerator. I was developing serious concerns. We had just turned on Hood's street when Jerry's phone chimed. I looked at the caller ID. It read Restricted. I answered. It was Chief Webb.

"I got it and made the call myself. No answer. I tried West's home and cell phone. No answer there either. What aren't you telling me?"

My guts twisted. "I think you better send some officers to Hood's home. I think there may be trouble." I hung up before Webb could ask any more questions.

"What kind of trouble?" Jerry said. I couldn't hang up on him. He was sitting right next to me.

"We're coming up on the house. Kill the lights and drive slow." He did and the obsidian night swallowed us. "Pull over and park."

"That's the best idea you've had all night. I think you need to fill me in."

The car rolled to a near silent stop. Parked a hundred feet ahead was West's car. The driver's door was open, and the dim dome light proved that the car was empty.

chapter 40

I'm waiting," Jerry said.

I stared at West's car and tried to ignore the growing sense that something was horribly wrong. "The problem has always been why. The motivation has bothered me from the beginning. It wasn't just that people were being killed. It was that they were killed in a horrible way and because they provided some loose connection to Hood. Why? Why do that? You asked it yourself. Why not go after Hood directly? The answer was obvious: Hood is difficult to find, but the police could find him faster than anyone else. Once they made the connection between the murders and Hood's program they would naturally hunt down Hood for questioning. The killer—Harper—created a scenario where the police would do what he could not. The police led him to his prey."

"But Floyd found Hood easily enough."

"It wasn't that easy, Jerry. Floyd tried all the public records. His break came because he had a friend who delivered to Hood's neighborhood. That's where he got lucky." I stopped. Was it luck? Maybe it was Providence. "Harper could have asked the same kind of question of the delivery service but he would have encountered the same kind of stone wall as he did with the network. Floyd had an in. Harper didn't."

Jerry looked out the windshield. I could tell he was putting it all together. "That's West's car out front, isn't it?" I said it was. "You stay here and wait for the police."

"Where are you going?"

Jerry was out of the car without answering. He walked quickly, crossing the distance between his SUV and the sedan in less than thirty seconds. As he approached, I could see him look in the car from the passenger side, then round the front to the open driver's door. He bent down and then rose a moment later. He held up a small object. It looked like a cell phone. Jerry looked at me, then looked in the direction of the gate. He tossed the object onto the front seat and walked through the gate and out of my sight.

I waited. I told myself to be patient, to wait for the police. I was in no shape to face anyone stronger than a newborn. The police would be here soon, I told myself. Jerry is wise and won't do anything stupid, I told myself. I could wait. I should wait. I exited the car.

I had no thoughts as I crossed the same distance that Jerry had covered. I forced them aside. Thinking only raised my level of fear. Instinct was my choice for now. Like Jerry, I looked in the car. On the seat was the cell phone. Not good. I turned my attention to the automatic gate and found it open. Considering Hood's paranoia, I could only imagine one reason why the gate would not be closed.

Jerry was gone. I could see the massive house. Every light was blazing, pushing against the darkness. Images of haunted houses in movies came to mind. I looked down the street, hoping that any second a police unit would roll up. One didn't. Jerry's car beckoned to me. No one would blame me, a badly beaten woman, for going back and hiding in the backseat.

There was a gunshot.

My nerves fired at random, and my knees weakened. "Oh, God," I said. It was the longest prayer I could utter. I moved through the gate and fast-stepped my way toward the front door. I wanted to feel courageous. I wanted to be brave and heroic. Instead, I was fighting to keep Mom's taco casserole where it belonged.

Somehow I made it to the front door. Images of dead bodies lying in puddles of thick blood began to play in the theater of my mind. The door was open a few inches and light poured out of it like water. Heart tripping, lungs laboring, mouth dry, and hands shaking, I put my ear near the opening. I could hear voices.

I peeked in and saw no one. I moved along the front wall and looked through the window at the large living room. I could see expensive furnishings and art but saw no people. Going back to the door, I pushed it open in a single slow motion. I prayed that Hood was fastidious about home maintenance. A squeaky hinge could be deadly. It swung freely.

One deep breath, then another. I stepped inside and listened.

"... apologizes won't do it, woman." I recognized Barry Harper's voice. It was coming from the dinette. "Words can't undo what you've done. You dumped me. You dumped the business. And you did it for this ... this string bean."

"We've been over this for the last hour," a woman's voice said. Katie Lysgaard. "You want me; you got me. Let's go."

I saw Jerry peeking around the corner of the kitchen. He had a fireplace poker in his hand.

"You don't need them," Katie said. "The cop has nothing to do with this. Hood's no threat to you. It's me you want."

"SHUT UP!" Harper was no longer sane—if he ever was. I stepped beyond the suit of armor, beyond the stairs, and skirted the plant-filled great room. My motion caught Jerry's attention. His eyes widened, then narrowed. He waved me off.

The phone rang and I tried to leave my skin.

"Why does that phone keep ringing?" Harper shouted.

"It's my producer. I'm supposed to be on the air soon. Let me talk to him." To his credit, Hood sounded calm.

"Your broadcast days are over," Harper said.

"Let me tend to the man's wounds," Katie said. "He's bleeding to death."

"I don't care. It's one less witness. There will be no witnesses. He was just my key to getting into this place."

I held my breath. West was bleeding. I couldn't see him, but Katie made it clear. How long did he have? I looked at Jerry, and his expression brought no encouragement. His eyes darted, and I could tell he was weighing his options. He was a man dedicated to preserving life. A man was a few steps away who would die in minutes if he didn't receive help. Logic said to wait for the trained men with guns to arrive, but that might be too long. Five minutes might be too long.

"Then finish it," Hood said. "You came to do me in; well, do it. I just can't believe you're hiding behind a gun. Afraid you can't break my neck?"

That brought a laugh from Harper. Hood didn't look like he could win an arm wrestling match with a sixth-grader. My guess: He was attempting to get Harper to drop the weapon. Maybe he thought that Katie and he could handle the man.

Jerry looked at me, then handed me the poker. I gave him a quizzical look. He mouthed, "Get out. Now." With that, he stepped around the corner and into view of the others.

"You!" Harper said.

"Yeah, me. Like your handiwork?"

"How did you—"

I took the spot Jerry had occupied and could see the others. Harper had his right shoulder to me. He held the gun on Jerry. I could see Katie a few feet away, standing in front of Hood, interposing her body in front of his. She was one dedicated woman. I looked down and saw a tiny sea of blood. West lay on the floor, his face pale and his breathing labored. The blood seemed to be oozing from his left side, the side he was lying on. Jerry went straight for him, kneeling by his side.

"I should have finished you last night." Harper's words were hot.

"Yeah," Jerry said. "It wasn't like you didn't try. How many times did you shoot this man?"

"The same number of times I'm going to shoot—"

There was a crash. I looked around the corner again and noticed that Hood was standing by himself. There was a dull thud, then another. I risked it all and stuck my head around. Katie had both hands on Harper's wrist, trying to control the direction of the gun he still held. She kicked, driving her knee into his thigh. He shouted something, but it was cut off by another kick, same knee, same spot on his leg. She spun him around.

"Get out! Get out!" Katie shouted.

I rounded the corner, the poker still in my hand and just in time to see Harper head-butt his former partner. Blood squirted from her nose, but she didn't let go. With a spin, Harper turned Katie like a dancer sweeping his partner off her feet. She lost her footing. He jerked the other way. That's when Hood made his move, charging forward. Harper saw it and pointed the barrel his direction.

The shot sounded louder than I would have thought possible. The acrid smell of spent gunpowder filled the room. My ears rang with the retort. Hood screamed and went down.

"Nooo!" Katie said.

With her attention snatched to her love, Harper gave another jerk and freed his hand. He swung the gun in a backward motion, catching her across the face. She stumbled back. Jerry sprung to his feet, but he was two steps behind. Before he could do whatever it was that had crossed his mind, I swung the poker.

In high school we were forced to play softball, a sport I didn't enjoy or have talent for. I never developed a decent swing or an eye to track a moving target. My eye-hand coordination was no better now. I aimed for his wrist; I caught him in the crook of the elbow. My aim was bad but the effect was the same. There was a scream, and he dropped the gun. It was all Katie needed.

Bodyguard that she was, endangered woman that she had become, she shot forward. Fists flew, elbows were thrown. Kicks were launched. But Harper had left his sanity some weeks before. He refused to go down. He fought back with a fury fueled by bitter hatred and made a comeback. He took several blows, recovered, then caught her on the side of the head. She crumpled like a house of cards.

Harper turned on me. I raised the poker, holding it with both hands. The cast on my right wrist made it impossible to get the grip I wanted, and that same wrist burned with pain. I had injured it again. He took a step in my direction.

Jerry charged, both hands extended, and then launched himself at Harper. They collided. Jerry was no match for the likes of Harper even if he had been in the best shape of his life. But Jerry didn't throw a punch. Instead, he wrapped his arms around Harper in a battle hug and tried to lift the man from the floor. The United States Army had trained Harper too well. He broke Jerry's hold and brought the heel of his hand to Jerry's chin. I saw Jerry's eyes roll back. He staggered and dropped to his knees.

I took my second at bat, but it was a weak one-handed swing. Harper took a blow on the shoulder I was sure would leave a bruise but it wasn't hard enough to do any damage. He seized the poker and yanked it from my hand. In a single motion he raised it above his head and started it toward my head. I had the feeling he was better at softball than I was. I ducked away.

There was another explosion and more acrid air.

Harper stumbled to one side.

Another bang.

Harper convulsed. A half second later he fell backward on the tile floor. This time it was his blood that pooled. On the floor, just five feet away, lay Katie, blood trickling down her face, her nose bent to one side, and Harper's gun in her hand.

Jerry groaned and rolled on his back. He opened his eyes. I was hovering over him. Suddenly his eyes widened. He sat up, then pushed to his feet, hunting for Harper. He found him. He looked around the dinette. Four people lay on the ground, although Katie was inching toward Hood.

Victim Jerry became Dr. Jerry. "Get on the phone. Call 911. Tell them we have multiple gunshot injuries." I looked at West. He was struggling for breath, his face was pale, and he was barely conscious. "Go. Do it now!"

I did exactly as I was told and raced back. "Done. I can hear sirens."

"Come here." He was hunched over West. He had already laid him on his back and ripped open his shirt. "Good news—blood loss is not life threatening unless he's bleeding internally. Bad news is, he has a traumatic pneumothorax."

"A what?"

"His lung has collapsed." Bubbles were in the blood that oozed from his chest. "Get me a towel from the kitchen."

I was back in seconds. "Here."

He took the small white towel and folded it several times. Then he took it in his hand and pressed it against it the wound. Immediately West began to gasp for air. Jerry removed the towel, timed West's breathing, and placed the towel over the wound, pressing hard enough to make the detective groan. His breathing immediately improved.

"Put your hand where mine is," Jerry ordered. I stared at the blood-soaked towel, then at West. My hand replaced Jerry's. "Press. The trick is not to let air slip in through the wound. I checked his back. I didn't find an exit wound." He waited a moment to be sure I was doing it right. "Stay put."

I watched Jerry move to Hood who was writhing in pain. Katie was by his side. "Left hip," she said.

Hood was wearing baggy shorts and a T-shirt. West pulled the back of the shorts down. "Exit wound," he said. "Help me roll him over." He looked at Hood. "This is really going to hurt, but it can't be helped."

There was a scream. There was some language. But Hood was soon on his back. Jerry gently pulled the man's shorts down around his thighs. "Caught him in the hip. It looks like the pelvis diverted the course of the bullet. No arterial bleeding. He'll live."

Jerry looked at Katie. "Are you okay?"

"I'm fine." She sounded nasal. A broken nose will do that.

"You'll need to be looked at, too. Once the adrenaline wears off, our perspective of our injuries changes. Trust me on that."

He rose and stepped to Harper. He stood next to the unmoving body. Most men would have turned and walked away, but Jerry squatted down once more and examined the last of the injured. He placed two fingers on the carotid artery. He left them there for a while, the victim wondering what help could be rendered toward his attacker.

The sirens stopped. Soon, uniformed men with guns at the ready stood with us. Their faces revealed their unspoken emotions. The carnage wouldn't soon be forgotten.

epilogue

Jim Fritz was buried the next Wednesday. Pastor Lenny spoke with compassion at the memorial service held in the mortuary's chapel. The room was crowded. Every council member except Titus Overstreet was present. Titus was recovering and had just returned home to convalesce. The city executives, none of whom could claim a longer tenure than Fritzy, were present. We sat in respectful silence. Tears were shed and hearts broken. Following the memorial service, we trailed the hearse to the spot where Jim's walnut casket would be lowered into the open maw of the grave. Again, Pastor Lenny spoke words that brought comfort and read passages from the Bible that had never meant anything to me before. Now they meant a great deal.

Fritzy was a rock. Tears rolled freely, but she held her head high. Grief was evident, but so was the evidence that love spans even the dark chasm of death. Pastor Lenny invited everyone to attend a potluck at the church.

Jose Lopez was buried in Camarillo two days later. The family he had left months before lacked the finances for a proper burial. He received one anyway, as did security guard Carl DiMaio, all courtesy of Mr. Robby Hood. The Atlas Security Guard was buried that Friday.

I attended that service. Fifty men in the white shirts and black pants of the company were there. Six of them served as pallbearers. I didn't know the minister who performed the service, but his heart seemed to be the same as Pastor Lenny's.

Harper Barrymore's—Barry Harper's—body remained unclaimed in the coroner's freezer.

Detective Judson West had surgery the night he was shot. He hoped to return to duty in a few months. Webb did the final write-up for the district attorney. There was more investigation to be done, but no trial was needed. Corpses were hard to convict. There was a different judgment for Harper to face.

Doctors were able to straighten Katie Lysgaard Hoddle's nose. She and Hood were no longer reluctant to talk. Katie had been watching her partner slip slowly into madness. He began to see them as lovers as well as business partners. He became aggressive not only toward her but toward clients. The business was headed down the drain. Hood had hired Katie for protection, and the two had fallen in love. The attraction was, in her words, psychic. I wasn't sure what that meant, but it fit with Hood's personality.

Hood announced the wedding on his show. Then the threatening calls began. Since he used a screener and a tape delay, the threats were never aired. Had Hood not been as paranoid as he was, Barry Harper would have tracked the two down and killed them before all the wedding presents were open. The wedding was small, held in the California desert, and only a handful of trusted friends were in attendance.

What remained a mystery, and would forever be a mystery, was how Barry Harper approached his victims. West believed that he used Robby Hood's Web site against him, studying upcoming shows and setting up his victims. Most likely he had several victims in mind. A few strands of Harper's hair were found in Jose Lopez's Gremlin. A downtown bartender came forward after seeing Harper's picture in the newspaper and said that the two men had been chatting it up late Sunday night. He said Harper bought the beer. The two walked out together. Best guess: Harper claimed to need a ride somewhere. In my mind, I could hear him saying, "Just drop me off at city hall."

As with Lopez, we were left guessing how Harper had approached Jim Fritz and Carl DiMaio. Perhaps he said he needed directions, or that he needed to use a phone for some emergency or another. It didn't really matter. Knowing the details changed nothing. There were a thousand permutations and no way to prove any of them.

H. Dean Wentworth had come to see me on the first of the week. He studied my face, which was no longer swollen but still bruised enough to cause puppies to run the other direction. He also looked at the cast that would be on my arm for the next six weeks.

"I can't tell you how sorry I am to hear about all your troubles," he said. He was seated in my office, and like Harper, he didn't wait for me to invite him to sit.

"I'm sure you are," I said. "Can you excuse me for a moment?" I paged Floyd. He arrived in a second. "Please ask Tess to come in here."

Tess arrived faster than I expected. Perhaps Floyd told her who sat in my office. When she arrived I introduced them although I knew they had met once before. "As you know, this is Tess Lawrence."

"Yes, we've met." He looked uncomfortable.

"Very soon, she will be the deputy mayor so I want her to hear this conversation."

She looked at Wentworth with a gaze that could wilt flowers. "You have something to say to us?"

"Well." He shifted, then seemed to find his cold heart. "It's just that with all the trouble the city has had with these horrible murders and their connection to the mayor ... I just wanted you to know that we at Howard Enterprises want to help you regain your good name. If you are able to proceed with the eminent domain process, we can bring a viable and popular business to the blighted property. Of course, we could keep it all out of the courts if you'll just see the wisdom in what we propose. Already some of your colleagues have committed to—"

"I've had enough," Tess snapped.

I knew the tone. I knew the look. This was going to be good.

"The only colleague you've made headway with is Councilman Overstreet. You approached him at one the worst times in his life and the report you gave him was a bundle of lies and fabrications. I spoke with Titus this morning. He's not ready to run with you or anyone from your organization. The property is not blighted. The business on that corner has been passed down through several generations. I see no reason to change that."

He laughed. "You seem a little defensive. Well, then, if you won't take the reasonable approach we'll just have to bring in the courts."

"I've been thinking about the courts a lot lately," I said. "I've been talking to the city attorney, to the district attorney. I've got a few more people on my list. They're interested in the bribe—I mean the bundled contributions—you offered. I also have a call in to Mr. Rutger Howard."

He blanched. "About what?"

"You remember that photo you had taken of us. The candid shot taken by a man pretending to be a stringer for the *Register*. Turns out he killed four people that we know about and physically attacked me, the mayor of this city, and a friend of mine. He held a gun on a police officer, disarmed him, and used him to gain entrance to a home where he shot two people. I was wondering how Mr. Howard felt about one of his employees hanging with a serial killer. Do you think that might tarnish his good name?"

"I didn't know he was a killer. I just met him on the pier. He said he was a reporter. I promised him a story. That's the only dealing I had with him."

Tess leaned close to him. "Do you think that will make any difference? He was there because he was stalking Mayor Glenn. Your encounter may have been accidental, but no one is going to believe it." She stood erect again. "Go away, Mr. Wentworth. Go away now."

He did.

As Tess started to leave I stopped her. "Tess, when we have some time, I'd really like to see some of your other paintings."

Then something surprising happened. She smiled.

I was back in the home that I never thought I'd see again. Upstairs, I took a seat and Robby Hood put earphones on my head and adjusted the microphone to my mouth. He smiled as he sat on a heavily padded stool, one stiff leg hanging to the side. He had weeks of therapy to get back in shape, but he had been a lucky man. The bullet just grazed his pelvis instead of shattering it.

He looked at his computer monitor, then his clock. He cleared his throat and spoke into the microphone. "Greetings to my fellow denizens in the darkness, you who prefer moon to sun, and a walk on the weird side to the safety of television and popcorn. As you know, the strange story is my bread and butter, and folks, we have a story that I'm having trouble believing myself—and I lived it. Stay tuned because tonight's guest is the mayor of Santa Rita and candidate for congress, the Honorable Madison Glenn. She has my vote and after you hear her story, she'll have yours, too. Welcome, Mayor."

The hour passed before I knew it, and Katie walked me down the stairs to the deck that overlooked the city and the ocean. Waiting for me was Jerry Thomas.

"Ready?" he said.

"Absolutely." He took my hand, led me to the door, and then to his car.

The Incumbent

Alton Gansky

*An abduction ... a trail of disturbing clues ...
Politics are about to become deadly.*

As the controversial mayor of the beautiful coastal community of Santa Rita, Madison "Maddy" Glenn likes to face things head-on. But nothing can prepare her for a hostile visit from the chief of police—or his terrible news. Lisa Truccoli, Maddy's friend and the treasurer of her last campaign, has been kidnapped. All that remains at the crime scene is a shocking clue ... with Maddy's name on it.

The ensuing hunt for answers only turns up more sinister clues in a terrifying game the abductor wants to play ... with Maddy. Caught between a haunting past and a dangerous present, Maddy finds the walls that keep her from faith beginning to crumble.

The stakes turn lethal with a second abduction and a clue that reveals inside information about Maddy's run for Congress—a decision she has not made yet. Someone is going to dangerous lengths to make the choice for her ... but is it a choice she'll survive?

Softcover: 0-310-24958-9

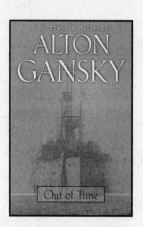

We want to hear from you. Please send your comments about this book to us in care of zreview@zondervan.com. Thank you.

GRAND RAPIDS, MICHIGAN 49530 USA

WWW.ZONDERVAN.COM